Praise for Vickie Taylor's
Carved in Stone

"Taylor's fascinating premise provides an atmospheric setting for an accomplished romance between two strong but prickly and suspicious protagonists. Fans of Christine Feehan's Dark series will find much to like in *Carved in Stone*."
—*Booklist*

"Taylor charts a clever and unique new path by unveiling the dark world of gargoyles—an exciting and new world with plenty of opportunities for exploration. *Carved in Stone* is a sexy, sensual, and dangerous romance."
—*Romantic Times*

"*Carved in Stone* offers paranormal fans something new, introducing a universe built around atypical supernatural creatures for the genre: gargoyles . . . An intriguing premise . . . a fascinating read . . . Complex and very well thought out. The way this story unfolds offers a smooth introduction to their world and allows us to get a feel for these creatures and their society without being too overwhelmed . . . The way the story finally comes together is effective, with a suspenseful and frightening climax . . . I hope this is just the beginning of a series."
—*All About Romance*

"[A] promising first book in a new paranormal series . . . There is a whole lot to like here, first and foremost being a truly outstanding and creative story . . . Taylor also has a way of writing about the city of Chicago that gives this story a bit of a crime noir edge . . . Taylor introduces plenty of interesting characters . . . The paranormal subgenre allows authors to be creative, break rules, and stretch boundaries in fantastical ways." —*The Romance Reader*

FLESH and STONE

Vickie Taylor

BERKLEY SENSATION, NEW YORK

THE BERKLEY PUBLISHING GROUP
Published by the Penguin Group
Penguin Group (USA) Inc.
375 Hudson Street, New York, New York 10014, USA
Penguin Group (Canada), 90 Eglinton Avenue East, Suite 700, Toronto, Ontario M4P 2Y3, Canada
(a division of Pearson Penguin Canada Inc.)
Penguin Books Ltd., 80 Strand, London WC2R 0RL, England
Penguin Group Ireland, 25 St. Stephen's Green, Dublin 2, Ireland (a division of Penguin Books Ltd.)
Penguin Group (Australia), 250 Camberwell Road, Camberwell, Victoria 3124, Australia
(a division of Pearson Australia Group Pty. Ltd.)
Penguin Books India Pvt. Ltd., 11 Community Centre, Panchsheel Park, New Delhi—110 017, India
Penguin Group (NZ), Cnr. Airborne and Rosedale Roads, Albany, Auckland 1310, New Zealand
(a division of Pearson New Zealand Ltd.)
Penguin Books (South Africa) (Pty.) Ltd., 24 Sturdee Avenue, Rosebank, Johannesburg 2196,
South Africa

Penguin Books Ltd., Registered Offices: 80 Strand, London WC2R 0RL, England

This is a work of fiction. Names, characters, places, and incidents either are the product of the author's imagination or are used fictitiously, and any resemblance to actual persons, living or dead, business establishments, events, or locales is entirely coincidental. The publisher does not have any control over and does not assume any responsibility for author or third-party websites or their content.

FLESH AND STONE

A Berkley Sensation Book / published by arrangement with the author

PRINTING HISTORY
Berkley Sensation mass-market edition / February 2006

Copyright © 2006 by Vickie Spears.
Cover art by Franco Accornero.
Cover design by George Long.
Hand lettering by Ron Zinn.
Interior text design by Kristin del Rosario.

ISBN: 0-425-20905-9

BERKLEY® SENSATION
Berkley Sensation Books are published by The Berkley Publishing Group,
a division of Penguin Group (USA) Inc.,
375 Hudson Street, New York, New York 10014.
BERKLEY SENSATION and the "B" design are trademarks belonging to Penguin Group (USA) Inc.

PRINTED IN THE UNITED STATES OF AMERICA

10 9 8 7 6 5 4 3 2 1

ONE

Connor Rihyad stood over Nathan Cross's body with warm blood on his hands and cold, cold hate in his heart. Above him, murky clouds twined across a matte black Minnesota sky. Below, the silkier surface of the Whiteface River slipped silently past. On the old iron trestle railroad bridge in between, Connor's breath froze in the air as if he'd spewed ice crystals directly from his chest.

As children, he and Nathan had been friends. Then over the years, Connor had begun to envy the man's rightful position as future leader of their people, and finally to despise him for his ideals. For the strife Nathan brought to their congregation. But he'd never thought he would have to kill him. Never thought any of his kind would kill another.

He'd been wrong.

Shrugging off thoughts of just how wrong, he fisted his hands, still tacky with his brethren's blood, and turned his face into the wind. The coppery scent in the air had stirred the beast within him, and the bitter breeze helped hold the monster at bay until Connor was ready to release him.

He'd been told the weather was unusually warm this winter—for Minnesota, anyway. The thermometer barely dipped below freezing during the day. The ice in the middle of the river was hardly more than paper thin, and yet Connor shivered at the thought of the frigid water beneath. If this was warm, he didn't know how anyone lived through a cold year here.

Hell to some people was a fiery place, but Connor's idea of punishment was eternity in an arctic wasteland of ice where nothing lived, nothing grew.

A place not unlike the rural countryside he looked out over now.

His gaze rolled across the riverbank, up the fields of snow to the farm barely visible atop the hill. The tin roof of the massive barn gleamed dully in what little moonlight it caught. Two dark grain silos stood like sentries against the night.

Those who lived there were lawless, without morals or conscience. But they were powerful. They'd thrown aside the mantle of obligation that had shackled their people—his people—for a thousand years, and taken control of their destinies.

No longer would they be servants to the frail human race; they would be masters, and he would be one of them, the murder of Nathan Cross the price of his admission. A test of his loyalty.

The wind lifted his longish hair. Dark strands clung to his cheeks, covered his eyes. His lips moved, but no sound issued from his mouth.

Sound wasn't necessary. He heard the words in his head, and his voice was not alone. A thousand voices over a thousand years lifted to join him in the ritual chant.

E Unri almasama
E Unri almasama

Connor's skin shrunk, tightened until it felt as if his bones would burst through. His muscles contracted, and he fell to his knees beside Nathan.

This was the curse and the beauty of his people. The Awakening of the beast inside. Tears filled his eyes, and yet he embraced the pain. He was one of *Les Gargouillen*. A Gargoyle. Pain mattered not. Only the mission mattered. The purpose.

Calli, Calli, Callio

The words pulsed like a drumbeat in his skull. His blood pounded with each beat. The rhythm drew his arms inward. His bones hollowed to make him light enough for flight, then splintered. Humerus, radius, and ulna divided, radiating from a center point at his shoulder like spokes in a wheel, with skin that had blackened and turned leathery stretched between each spiney finger. His jaw and facial structure jutted forward. His forehead sloped back and elongated to a single point.

Somara altwunia paximi

The transformation complete, he rested for a moment, then stood, no longer a man, but a magical cre-

ation made in the image of a creature nearly as old as
Earth itself. A pterodactyl. A prehistoric beast with
wings like a bat's but many times larger, a lethal ser-
rated beak and sharp talons strong enough to snap a
human spine.

He tipped back his head and studied the farm in the
distance again, this time with round, bestial eyes. Only
his labored breath broke the still of the night.

There was his mission. His purpose.

He spread his wings, flapped once, and screeched
into the darkness. It was a predatory cry. A challenge.
He followed it with a shrill, ultrasonic blast far above
the hearing range of humans. Only *Les Gargouillen*
could hear the Calling. Only *Les Gargouillen* would
answer.

Mere moments passed before he heard them:
hooves beating frozen turf. The *whump* of heavy
wings. Dried, brittle grass rustling as some legless being slithered through the snow.

The newcomers stood in a semicircle at the end of
the bridge, some taking back their human form, some
still amalgamations of all imaginable beasts, modern and prehistoric, real and mythical. All watching
warily.

Connor morphed back into human form. With
feet spread and fists at his sides, he met the eyes of
each man or animal in turn. "I've done as you
asked," he called. "I've brought you the man who
killed one of your own. Now it's your turn to fulfill
your promise."

Devlin, a burly man with a round face and rounder
body, one of the ugliest and most unkempt sons-of-
bitches Connor had ever seen, took a step forward.

He'd been the first one Connor had met when he'd approached the Minnesota congregation and asked for admission, and the meeting had been almost enough to convince Connor to call the whole thing off.

"That's him?" Devlin asked, looking at the body at Connor's feet.

Connor put his foot on Nathan's shoulder and rolled him onto his back. The blood on his shirt, which had run thick and crimson a little while ago, had congealed to gelatinous black.

"This is the one who killed your brother," Connor said. "Emasculated him and then ripped his throat out."

Devlin's bushy eyebrows drew down. "Why should I believe you?"

"I can show you the memory if you want. I was there." He didn't have the ability to communicate in words or direct thought telepathically. None of his kind did. But they could make intent clear to one another, a skill that came in handy when fighting side by side. And they could share images, even memories. He would show Devlin his brother's death if he had to, though he'd be sure to edit out the part where he himself, not Nathan, had killed the second Minnesotan who had attacked the school. That wasn't likely to earn Connor any points here.

He still didn't know why the two Gargoyles had come to St. Michael's, the school where *Les Gargouillen* of Chicago raised their young, other than that they'd tried to take some of the boys. But in the months that had passed since, Connor had spent every waking moment—and many dreams—tracing the movements of the two intruders. Who were they? What did they want with the children?

What he'd learned was beyond anything he could have dreamed. Gargoyles are born with two tenets emblazoned in their minds, their very souls, by the ancient magic that created them: protect humankind, and propagate the species.

Never in his ten incarnations had Connor heard of a Gargoyle who could deny these basic drives. Even Nathan, who had sworn he would not produce children in this life—thus losing his right to reincarnate into another upon his death—had finally given in and taken a wife. It was the natural order.

Although it was definitely not natural for a Gargoyle to stay with a woman once the child was born, as Nathan planned to do. Usually, once a son was born, Gargoyles took the son and left the woman and any female children behind.

The Gargoyle magic did not pass to females, so girl children were useless. And human women would not understand when their male babies began to sprout horns or extend claws in their cribs.

For the best interests of all, *Les Gargouillen* remained a male society. At least they had until Nathan Cross came along, spouting ideas of admitting women into the congregation.

Even that seemed more believable than these Minnesotans' idea that they were no longer responsible for protecting humans. That in fact, they preyed on the very race they'd once sworn to protect.

With bile rising in his throat, Connor pushed a single image from Nathan's fight with Devlin's brother toward the burly Gargoyle, but he felt Devlin reject the connection.

Devlin spit noisily, his arms growing a thick pelt of

brown fur, his teeth and nails elongating as he changed into the form of a bear, the same form his brother had taken when he'd attacked the school. The man-bear advanced another step, snarling. "Maybe later. First I'm gonna tear him apart with my bare teeth."

"This piece of garbage? You'd probably choke on his putrid flesh." Connor sneered and shoved the body carelessly off the side of the bridge with his foot. The river swallowed Nathan with a crack of thin ice and a quiet splash, an inauspicious end to a life that had created such controversy, such division, in his congregation.

Devlin growled his outrage. Connor walked slowly toward him. "I've done as you asked," he repeated. "Now does the Council of the Minnesota congregation of *Les Gargouillen* accept my petition to join them, or not?"

"Council? We don't got no stinkin' Council! And since you just tossed my dinner into the water, maybe I'll chew on you instead."

Connor's stomach turned. Years ago, he'd heard stories of *Les Gargouillen* who ran in the form of their beasts even when they weren't in battle. Who lived and hunted and ate as animals for the blood sport of it. He thought they'd only been horror stories the older boys told to scare the little ones.

With a popping of bones and ligaments, he quickly Awakened his own beast, leaving only enough of his face human to be able to speak. Six-inch talons with razor edges extended before him. "You can try," he said in a voice laced with menace.

A thinner man, much better groomed with dark blond hair and a mustache—Jackson, Connor remembered his name—who seemed to be the informal leader, stepped from behind Devlin with a slap and squeeze of the bigger man's beefy shoulder. "Relax, Dev. We could use some fresh blood in the congregation."

The blond man stepped forward. "Did you learn where the Chicagoans have hidden the children since their school burned?"

"I didn't have time to do a lot of talking."

Devlin scowled. "I don't trust him."

"Trust is earned, not given." Jackson peered at the dark hole in the ice covering the water below. "He's taken a good first step toward earning ours."

"I still don't like it," Devlin growled.

"You don't have to like it." Jackson's voice was sharper now. "We have our orders."

Connor stilled his reaction to the last comment. *Orders*. So there was some sort of command and control structure above Jackson in the renegade band, even if they didn't have a Council. He wondered who their leader was, and where—not to mention what sort of orders he'd issued. What were they up to? Why had they tried to take the children?

Jackson held his arms wide and gestured at the winter landscape. "Welcome to the frozen tundra, Connor." He dropped his arms. "Come inside and get warm."

A moment of indecision—hell, of panic—froze Connor in place. The lure of what these men offered was seductive: a life spent living for himself instead of serving a population of thankless humans who didn't even know those like him existed.

It was also very, very dangerous.

He let out a slow breath and forced his shoulders to

relax. He'd made his commitment. He'd sealed it with the blood drying on his palms.

He seriously doubted Devlin and his friends would let him walk away now, anyway. He'd passed the proverbial point of no return, and so he walked with his head held high to the end of the bridge. Without so much as a backward glance at the dark, cold waters where the body of Nathan Cross, the rightful next Wizenot of the Chicago congregation of *Les Gargouillen*, had sunk, he stamped his feet to restore circulation, blew on his hands to warm them, and marched up the hill toward the farm with his new brethren.

Tonight was the night.

Mara Kincaide kept her gaze lowered, but still soaked in every detail of the scene as she picked up the dirty plates that sat in front of the men in the dining room. They were drinking more than usual, welcoming the new guy with wavy hair that fell past his collar, a jagged scar on his cheek and eyes not yet dulled by alcohol and hedonism like the rest of them.

He seemed different. More human, the way he'd actually mumbled "thank you" when she'd set his dinner in front of him and managed to close his mouth when he chewed.

She wondered where he'd come from, why he would come to a place like this, but didn't puzzle over it long. Where he'd come from didn't matter. To her, he was just one more monster in a house of horrors.

The thugs laughed too loudly at bawdy jokes and sloshed beer on the floor when they crashed their mugs together for a toast. None of it mattered, she told herself, as long as she was out of the little cage she'd lived in for six days without respite when she'd first arrived. She was now free to check the layout of the farmhouse. Free to make plans, even if she had to do it while they slapped her ass and grabbed at her crotch as she served the slobs like a slave.

At least she had only been tasked with kitchen duty so far. She had a feeling the women assigned to work *upstairs* were being forced to perform acts much more degrading than carting stacks of plates full of ribs gnawed to the bone into the kitchen.

Despite the fire roaring in the stone fireplace in the corner of the dining hall, a chill crawled over her skin.

Tonight was definitely the night.

Walking out of the kitchen to pick up another load of dishes, she wiped her hands on her apron and stole a glance out the window. The farmhouse was huge, from what she'd seen. Several of the eight or ten outbuildings were even bigger. She thought the place might have been an old work farm. The correctional system had tried that for a while, bringing low-security inmates to the country for fresh and air and hard work instead of penning them up in eight-by-ten cells where they learned all the really good ways to steal a car. That or the place had been some sort of commune.

But there weren't any livestock or crops here now. The place was a slave camp, and she was one of the slaves.

She had to escape. Tonight.

She rehearsed the plan in her mind while she collected the last of the plates: Around the west wing of the house to the empty dairy barn. Through the chutes to the corral. Along the backside of the henhouse. She and the others would take their blankets to lay over the barbwire on top of the fence so they could climb over without injury. Then down the slope where they could make their way to the river without being seen from the house. She hoped.

"Hey, you." A bald-headed man she'd noticed eyeing her the last few days but whose name she'd yet to over-hear grasped her arm. Her momentum spun her around, and the plates she was carrying crashed to the floor. A hunk of mashed potatoes splattered on his thigh.

"Shit!" He shot to his feet.

The two other women cleaning up in the room scur-ried to the kitchen like rats who'd heard the cat meow.

Mara dropped to her knees and frantically picked up pieces of the shattered dishes. Her heart jumped wildly.

The bald man swiped at the goo on his jeans and then backhanded her, sending her spiraling to the floor. Lumpy potatoes smeared across her cheek. She left them there, going still and bracing for another blow. Moving would only make it worse. Minor trans-gressions were punished harshly here. Attempting to avoid the fist or boot that was bound to come at her next would only make matters much worse.

She felt as much as saw the man's hand rise above her head, but the blow never landed. She heard the slap of skin on skin. Instinctively she looked up, though she knew better than to make eye contact with any of them.

The new guy held Baldy's wrist in midair. The two men's gazes locked. She held her breath, waiting for a brawl to break out. It wouldn't be the first she'd seen in this place.

"Is this the way you treat your women?" the new guy asked. A muscle ticked in his jaw.

Baldy sneered. "Yes."

Mara edged backward toward the door on her hands and her heels.

New Guy's face hardened. The scar running the width of his cheek reddened a shade, then he turned and let his gaze linger on her. His look swept over her from head to toe, appraising her and raising goose bumps of fear on her arms before he turned back to Baldy. "Is she yours?"

"She's ours." He belched and grinned. "We believe in sharing, here. Why? You want her?"

"I might. But I don't like them marked." He slowly forced Baldy's hand down, then released him. "And I don't share."

A moment of tense silence passed. Baldy chuckled, and then laughed. He hooked an elbow around New Guy's neck and swung a fist at him in a mock blow, stopping just short of breaking his nose. "I think I'm gonna like you."

The others in the room, all of whom had come to their feet, laughed too, and scraped their chairs back to the table as they sat, the tension subsiding as quickly as it had risen.

With one quick glance at the new guy, whose eyes were as cool watching her now as they had been hot when he'd faced down Baldy a moment ago, Mara cradled the broken plates against her chest and hurried into the kitchen. She felt his eyes on her back long after she'd cleared the doorway.

In her basement cage hours later, when the voices upstairs had gone quiet, she reached under the single, thin blanket she'd been given to sleep on and pulled out the fork she'd stolen the day before yesterday, her first day in the kitchen. She'd broken off all but the center tine, and last night she'd filed it down bit by bit to the shape she wanted.

Her captors were arrogant. They didn't even search the women as they finished their chores and were ushered back to the basement prison each night. They'd made it almost laughably easy to formulate her escape. Men like that wouldn't believe a mere woman would dare defy them.

Gingerly, she fingered the welt on her cheek.

The fools were due for a lesson on the strength of the female spirit.

Holding her breath while she checked once more that the house was quiet, she squeezed her fingers, with the fork, through the metal bars of her cage and felt the lock from the outside.

It should take her two minutes to pick. Maybe less. Back in her day in the old neighborhood, she probably could have done it in thirty seconds or less.

All the same, when the lock snicked open, tears of relief sprang to her eyes. She sniffed them back. Cringing at the squeaking hinges, she tiptoed into the aisle that was lined with cages just like hers.

Tonight was definitely the night. It was a stroke of luck that none of the girls had been dragged upstairs as the men shuffled off to bed. They were too drunk, too tired.

Hopefully they'd sleep soundly. She'd get the others out first, then follow them to safety later.

After she found out what had happened to Angela.

TWO

"It's okay. Come with me." Mara held out her hand.

Theresa, the youngest of the six women held captive here, cowered in the corner, her long dark hair a curtain over her pale face. "No."

"Come on, Theresa," Mara coaxed, reaching farther. "We're getting out of here. All of us."

Theresa's dark eyes were as round as quarters. Finally she reached out with a shaking hand, and Mara pulled her toward the door of the cell. Quickly she explained the plan. Theresa was the last. The others had already stacked a pile of crates under the cellar window, which came out at ground level. Four of them had already shimmied through and were slithering across the yard on their bellies so they wouldn't cast shadows that might be seen from the house.

Mara nudged Theresa up the pile of crates. "You go. Catch up to the others." She gave the girl's hand a reassuring squeeze before letting go and stepping back.

Theresa wiggled through the window and turned to peer back inside. "What about you? Aren't you coming?"

"In a minute. Don't wait for me."

Theresa reached back inside. "No, you have to come." Panic raised the pitch of her voice.

"Shhh. Don't worry about me. I'll be along. Go now. Quietly." She made a shooing motion. "Go."

The basement seemed colder once Mara stood there alone. She rubbed her arms to ward off the sudden chill, then made her way to the bottom of the stairs. With her lock pick in one hand and the other hand on the wooden rail, she made her way up.

Each step was an agony. Would a board creak? Would her footstep be heard? But the house was still dark and quiet after she'd reached the top and worked the lock on the stairway door.

The LED light on the kitchen stove read 2:30 A.M., illuminating the room just enough for her to see the doorway into the dining area. Beyond the big table, the living area opened up in a sea of black space. That room was carpeted. If she could make it there without being heard, she stood a good chance of getting past the stairway that led up to the bedrooms and into the office that opened off an alcove just beyond them.

She'd seen Jackson come out of the office twice. Before he'd closed the door, she'd glimpsed a desk with a phone and blotter on top. A computer sat on the credenza behind the desk, and sheaves of paper littered the workspace around it.

Mara had questioned the other women about Angela. None of them knew her. Either her friend had never been here and Mara was risking her life for nothing, or she'd been moved—or, God forbid, killed—before the others arrived. If there was any record of her friend in this place, or what had happened to her, it was in that office.

Silently she blessed herself with the sign of the cross, something she hadn't done since childhood, and treaded lightly into the kitchen and through the dining and living areas. As she passed the bottom of the stairs she thought her heart would pound right out of her chest. Surely the whole house could hear it. But the house was quiet, as far as she could tell.

With any luck, it would stay that way.

Connor paced the length of the interior bedroom he'd been assigned on the second floor—a strategic move, he figured. No window to sneak out of, a door that locked from the outside. Congregation members on either side of the thin walls.

They still didn't trust him, even after they'd seen Nathan's body with their own eyes. Not that he'd expected them to.

It wasn't their lack of trust that disturbed him. It was the women. It appeared Gargoyle children weren't the only things the Minnesota congregation had been kidnapping.

Could he really stand by while the women were held captive? Mistreated? Hell, he was sugarcoating it. Trying to somehow make it acceptable by using nice words.

While they were raped and abused.

There, he'd said it. Or thought it, at least.

He sank to the edge of the twin bed against the wall and scrubbed his face with his hands.

Information. What he needed was information. Who was their leader, the great Wizenot that even these unruly jackasses showed so much deference to that they wouldn't speak of him above a whisper? Where was he?

Connor couldn't even be sure that the dozen or so men living here in the compound were all of the congregation. There could be more elsewhere.

How many women were there in the cellar? He'd seen guards lead the servingwomen down the back stairs after dinner. He pictured the small-breasted woman with the close-cropped red hair sitting down there in chains, and his jaw tightened.

She had grit, that one. She'd put on a good act of subservience, but he'd seen the hatred in the stubborn set of her fine jaw, the fire in her amber eyes. She'd tried not to draw attention to herself, but she'd been watching every move in the dining hall.

Listening to every word.

Maybe she would be more forthcoming with information than his new brethren.

Decided, he stalked across the room before he changed his mind. He could ask her questions and be pretty sure she wouldn't rat him out to the other men. She didn't seem to want any more interaction with them than she was forced to endure.

Then again, she might see selling him out as a way to gain favor with her captors, maybe earn herself a little easier time. It was a risk he was willing to take. He needed to understand the rules of the game here.

Besides, it would get her out of the damn basement, at least for the night. After that, God knew what would happen.

He crossed the hall outside his room and rapped on the opposite door.

"What?" Barefooted, bare-chested, and with his jeans unsnapped, Jackson yanked the door open and scowled at him.

"The redhead who dropped the plates at dinner," Connor said without preamble.

"What about her?" Jackson smoothed his mustache with his thumb and forefinger.

"I want her."

The office door opened as easily as the others Mara had picked. *These guys really should invest in decent locks*, she thought. Leaving the door cracked open an inch rather than risk the sound of the jamb catching, she tucked her pick under the cuff of her blouse, stepped inside, and went to work.

The light of the moon shone off the snow outside and illuminated the blotter on Jackson's desk. She scanned it quickly and found it clean except for doodled images of swords and castles. Moving behind the desk, she flicked on the computer on the credenza and rifled through papers while she waited for it to boot up. The papers in the first stack were common bills, electricity and water.

The pages of the second pile brought bile to her throat. They held lists of names, each with a date and a city next to it. Women's names. Dozens.

Feeling like a balloon was expanding in her chest,

making it impossible to breathe, she squinted and held the papers closer to the dim light that emanated from the computer monitor, looking for Angela's name. She was so intent in her search that she almost didn't hear the footsteps at the top of the stairs until it was too late.

Her pulse spiking, she reached for the computer monitor and killed the light, but just as her fingers left the on/off button, the CPU chimed in a cheery voice, "You've got mail!"

Mara's skin went as cold as if she'd been dropped into a cryogenic freeze chamber. At the masculine sound of "What the fuck?" from the bottom of the stairs, she dived for the door, still clutching the list of names in one hand.

As she launched herself through the doorway, the alcove light flicked on, nearly blinding her, and silhouetted two men for an instant before one of them grabbed her.

"What the *fuck*?" Jackson growled again. Mara squirmed in his grasp, but his arms were like steel bands holding her in place. He yanked the papers from her hand and tossed them to the floor.

She used his momentary distraction to elbow him in the gut and stomp on his foot.

"Ow, shit!" Hopping and limping, he loosened his grasp just enough for her to pull free. Before she could run, though, he snatched at the back of her shirt. When he had hold of her, he pushed her to her knees. His fist cocked over her head.

The second man, the new guy, appeared from nowhere and stepped between them. He held Jackson back with a stiff arm and a fist wrapped in the collar of the shirt under Jackson's chin. Once again, Mara pulled free. She leaped to her feet, but this time, rather than run, she stood with her back to the wall, frozen in place like a small animal in the path of a speeding truck.

Jackson's face twisted. "What do you think you're doing?"

The new guy's blue eyes turned smoky gray. "I said I don't like them marked."

"Are you crazy?" Jackson pulled himself loose and smoothed his shirt. "The bitch nearly broke my foot."

He still wasn't putting weight on it, she noticed. Score one for her. It would probably be the only point she ever got, as they were likely to kill her now. Or worse.

With that thought, a little of the numbness that had held her immobile the last few seconds faded, and her knees wobbled. She couldn't seem to draw enough air into her lungs.

The new guy stepped close to her, but wisely didn't try to touch her. She might be hyperventilating, but that didn't mean she would go down without a fight, however weak it might be.

But his gaze locked on hers and took the fight right out of her.

"I like her fire," he said.

To her ears, he almost sounded like he meant it. She tried to read something in his blue eyes, but they were like mirrors, just reflecting back her own pale complexion. Her fear and her rage.

Jackson heaved a deep breath, grumbled something under his breath, then spoke up. "Just be careful you don't get burned."

He hobbled toward the kitchen, looked down the

stairs to the basement, and shook his head. "They're all gone. Take her to your room and make sure you keep her there. I've got to rouse the troops and chase down the others."

As Jackson left, the new guy reached toward Mara's face. She flinched, shrinking back even as she cursed herself for letting him see her fear. With a look of something close to compassion on his face, he stepped well to the side and gestured for her to pass him.

Mara tried to look unaffected as she preceded him up the stairs and through the narrow halls of the farmhouse, all the while looking for a way out. But there was nowhere to run. Nowhere to hide.

God help her.

"This one." Connor *pointed toward his door. She* turned the knob, pushed too slowly. It was that slight hesitation that gave her away.

He was ready when she whirled, and caught her easily. He gathered her against him, where she couldn't get enough leverage to do him any serious damage, trapped her arms at her sides, and backed her into the room.

He kicked the door shut behind him. "Be still." She squirmed harder. "Be still— Ow!"

Her teeth sunk into his collarbone.

He shoved her away, grimaced, and grabbed his shoulder. Blood seeped through his shirt onto his palm. "Goddamn it."

"Stay away from me." She stumbled backward until she hit a wall.

"Gladly." Once, as a boy, he'd trapped a feral cat,

thinking to make it a pet. It'd had the same wild look in its eyes. Damn thing took a chunk out of his forearm, and he'd ended up having to go through rabies treatments because they couldn't catch the animal again to test it.

It wasn't an experience he wanted to repeat.

She slid along the wall to the farthest corner, never taking her eyes off him.

He made no move to stop her, or to follow. "What's your name?"

Her nostrils flared as if she sensed danger in the simple question but couldn't quite figure out the trick of it. He leaned back against the door, folded his arms across his chest. "Should I just call you 'Woman,' as in 'Hey Woman, get me another beer'? Or 'Hey Woman, get on your knees, now'?"

He'd thought he could shock her out of her resistance, but her back only stiffened further.

Good for her. He hadn't been lying to Jackson; he liked her fire. He didn't want to see it extinguished.

He also didn't want to go down in flames.

He turned his back to her, pulled out the desk drawer where he'd put the meager possessions he'd brought with him to Minnesota in his backpack—a few clothes, a book, and a bottle of scotch—and poured half a shot into a glass on the nightstand. He left the glass where it sat and backed away.

"For you," he said. "I don't drink."

She looked at the glass, then at him. Then back at the glass, then back at him. "Then why do you have a bottle of booze in your drawer?"

So, she was a curious thing, too. It might just be her undoing.

"In case of emergency." He smiled. "Which is a good thing, because you look like you're in dire need."

"I don't drink, either."

That was a bald-faced lie and he knew it from the way she eyed the glass, but he didn't press the issue. "Suit yourself."

He pulled aside the collar of his sweater and used the mirror over the desk to study the wound she'd inflicted. In the reflection, he watched her watching him. "My name's Connor, by the way."

No answer. It didn't matter. He'd heard the others call her Mara. He just would have preferred it if she'd told him herself.

Okay, so he'd try another tack. "What do you want most in the whole world?"

"To kill every one of you bastards and get out of here." She answered that one fast enough.

"What if I could make that happen? The getting out of here part, anyway. In return for a little . . . cooperation."

Every muscle in her body coiled to flee. Or strike. "You'll have to kill me first."

"Not *that* kind of cooperation."

What the hell? He picked up the glass of scotch and swallowed it in one gulp. When he stopped coughing, he added, "All I want is a little information."

"What kind of information?"

He shrugged. "Just tell me what you've seen here. Tell me what you've heard."

He could see her considering. Processing. The shoulders she'd been carrying hunched nearly to her ears dropped an inch as she thought.

When she wasn't terrified, she was really kind of

attractive. Not in the cover model way, but as a *real* person. Her straight, deep-red hair appeared to be natural, and the boyish cut, shorter than his, gave her a no-nonsense look. Her limbs were lean and long. She looked fit. Strong inside and out.

"Who are you?" she asked. Her amber eyes held caution.

Add smart to the list of her finer qualities.

He shifted on his feet. "Just a guy who's trying to figure out the rules of the game in this place."

"You think this is a game?"

He shrugged. "Poor choice of words. I'm trying to figure out what's what and who's who."

"You and your friends are the bad guys and me and the other women, we're the innocent victims."

The beast within him cried out at the knowledge of what she and her friends must have endured. The urge to kill flailed in his chest. He was born to protect people like her.

It was a hard habit to break.

He cleared his throat and avoided looking her in the eye. "How many men have you seen around? Just the ones here tonight, or are there more?"

"I don't know."

"Who is their leader, besides Jackson? Who is his boss?"

"I don't know."

"Have you heard them talk about Chicago? Children?"

"Children?" Her face paled. "I—I don't know."

"What the hell *do* you know?"

She flinched. "I know those women out there are being hunted down like dogs."

His stomach plunged.

"I know I would have escaped tonight if you hadn't ruined it," she added.

"You would have been hunted down just like the others."

"We would have made it."

"You never had a chance."

She turned her head away.

He raked his hair back from his face in a jerky swipe. *Christ*, how could he make her believe him without telling her more than she needed to know? More than he could allow her to know?

These were more than mere men she was dealing with. They were *Les Gargouillen*. In their beast forms, with their animal senses, they would have tracked her like bloodhounds on an escaped convict's trail. Already, booted feet stomped up the stairs from the first floor, meaning the escapees had been corralled.

"Connor, you in there?"

He recognized Jackson's voice and tensed. "I'm here."

"You still got the girl with you?"

"Yeah."

The hallway outside his door erupted in catcalls.

When the din quieted, Jackson spoke up. "It's awful quiet in there. What's the matter, she turn out to be too much woman for you?"

The doorknob shook as if a hand had settled on it on the other side. Suddenly realizing his mistake, Connor lurched across the room, yanking his sweater over his head as he moved.

The woman's eyes widened. She put her arms out to defend herself, but he was too quick for her. Too strong. He ripped the sleeve of her blouse, tore the front open, popping all the buttons in the process, then took her by the shoulders and threw her down on the bed, landing on top of her a fraction of a second later.

His brethren took what they wanted, when they wanted it, with no respect for rights. No concern for suffering. They expected no less from him.

Grunting, he unbuckled his belt and opened his fly with one hand. The other splayed across her forehead, holding her still.

Her slim body shook beneath him. Her eyes glassed over. She tried to bring a knee up between his legs, but the effort was weak. He stopped her with ease.

"Get off me!" she squeaked.

He hissed in her ear. "Quiet!"

She squirmed and pushed ineffectually at his chest. "I'm not going to be one of your sex slaves. I'll kill myself first. I'll kill you!"

"What?"

"You heard me. I'll kill—"

He didn't have time to tell her he'd understood the killing herself part—not with Jackson standing outside his door. He wanted to know what she'd meant about being a sex slave, but she needed an answer.

With sudden insight into just how twisted his new brethren were, Connor understood why they were kidnapping women.

His stomach sickened at the knowledge.

"Sounds like you're having a little trouble there, brother." The sound of men chuckling reverberated through the door. "You sure you don't need a little help with her?"

Connor clamped his hand over her mouth.

"Hell, no." With his shoulder, he knocked the bed against the wall once. Then again, and again. A little faster. "I'm doing just fine."

He'd be doing even better if he could ignore the part of his brain that insisted on acknowledging that the friction of his body sliding over hers felt good, that they fit together like a key in a lock.

"Uh-oh," someone outside said. "Don't come knockin' when the headboard's rockin'."

Laughter rumbled on the other side of the door, but he didn't hear the men moving away.

He brought his mouth down close to her ear and slowly removed his palm from her lips. Her breath warmed his skin in hot little puffs.

"Scream," he breathed, throwing the head of the bed against the wall again.

He'd locked one thigh over hers to hold her down. One hand pressed down on her midsection. Where their chests brushed, he could feel her heart pounding like a basketball, but she didn't seem to be breathing. Again he rammed the headboard.

"Scream, damn it!"

THREE

"Nathan!" Rachel Vandermere Cross jumped from her chair when her husband walked through the door of the makeshift office the Chicago congregation of *Les Gargouillen* had set up in an old YMCA after their school and home, St. Michael's, had come under attack two months ago. The building had suffered major fire damage, and since the goal of the attack had seemed to be an attempted kidnapping of some of the boys in residence, Nathan and Teryn both felt it was better to keep the children hidden until their safety was assured.

Across the room in three long strides, she flung herself into Nathan's arms and held on like he was a life preserver and she'd gone overboard in stormy seas. "Oh, I'm so glad you're back. And all in one piece."

He kissed her hair, then pulled his head back to look at her. "I've talked to you on the phone twice since last night. You knew I was okay."

"I had to see for myself."

She let go of him and held him at arm's length to look at him. "Yep. Two arms, two legs, wicked green eyes. Definitely all in one piece." She hugged him again.

Teryn Carnegie, Wizenot of the Chicago congregation, stepped up beside her and removed his wire-rimmed glasses. "So, Connor is in."

Nathan confirmed what they all already knew with a nod.

Rachel's husband hadn't been crazy about this plan for Connor to infiltrate the group that had attacked them. Neither had she, after she'd learned Nathan had to pretend to be killed and dumped in a freezing river to make it work. But they hadn't come up with a better option. Or any other option.

After weeks of tracing the two Gargoyles who had tried to take their children and nearly killed everyone else in the process, and more weeks of spying on the Minnesota congregation once they'd located them, Connor had approached the renegade group as a disgruntled Chicagoan. He claimed to be unhappy with the leadership of the congregation—which wasn't far from the truth, since he and Nathan didn't see eye to eye on many things. He told them he'd been excommunicated, and that he wanted to join the renegades.

At first they'd refused. When Connor pushed the issue, they'd set a test before him. One of them said they would accept him when he brought them the body of the man who'd murdered his brother, one of the attackers on St. Michael's.

Nathan's body.

So they'd made it look as if Connor had killed Nathan. Evan Cain, a doctor and a Gargoyle, had even drawn a pint of Nathan's own blood to pour over him for effect—Gargoyles could smell blood, and would never have been fooled by a substitute for the real thing.

Connor dumped the body in the river, where Nathan had changed to Gargoyle form and swum to safety behind a rocky point. Two of the brethren more suited to amphibious activities were waiting below the surface with scuba gear just in case.

The plan was full of risks, but it had worked.

Teryn had watched the scene on the bridge through the Second Sight, the self-hypnotized vision that allowed Gargoyles to see beyond their physical realm. He'd even shared the vision with her—a little trick they'd perfected over the last few weeks.

As a female, Rachel didn't possess many of the Gargoyle gifts. But as a first-generation daughter of one of the Old Ones, the original townsmen of Rouen, her Gargoyle blood was stronger than any female's in many generations.

She could hear the Calling, and her mind operated on a frequency similar to that of her kinsmen. She could brush the thoughts of *Les Gargouillen*, sense their intent. She could share images, as she had with Teryn.

She'd watched, albeit from a distance, as Nathan climbed out of the river and his brethren wrapped him in heated blankets to fend off hypothermia. Still, it was a relief to see him in the flesh.

Nathan threw his black leather jacket over the back of a chair and sat. "Have you been able to get any idea of what's going on since he went in?"

Teryn took his place behind the desk and put his glasses back on. "I don't dare try while he's so close to them."

The "tunnel" of Second Sight, as it had been described to her, was a two-way conduit. A Gargoyle on
the far end could sense its presence if he was paying attention, and follow it back to the source of origination.

Teryn couldn't allow that to happen. For the safety
of the children, the Chicago Gargoyles' new location
must remain a secret. They had set up contingencies
for communication.

Two of the congregation were watching the Minnesota compound at all times. Connor could pass basic
messages to his brethren using primitive methods like
hand signals, assuming he could get out in the open
where the signal could be seen. And a designated drop
zone had been selected for written communication, assuming Connor could get to it.

All those assumptions made Rachel nervous.

Needing something to calm her nerves, she poured
three cups of homegrown herbal tea—spearmint,
today—from the ever-present pot behind Teryn's desk
and passed them around. "What do we do now?"

Nathan sipped and settled his cup back on its
saucer. For a moment, Rachel was taken with the
contradiction—such a strong man, primitive in some
ways, with animalistic instincts. And yet he was such a
lover of art, and his fingers clutched the fine china
with the delicate grip of a courtier.

"We watch," he said. "And wait."

"What if he gets in trouble?"

"Christian and Mikkel are nearby, along with Noble and Rashid. If he Calls, they'll help him."

She set her tea on the corner of the desk. "Five
against twelve?"

"It's all we could spare." Teryn sighed. "We can't risk taking guards away from the children."

"It's the best we can do. Maybe more than we should." Nathan stared into his teacup, looking troubled. He and Connor had a history of bad blood between them, but lately they'd forged a truce of sorts, at least while the congregation was under fire.

Still, his brow drew down. "He knew the risks when he took the job."

Mara opened her mouth to scream, but no sound came out. No words. No demands. No pleas. Those were beyond her. Her body was in Minnesota, but her mind was in Los Angeles, on the south side. The bad side.

Another new social worker. It seemed like they quit every other week. Couldn't really blame them. Most of those white-bread college-educated types were scared to even come down to this part of town.

She'd missed her four o'clock appointment. She'd almost blown it off altogether, but she had three strikes on her record after getting caught lifting that CD player. She was seventeen now. If they decided to lock her up again, they might not send her to juvie.

When she opened the front door, she checked the clock on the wall. Five fifty-eight. They weren't supposed to close until six, but the place was empty.

Crap. Just her luck, he'd be gone, and report she'd missed her appointment after she'd taken the bus all the way from the valley—where she wasn't supposed to be—to get here.

Her sneakers shooshed *across the polyester carpeting as she walked through the building. There was a light on at the end of the hall.*

Maybe. Maybe he was still here.

The handwritten sign on the door read STEVEN THURLESON, and a heavyset, balding man with a sweaty forehead sat at his desk scribbling in a folder.

She cracked her gum. "Mr. Thurleson?"

His head snapped up like she'd sneaked up on him.

"Mara Kincaide, your four o'clock?" she said hesitantly.

"You're late."

"Sorry." She shrugged. "Couldn't get a ride."

He set his pen down and looked up. She had a feeling he was about to tell her to get lost, that it was too late, and he was ready to call it a day. But on the way from his desk to her face, his gaze caught on her breasts.

Not that she knew why. She didn't have much in that department. He didn't seem to mind, though.

"I guess I can stay a few minutes late," he said, sighing as if he were doing her a big favor. "Come on in."

For a minute she was weirded out by the way he was still looking at her chest, and didn't move.

But he said, "Come on in," again, stood up and walked toward her, gesturing to the chair opposite his desk, and added, "Close the door behind you."

So she did.

Then he reached around her and locked it.

Mara's head lolled forward and then back, forward and back. It took a few moments for the realization that someone was shaking her by the shoulders to sink in. Then, just like that, Los Angeles was gone.

Behind her, where she'd put it years ago. Or so she'd thought.

She was in Minnesota, in an old farmhouse. Her tattered blouse hung off her like rags. The weight of a man bore down on her. The smell of his body, his arousal, suffocated her. His hands groped her.

Her blood surged. Rage gave her strength, and she pushed against him, rising up and flicking the lock pick from her cuff into her hand.

He had only a moment to look surprised before his expression tightened in pain as she drove the sharp point of the pick into his forearm. It wasn't much of a weapon—not big enough to do any real damage unless she hit him in the eye or the neck, but it was sharp, and she put all the force she had behind the blow.

"Damn!" he cried.

In that first shocked instant, she could have sworn the whole shape of his face changed. His eyes seemed to glow.

Then he lashed out with his good arm, knocking the weapon from her hand.

"What the hell was that?" Jackson asked from the hall. The doorknob moved a fraction. "I smell blood. What're you doing in there?"

His face screwed up in what looked more like anger than pain, Connor flung her arm out of his grasp and slapped her hard on the face. He grazed the wound on his arm with his left thumb and then smeared the blood at the corner of her mouth just as the door swung open and Jackson stepped through.

Both Connor and Mara turned toward the intruder, breathing heavily. Connor kept his hand at his side, his bloody forearm pressed against his hip where Jackson couldn't see it.

Mara tasted his blood on her tongue. The warm print of his hand stung her face, the mark no doubt visibly red.

Connor brushed at her cheek with the same thumb he'd used to bloody her. Gaze locked on Jackson's, he lifted the digit coated in crimson to his mouth and sucked it clean. In a low voice that belied the tension she felt in his rock hard muscles, he said, "Get the fuck out of here."

A long minute passed after the door shut quietly and several sets of heavy footsteps shuffled down the hall. He eased his weight off her.

Like a mouse sprung from a trap, she scooted backward across the bed, gathering up the chenille bedspread and wrapping it around her shoulders as she moved.

Connor stood and fixed his pants. "Are you all right?"

Her mind was finally beginning to process what had happened.

And what had not.

She watched the muscles of his shoulders and upper arms play as he pulled his sweater back on, fascinated at the coiled strength. The tension.

He began to pace wall to wall, but kept as much distance between himself and her as was possible in the tiny room, as if he understood her need for space. As if he needed some himself.

While he walked, she took her first good look at him. He was tall, but not a giant. Maybe six feet. And solidly built. Broad shoulders and thick biceps pushed at the seams of his hunter green sweater. The hard muscles of his thighs bulged beneath his blue jeans with each step he took, and yet he didn't stalk the room like a predator, or saunter like a victor letting the anticipation build before he pounced on his spoils.

He shuffled across the room with a heavy step, like a man with the weight of the world on his back.

Or on his mind.

The chill that had gripped her moments ago receded. In fact, her skin felt flushed, but she wasn't ready to let go of the bedspread yet. She felt safe inside the folds of its soft cocoon. Protected.

"Why didn't you . . . ?" she asked, her voice sounding small.

"I don't rape women," he snapped.

"You just want your friends to think you do?"

Maybe he wasn't capable of rape, she thought. Maybe he couldn't keep it up, at least not without pharmaceutical help, and he didn't want them to know.

The thought almost made her giggle. Not because she wasn't sensitive to the suffering of men with erectile dysfunction, but because she was barely holding back hysteria as it was, and because she could just picture her friend Angela wailing in protest, proclaiming how unfair it was that women should be denied a good-looking piece of man-flesh like him.

Mara's heart twisted and her smile fell. Angela wasn't here. Mara didn't know what had happened to her, which was what had gotten Mara into this predicament in the first place.

Connor turned sharply toward her. His blue eyes were filled with such agony that her breath caught in her throat at the sight of it.

"I'm sorry I scared you," he said. His usually smooth voice had gone husky again, and this time she didn't think it was because he was trying to convince anyone he was in the throes of passion. "There wasn't time to explain."

She shrugged, unsure of her footing in this conversation, as if she'd been standing on the bow of a rocking boat. "It wasn't you, really. You just pushed some buttons. Brought up some bad memories."

"Christ." He shook his head. "Did one of them—?"

"No," she said quickly. "It was a long time ago and anyway, he didn't really." She was feeling braver now, more confident. She wanted him to know what she was capable of, in case he didn't need those pharmaceuticals after all. "I killed him first."

"Jesus."

"Funny, that's what he said just before I planted his letter opener in his heart."

"Son of a bitch deserved what he got. And worse."

"That's not what the judge who tried my case said. But then I was just a poor kid with a rap sheet from the inner city, and he was college educated. Had a family in the suburbs. I got twelve years. Served eight before the parole board sprung me."

"Jesus," he said again, this time muttering a few more choice words to himself afterward as he stalked over to the desk and poured himself another scotch.

"Only in case of emergency, huh?"

"Dire," he said, and threw the shot back. This go-round, he didn't even choke. Fast learner.

Fighting back a smile, albeit a shaky one, she let the bedspread slip off her shoulders and automatically started smoothing it in place across the bed, careful not to completely turn her back to him. She still didn't trust him that much.

He stepped up and caught her hands. "Don't."

She had no idea what he meant.

"You're not my servant."

A warm ball settled in her chest. Its glow radiated all the way to her toes. "Do your friends know about this little problem of yours?" she asked. She spoke quietly, mindful of the thin walls.

"What problem?"

"That shred of decency you seem to still have left in you."

"No." He released her hands. Her wrists tingled.

She finished making the bed, not because she felt she had to, but because it kept her hands busy. "Who are those guys? Some kind of freaky religious cult?"

He tugged down the corner of the sheet they'd mussed and folded it perfectly square. "Something like that."

The bed done, she straightened. They faced each other awkwardly, as if neither one of them quite knew what to do next. "And what about you? Who are you?"

"Just a guy looking for the truth."

"Which truth would that be?"

"What were you looking for in Jackson's office?"

She sat on the edge of the bed and twisted the fringe on the spread.

"What was on the papers you found?"

Did he really not know what kind of men his friends were, or was this some kind of test?

She lifted her chin, met his questioning eyes steadily, though it took all the willpower she pos-

sessed. "A list of names, dozens of them. Women I
think were kidnapped like me. I think they're selling
them or something. Like some kind of slave ring." She
pressed her lips together. "Sex slaves."

The same strange change she'd seen when she'd
stabbed Connor came over him again. His eyes became more vivid. His jaw popped and the veins in his
neck bulged.

She took a step back without even realizing she'd
done it until her calves hit the side rail of the bed.

Connor's arm shot out. She ducked reflexively, but
the glass he threw sailed in the opposite direction from
her. It shattered against the far wall, and he stormed
out of the room without another word.

Connor stomped through the living area. He'd
thought everyone had gone to bed after the excitement
of the night, but he'd been wrong. Devlin sat in a chair,
peeling an apple.

"Done already, Rihyad?" He glanced up the stairs.
"Maybe I'll go see if she has anything left for me."

Connor snatched the big man out of the chair by the
collar. "Touch her and I'll kill you."

Suddenly the big man held the paring knife at Connor's throat. He didn't even blink.

"You want to fight? I'm game." He glanced point-
edly at the blade in Devlin's hand. "But let's forget the
knives. Go man-to-man. Or should I say bear-to-bird?"

The woolly mammoth looked uncertain. Connor
stared him down, then turned and marched away. He
half expected to feel the blade of a paring knife sink

into his back, but the door closed behind him without the flow of blood.

The frigid air outside hit him like a slap in the face.

Good. Maybe the cold would push the beast inside him back into its cave. For a minute, when Mara had reminded him the Minnesotans were kidnapping women into sexual slavery, he'd thought she was going to see the Awakening right then and there. The chant had echoed in his head. Fire had burned and lightning had crashed in his veins. Protect. Protect.

Kill.

It had taken all his will to beat the monster back.

His fingers clenched the porch rail he leaned on. Sex slaves, his ass. If the Minnesota Gargoyles were taking women as sexual slaves, they could only have one purpose: to spawn sons. Sons that would guarantee their fathers' reincarnation after death in this lifetime.

Sons that would grow up to be just like them.

But one son apparently wasn't enough for these guys. Not with the large numbers of women they'd taken. Dozens, Mara had said.

Hell and angels, now he knew why the Minnesota congregation had tried to take the children from Chicago, too. Kidnap boys young enough, their minds would still be malleable. They could be turned into soldiers in a matter of years. Add those to the numbers they were able to produce biologically, and they would indeed have an army. An army of Gargoyles.

And an army of Gargoyles without morals or conscience could rule the world.

He had to find out more about them. Where did

they take the women to give birth? How many more men were there? Where did they raise the children?

He had to get word to Teryn and Nathan in Chicago.

And in the meantime, what did he do about the six women here? Mara was safe enough for the moment, but he couldn't protect her every minute. And who knew what tortures the other five were enduring daily?

How could he leave any of them victim to rape and torture, to serve as . . . as *broodmares* for an evil empire while he played his spy games, even if his mission was to protect his congregation?

How did he choose one oath over another?

And if he chose his people, how did he live with himself afterward?

FOUR

Connor sat on the floor across from the bed in his room, his back propped against the wall, his book open on his chest, but tipped forward to his chest to hold the page. Normally he liked to read. Words soothed him, especially the words of the masters. The rhythm and the imagery filled his mind until there was no room left for the stresses and doubts of the day.

But the image that held his attention at the moment was one far more tangible. He'd been watching Mara sleep since dawn, fascinated with the gentle rise and fall of her breasts, the way her fingers curled against the pillowcase. The occasional soft flutter of her eyelashes over her pale cheeks.

For a woman with a core as strong as any he'd ever known—strong enough to kill a man—she looked incredibly soft in sleep. Incredibly vulnerable.

It had been a long time since he'd been with a woman. At sixteen, he'd impregnated a girl. He'd been in a hurry to produce a male child, to offer his heir to the congregation. To do his part for the propagation of his species as the magic that created him demanded, and to be rewarded with a renewal of the soul. A guarantee that he would be granted reincarnation into another body, a new life, when this one ended.

The girl, though, hadn't wanted to be an unwed teenage mother. She'd had an abortion without telling him until it was over.

There had been a few others over the years, but modern women were much more in control of their bodies than they had been a thousand years ago when the crazy spell that made him what he was had been concocted. He'd lived with one woman for nearly six months, wondering why they hadn't conceived—they'd certainly rutted like rabbits—until she finally confessed she'd been on the pill. Others refused to have sex at all unless he used a condom.

Eventually, he'd just quit trying to change their minds. Or maybe Nathan and his traitorous ideals about women had more of an effect on Connor than he'd thought. Propaganda like that had a way of sinking in even when a person didn't believe it.

Damn Nathan Cross. He was going to be the ruination of their people yet.

If they still had a people once the Minnesota congregation got through with them.

He scowled and stood, keeping his place in his book with a finger between the pages of the leather-bound hardback.

Mara's lids lifted. Her amber eyes shined beneath.

She stretched, studied him a moment, and then asked, "Something wrong?"

"No." He cleared his throat. "I was just reading."

She squinted at the leather-bound book cover. "You read poetry?"

"I read Wordsworth."

"Who's he?"

"You've never heard of William Wordsworth? *The Prelude*? 'Imitations of Immortality'?"

She sat up and plumped the pillows behind her. "Hey, the closest thing to literature we had where I grew up was graffiti and rap lyrics. Cut me a break."

She reached for the book. He handed it to her and she fanned the pages. "So, is he any good?"

"Keep it. Find out for yourself."

Her smile fading, she set the book on the night-stand. "They won't let me take it to the basement. It's too big to hide."

He jerked the book off the table and set it softly beside her, then crouched so they were at eye level and smoothed the unbrushed hair at her temple. "You're not going back to the basement."

She didn't dare hope. It would hurt too much when she found out he'd lied. "Really?"

"This is your room now." He stood, rubbing absently at the knot that tightened in his chest. "Stay here until it's time to go down and help with breakfast. I'm going to go for a run, but I'll be back in time to eat."

"A run?"

He pulled sweatpants and a sweatshirt out of his drawer. "You know, jogging?"

She wrinkled her nose. "In this cold?"

"I need to burn off a little steam."

He looked around for a spot of privacy to change.

Finding none, he turned his back on her, slid his jeans off and pulled the sweats over his Jockeys. As he was trading his sweater for the sweatshirt, he turned back to her.

"Maybe you could do me a little favor. Keep an eye on the clock in the kitchen. At exactly eight o'clock, make some kind of commotion. Drop another load of dishes or something. Anything noisy that'll draw everyone's attention."

She frowned. "Why?"

Because I need a diversion so I can make contact with my people.

The words wanted to come out of his mouth, but he held back. It was too soon to trust her, though if he were honest with himself he'd probably find he already did. He didn't *want* to trust her.

Trust meant more than two people thrown together by circumstance. Trust was a commitment.

He shrugged casually. "I'd just like to get a look around out there, and I'm tired of these guys watching me every second."

She paused a moment, then nodded.

Before he walked out, he warned her, "Don't forget you're supposed to be traumatized and terrified of me." He glanced over his shoulder and his pulse missed a beat at the sight of her soft, sleepy, definitely untraumatized, unterrified face. The beast slumbering inside him opened one eye in lazy wakefulness. And awareness.

"Try to look the part," he said, and walked out while he still could.

In the entryway, Devlin grabbed him by the collar from behind. "Where do you think you're going?"

Connor turned and brushed the man's meaty fore-arm away. "For a run. That all right with you?" His tone made it clear he didn't really give a flip one way or the other.

"Hmmph." He let him go. "Freeze your nuts off if you want. Don't matter to me."

Connor turned again and paused to wrap the towel he'd stolen from the bathroom around his neck and tucked the ends into his sweatshirt.

"But stay inside the fence. Leave the compound and I'll take great pleasure in dragging you back myself."

"I'll try to remember that."

"Fuckin' crazy," Devlin grumbled again as Connor closed the door behind him. "Guy's freaking insane."

Connor took a moment to stretch on the porch and check out the property, making sure no one else was out and about. He didn't see anyone, but that didn't mean they weren't watching from the windows.

The snow crunched beneath his running shoes as he tentatively jogged away from the house. It was slippery, and his toes were already going numb. By the time he'd made it three-quarters of the way around the enclosure, he'd lost feeling in his nose, his cheeks, and his arms up to his elbows, yet his chest was on fire. Running was really not his thing. He really preferred a clear sky and a light breeze to glide on for his exercise.

At exactly eight o'clock, he hopped and drew up near a clump of trees, then flattened his palms against one trunk and leaned forward, balancing on his toes as if stretching out a cramp in his calf. Then he moved away and bent to touch his toes.

As he doubled over, he shook his right arm and curled his fingers back under his wrist to work from his sleeve the note he'd written on the title page he'd ripped out of his book. It was a shame to deface a masterpiece like that, but desperate times called for desperate measures, as they say.

Trying not to look obvious, he cupped his message for Teryn and Nathan in his hand until his fingers reached the tips of his shoes, then he slid it under his foot and mashed it down beneath the surface of the snow and against a bare tree root.

Straightening up, he lazily scanned the area again, checking to see if anyone was watching while trying not to *look* like he was checking to see if anyone was watching, then set off at the best pace he could manage and just hoped he could make it back to the house before he keeled over or froze solid.

He was confident Mikkel, or whoever was on watch at the point they'd designated as a drop spot, had seen him place the note, even if Connor hadn't seen them. But his brethren probably wouldn't be able to retrieve the note before dark.

Hopefully no one else would find it first.

Mara managed to fake a tremble strong enough to slosh coffee over the rim of every mug she set on the table at breakfast. She flinched if anyone touched her, even accidentally, kept her head down and met no one's eyes.

Yet she could feel eyes on her. Connor's eyes. She could feel the rage roiling in him like a violent weather system ready to spawn a cyclone every time he looked at her. She had a pretty good idea why, too.

She touched the new bruise under her eye. It was

tender, but not really painful. No permanent damage done, not that severity—or lack of it—seemed to matter to Connor. Lightning flashed in his sky-blue eyes.

How could she read him so well when the men in the room were so obviously oblivious to his temper? It didn't seem possible that she'd only known him less than a day.

"You, get me some butter," Devlin demanded.

Mara jumped and hurried into the kitchen. She'd just unwrapped a new stick and set it on the butter dish when hands grabbed her from behind, spun her.

There was nothing fake about the way she jumped at the touch this time.

She gasped, nearly lightheaded with sudden relief. "Connor!"

He stepped her backward until her back hit the countertop, then tipped her chin up and turned her head sideways to get her face into the light.

"Who did this?" he growled.

She twisted out of his grasp and brought her fingers to the sore spot by reflex. "It doesn't matter."

"Hell it doesn't. Who did it?"

She pressed her lips together and shook her head. For what reason, she didn't know, but apparently he had appointed himself her protector. It wasn't that she didn't appreciate his help, but some battles she needed to fight herself. When the time was right, Devlin would get his due for slapping women around. Until then, she didn't want to create any more animosity between him and Connor. Devlin wasn't just big and ugly. He was mean as a water moccasin as well. She held no doubt he was capable of killing Connor just because he didn't like him.

Mara wasn't sure exactly what Connor was up to here. She didn't have any proof that he was up to something, even if she was pretty sure things weren't exactly what they seemed with him.

She was way too street-smart to trust him blindly, but right now, he looked like her best shot at surviving this nightmare. And maybe even finding Angela.

She needed him alive.

She raised her head for the first time all morning. His blue eyes were cold, but his body was hot against hers. "Did you get your personal business taken care of this morning?"

He nodded.

"Then it was worth it."

"Damn it, I should have known you'd pay the price. I shouldn't have asked—"

"Forget it, Connor. It's done."

He took her chin in his hand again, tipped her head up farther. This time he wasn't looking at her cheek, though. He was looking into her eyes.

She met the stare with equal resolve, though it felt like staring at the sun. His intensity blinded her.

Then a hand thudded against the swinging door behind him. A heavy footstep followed. "Woman, where the hell is my butter?"

Connor flicked a quick glance over his shoulder. Panic leapt in Mara's throat, but before she could even squeak, Connor turned back. Just as Devlin cleared the doorway, Connor covered her mouth with his, and plunged deep.

The footsteps stopped. "Son of a bitch. Can't you leave her alone long enough for us to eat a little breakfast, Rihyad?"

Mara doubted Connor had any intention of answering. At the moment, he was speaking to her with his lips and his tongue and little nips of his teeth.

Oh, what a statement he made.

His left hand caressed the column of her throat, up to her jaw to gently urge her mouth open wider. His right hand curved around the small of her back and dragged her close. Close to his heat and the pounding of his heart against hers.

He plundered her mouth, pushing as deep as he could reach, then pulled back to coax and cajole. Teasing her tongue to come out and play.

Despite nearly being raped at seventeen and spending most of the sexual prime years of her life in a women's penitentiary, Mara was no virgin. She'd had lovers. But she'd never been *made love to* like this.

She'd never responded like this, either. In gratitude. In awe.

She found her own tongue darting after his in a game of oral hide-and-seek. Only it wasn't a game at all. When she caught him, she held him gently with her teeth and sucked, imitating the act of fellatio and startled by the similarity of the arousal the act produced.

Connor no longer had to hold her to him. Her body felt as if it were melting into his.

"Shit. Just give me the damn butter." Devlin took the dish from her hand, which was a good thing, since she surely would have dropped it in another moment.

"Get a room, would ya?" he said as he tromped out of the kitchen. The door creaked shut behind him.

Gently, Connor disengaged and lifted his head. His breath shooshed out in a warm gust against her forehead. "He's gone."

She could only nod. She knew the kiss hadn't been real. She knew it was a cover to keep Devlin from wondering what they'd been talking about in here all alone, or to make sure the goon didn't whale on her again for being too slow with his butter. It was all part of this intricate charade Connor was putting on.

She knew that, and yet it was still disappointing to have her supposition confirmed.

Self-consciously she ran her fingers through her hair and squeezed out from between Connor and the counter. "I'd better get back to work."

He made no move to stop her, but when she glanced back as she walked out, his sky-blue eyes had darkened to indigo. His hands were clenching and unclenching lightly, and his chest still rose and fell like he'd only just then finished his jog.

Real kiss or not, there was no denying the chemistry between them.

FIVE

"He wants what?" *Nathan was still reeling from* the revelation that the Minnesota congregation had apparently tried to kidnap the young Gargoyles from Chicago to use them as some sort of soldiers in a war against humanity, and that they held six women there as well, to raise even more sons. His mind simply couldn't process the second part of Connor's note. It didn't make sense.

He held the phone closer to his ear to make sure he'd heard Mikkel right.

"Sumac. *Poison* sumac. Or poison ivy, or poison oak. Whatever we can find."

Yep. He'd heard right. He scribbled the names on a notepad and passed the message to Teryn.

"Where are we going to get that this time of year?"

"Ask Teryn. He's the herb expert."

"Poison sumac is not an herb."

As Teryn read the note, his brows, dark even though his hair had turned silver years ago, pulled down into a worried V. Rachel leaned over his shoulder to see what Nathan had written, her expression equally concerned.

"All right," Nathan told Mikkel. "We'll call you back when we have a game plan." Nathan hung up and sighed.

Teryn shook his head. "What could he possibly want with these plants?"

Nathan spread his hands on the desk. "Who knows."

"But if he risked getting a note out to get them, it must be important," Rachel said. "Do you have any idea where to find the plants this time of year?"

Teryn fiddled with the leaves of a newly transplanted mint on the edge of his desk. "Other than flying a thousand or so miles south? We could try the arboretum. They have indoor exhibits of most of the plants indigenous to this area. And some of the bigger nurseries may have had some weed intrusion in their greenhouses."

Rachel leaned over the computer on the stand beside Teryn's desk. Her fingers flew over the keys with purpose.

Nathan loved watching her work. He only regretted that they both had to work so much right now. He wished they had more time to enjoy each other.

Not that they didn't enjoy each other pretty regularly . . .

As he struggled to forget this morning in their bedroom and remember what they were supposed to be doing now, in the office, the printer started to hum.

"I'm downloading pictures from the Internet," she

said. "We'll give everyone we can spare a copy and fan out."

"It's going to take time."

He recognized the gleam in her eye. She was on a mission and there would be no stopping her now. She picked up handful of printouts and shoved them toward him. "Then we'd better get started."

Just in from his third day of jogging—one to plant the note and two looking for a response—Connor stood in the doorway of the living room in his sweats. If he kept this running thing up, he might actually get used to the cold—if it didn't kill him first.

He scanned the room. Three of his brethren, including Devlin, sat watching a European soccer game. Two more snoozed on opposite ends of the couch, one snoring loudly. Jackson sat in an upholstered chair, seemingly deep in thought.

That, or he was in a coma, Connor amended mentally. It was hard to tell the difference.

"So, what's the deal today?" he asked, aiming the question at Jackson. "You got something lined up, or are we going to sit around scratching our asses and farting again like we have all week?"

At this rate, Connor was never going to get the information his people needed to bring down this evil empire.

Devlin snorted without looking away from the soccer game. "I would'a thought you were getting enough action with your little hoochie upstairs to keep you from jonesing for a while."

Connor was dying to make a comment about how at least he *could* get a jones on, but he was afraid Devlin would then feel compelled to prove his virility on one of the women, so he bit his tongue instead. With any luck, soon none of the men would be caught dead anywhere near those girls. Until then, he'd keep his mouth shut.

"Give it a rest, Dev," Jackson said.

Devlin gave his boss the finger and turned his attention back to his TV screen.

Jackson pretended not to see the gesture. Or he just didn't care. Of all of the men here, he alone seemed to have some self-control.

It made Connor wonder what he was doing with the rest of these idiots.

"Getting bored, huh?" Jackson asked.

"Just ready to start earning my keep." Not to mention that getting involved in their operations, whatever those were, might be the only way he was ever going to find out exactly what they were up to and who their leaders were.

"All right, then." Jackson stood, walked over to the television area, and shut the set off. The three watching the game groaned and complained. "We could use some supplies. Benson, Hard Case, Devlin—" He jerked his head over his shoulder toward Connor. "You know the drill. Take the new blood with you. But keep an eye on him."

Mara was lying crosswise over the end of the bed, her bare feet kicked up in the air behind her, reading, when she heard a key slide into the door of the room she'd been locked inside for most of three days. Her only reprieve had been mealtimes, when she went downstairs to help cook and serve.

She wasn't complaining. It sure beat her cell in the basement.

The door swung open. A tingle zinged over her skin when she saw it was Connor, and that he was smiling.

"You're looking awfully chipper," she said.

"A run always perks me up."

"Liar. You've come back here dragging your shivering ass every morning." But she let the brush-off go at that. She had her secrets; he had his. Neither one of them trusted easily.

He unwrapped the towel from his neck and picked up his clothes. "You enjoying the book?"

She read him a passage:

> *Earth has not anything to show more fair;*
> *Dull would he be of soul who could pass by*
> *A sight so touching in its majesty;*
> *This City now doth like a garment wear*
> *The beauty of the morning; silent, bare.*

He finished it from memory:

> *Ships, towers, domes, theatres, and temples lie*
> *Open unto the fields, and to the sky;*
> *All bright and glittering in the smokeless air.*

"You really do like Wordsworth. And you're right," she said, still awed by the passage even after she'd read it three times. "His writing is beautiful."

Their gazes connected and a moment of frisson

passed between them. The kind of moment that, in different circumstances, shared with someone she knew better, would have made her think he was going to kiss her again. This time for real.

The moment passed, though, and he looked away.

"I've got to go shower and change. I want you to stay in the room today. The door will be locked."

Like she expected anything else. "Where will you be?"

He hesitated, then said, "Working."

She thought about demanding more of an explanation than that, but suspected she wouldn't get anywhere.

While she fretted in silence, he checked over his shoulder as if to make sure they were alone and that the door was closed. When he spoke, he lowered his voice. "I need you to do something today, too."

She cringed inwardly. "Another diversion?"

"No." He pulled a plastic bag from inside his sweatshirt.

"You want me to smoke pot?"

He grinned. "It's not marijuana. It's poison sumac. I want you to give it to the women and have them rub a little bit on their arms or the side of their necks. Just a little though. The stuff will make them itch like crazy."

"Why in the world do you want them to itch like crazy?"

"I don't. I want them to have a rash. Then I want you to tell a couple of them to cough through the day, and especially at dinner tonight. Maybe you could do something to make one of them look like she's got a fever. Tell her to play it up."

Understanding slowly dawned. "You're going to run a con."

He shrugged. "Poor girls, living down in the basement with the rats. Who knows what they could catch? Rashes, coughing, fever. Might even be contagious. Highly contagious."

A slow smile broke across her face, her first true smile in what felt like . . . forever. "In which case the men wouldn't want to get anywhere near them. Definitely wouldn't take them up to their bedrooms."

"Believe me, a guy sees a rash like that, he's not going to let his pecker within a mile of it. Think your girls can pull it off?"

"I know they can." She studied the leaves through the clear plastic. "Where did you get this stuff?"

His pause was telling. She didn't let on that while she peeled potatoes for hash browns in front of the kitchen window she'd seen him stop two mornings in a row at the same tree and dig his toe in the snow as if looking for something. "I have my sources."

"Then I'll see you tonight."

He carried his clothes to the door, but stopped just short of leaving. "One more thing. Make sure you don't get any of that on you."

"You don't think I can act?" She tried to sound offended, but didn't quite pull it off, she thought.

"Let's just say I don't want to have worry who my pecker gets close to."

She nearly choked.

As he walked out, smiling, she caught her breath and felt that frisson again. Just as she had felt when he'd quoted Wordsworth from memory.

This time, it lasted until long after he'd gone.

* * *

These women deserved Oscars, every one of them.

Connor had spent a frustrating day smashing ATMs for cash and burgling warehouses for everything from auto parts to beer. The Gargoyles hadn't even changed form to commit the crimes—they'd just pulled ski masks over their faces like common thugs.

The worst thing was, Connor hadn't learned a thing about the structure or leadership of the Minnesota clan of Gargoyles, where their headquarters were, or even how many of them there were. Every question he'd asked had been dodged.

After his rotten day, the ladies' performance was sheer joy to watch.

They moped around the dinner table, serving and cleaning and looking sadder and more distressed than in the four days Connor had been there combined. They coughed and scratched and massaged their temples as if their heads ached. So far, the ever-observant Gargoyles of Minnesota hadn't noticed, but the crowning moment was yet to come.

Jackson's fork went still over his potato casserole. "Do I smell something burning?"

Hard Case turned his shaved head toward the kitchen door and nearly spilled his beer. "Is that smoke?"

Twelve chairs scraped back from the table. In the kitchen, the youngest of the women, Theresa, lay sprawled on the tile floor. Her eyes were closed and her face was bright red. The milk she'd been boiling for some creamy dessert ran over the edges of the pot to hiss and steam on the stovetop.

Connor pushed his way to the front and knelt beside the girl, the back of his hand pressed to her forehead. "She's burning up."

The other women huddled in a corner.

"What's wrong with her?" the wiry man named Benson asked.

Geez, how stupid were these guys? Couldn't they see what was right in front of them? He was going to have to help them a little.

"I'm not sure." He checked her carotid pulse, lifted one eyelid and watched her pupil constrict perfectly normally. "But she's in bad shape. We'd better get her— Uh-oh."

"What?" Jackson asked.

Connor was most worried about Jackson. He wasn't nearly as dumb as the rest. If he bought it, the others should follow right along.

Running his finger along a line parallel to the girl's forearm without actually touching her, he pointed out the blistered, puffy skin. "Look at this."

"Aw, let's carry her downstairs and get on with dinner." Hard Case stepped forward. He reached for Theresa.

"I wouldn't do that if I were you," Connor warned.

"Why the hell not?"

"You have no idea what that could be. What if it's contagious?"

"Contagious?" As a group, they took a step back.

"Hell, it's just a rash." Benson didn't move any closer though, Connor noticed.

It was a turning point of sorts. Success or failure hung in the balance of the next few seconds.

Jaina, who'd apparently been here long enough for

her blond roots to grow out an inch, giving her a two-tone look, stepped out of the group in the corner. She coughed once and showed them her arm. "I've got it, too."

"And me," another piped up timidly.

"And me."

"Me."

All but Mara and one other girl—a nice touch to not make the outbreak appear too staged.

Jaina put on a stricken expression. "Is it serious? Are we gonna . . . die, or something?"

"Let's not get carried away here," Connor said, even though getting carried away was exactly what he hoped the Gargoyles would do.

Jackson leaned over Theresa. "Maybe we should get a doctor."

Connor's heart kicked. "And tell him what? That the slave women we hold captive in our basement have a rash?"

"All right, bad idea." He actually looked concerned. Connor hadn't expected *that* out of anyone in this group. "But she really doesn't look good."

He looked up at his new boss, of sorts. "We need to get her upstairs and into a bed."

"Oh, no." Benson issued the ultimatum. "No way you're taking any of them upstairs."

Connor cursed outwardly and smiled inside. "All right. Downstairs then. But we need to get her out of the kitchen."

"I'm not carrying her."

"Me neither."

"Make the girls carry her."

In the end, that seemed the best solution. Connor

put up a token protest, but he didn't want to give his brethren any reason to suspect he could have also been infected. The last thing he needed was to be quarantined. Then he'd never find out what he needed to know so he could get out of there.

Four of the women hefted Theresa up and carted her down the stairs, leaving only Mara in the kitchen with the men.

"Her, too," Devlin said.

The hair on Connor's neck stood on end. "No way."

"You said yourself, man. No way to know what they got."

"Mara hasn't been in the basement with them. She hasn't got it."

"How do we know that?"

He reached out to Mara's arm and pulled her toward the men. She cowered from him, exactly as she was supposed to, and then complied with her head hanging.

He pushed up the sleeves of her blouse, turned her head back and forth, showing them each side of her neck.

"That ain't nothin' man. How do we really know?"

Connor took in a deep breath. "Lift up your shirt," he ordered Mara.

She looked at him with such suffering that he almost couldn't do it. But he had to. They had to sell this. He needed an ally here. She was all he had.

All he *wanted*, he realized, and that alone nearly made him send her to the basement with the others.

He gritted his teeth. "Do it."

Slowly she pulled the hem of her blouse out of her slacks, lifted it to her shoulders. The plain white bra looked as sexy as black satin and lace on her. Despite his attempts to keep his distance from Mara, emotionally and physically, he'd found himself drawn to her more and more these last few days.

She was an obligation, he reminded himself, nothing more. Not an ally and certainly not a friend. But she was a woman and he was *Les Gargouillen*, driven to procreate. He couldn't help but be attracted to her.

His breath deepened at the sight of her. "Turn," he ordered.

She made a slow circle. He could feel embarrassment shimmering off of her, and caught himself reaching for her mind to console her. Ruthlessly, he cut off the mental connection before it had a chance to form.

"Pants, too," Devlin said. Connor suspected he wasn't worried about finding a rash. The man just wanted to see her legs.

Connor wavered a moment, undecided which way to play it, then looked the big man in the eye. "If she's infected, I'll bring her back down. You think I want to catch this thing?"

There was some grumbling and some posturing, but in the end he won out. He took Mara's hand and led her up the stairs, ears straining to listen with interest as Jackson explained to Devlin that he'd be going out tonight.

In the room, Mara closed the door and gave Connor a high five. "We did it!" Her squeal was quiet enough that it wouldn't be overheard, yet exuberant enough to make Connor smile.

"They won't be bothering those girls for a while."

"They might be locked up, but at last they're safe."

"How did you make Theresa's face so red?"

"Steamed towels."

He almost howled with laughter. "Perfect."

"Did you see how Benson was holding himself? Like he thought his penis was going rot and fall off any second."

"Men are very protective of that particular appendage."

He regretted the comment as soon as he said it. This was not a direction in which he wanted to take the conversation. He'd been having enough trouble keeping his mind on his mission lately without having to discuss penises.

"Thank you," she said. Her amber eyes shone.

Connor experienced the pleasant sensation of the slow southerly flow of blood in his body. He eased her toward him by her elbows. "You pulled it together. You were great."

"It was your idea." She tipped her head up, inched closer.

"Let's take joint credit," he breathed an instant before his mouth settled over hers.

This time there was none of the showmanship, none of the gamesmanship of their first kiss. It was slow, and hot, and wet. Sometimes deep and sometimes shallow, like nibbling a delicacy. One that he would have liked to taste a lot more of, but forced himself to pull away from.

The beast inside him was already restless. He was in a constant state of agitation, cut off from his home, his real brethren, the life he'd built in Chicago. Sharing a room with Mara was like waving a steak in front of a hungry dog just beyond the reach of its chain.

If he wasn't careful, his beast would break its tether.

Gently he eased her away from him and rested his chin on the top of her head.

"What are you?" she asked against his shoulder.

His heart tripped. She couldn't know about him. About the Gargoyles.

"What do you mean?" he countered.

She lifted her head and looked up at him somberly. "FBI? ATF? Local heat?" She squeezed his biceps. "No, you're not local. You're in too deep for that. God, you're not CIA, are you? Or one of those secret agencies?"

He felt as if someone was pumping helium into his chest: lighter. "You think I'm a cop?"

"You aren't one of them. You can't be. You aren't like them. You're undercover, right? I could help you. You need some backup in here."

His back stiffened. "No. No backup. This isn't your concern."

"Not my concern? Those creeps kidnapped me, and you're telling me to stay out of it?"

"I don't need your help." She was a human, for chrissakes. A woman. She had no business taking on *Les Gargouillen.*

She peered at him out of incredulous eyes. "You don't think I can handle myself."

"I didn't say that."

"I'm a lot tougher than I look, mister." She stabbed his chest with her forefinger. "I've taken everything these goons have dished out, and more. I told you, I—"

"You killed a man. I remember." He grabbed her wrist to prevent further bruising to his ribs, and lowered his voice. "How did you end up here, Mara?"

Her shoulders sagged and her puffed-up chest deflated. "I—I answered a job ad in a Duluth newspaper. The description said it was the perfect job for unattached single women who were free to travel. See the world. Good pay. No degree necessary, just a nice smile and good people skills. It sounded too good to be true."

"Turned out it was, huh?"

"There were a lot of questions on the application about family and other kinds of ties—property, businesses. I think they were trying to make sure no one would come looking for us once they took us. When I was hired, they had me pack up all my stuff and put it in storage in a warehouse they owned. They said I wouldn't need an apartment. They would put me up in four-star hotels wherever I went. Next thing I knew, they gave me a drink to toast my new career, and I got really sleepy. I woke up here. In the basement."

She shrugged, but her gaze hedged away from him. He got the feeling there was more to the story—she was too smart to fall for a scheme like that—but he didn't press her.

Finally she brought her eyes back to his, and her lashes were wet. "When I was seventeen, I swore I'd never be a victim again. I won't give in. Not to one sick man. Not to the unjust punishment of the system that was supposed to protect kids like me. Not to a group of wackos who think women are objects to be sold or traded for profit and pleasure. Not even to you."

She lowered her gaze a moment before continuing. "I might have fallen into these guys' trap, Connor, but I'm not helpless. As long as I'm alive, I have to fight back. It's in my nature."

For the first time in all his ten incarnations, the

knowledge that the human race had changed struck Connor with abject clarity. The species had grown stronger, more capable of protecting themselves. Especially the female gender.

So where did that leave him, and those like him?

Outdated, perhaps. Useless remnants of another time to be displayed in museums, or simply thrown away like horse-drawn carriages, steam engines, and eight-track tape players.

Maybe Nathan was right, and it was time for their people to change.

Or maybe *Les Gargouillen* of Minnesota were right, and it was time they quit catering to the ungrateful humans and took their due from the world.

Connor's mood darkened at the thought. Perhaps there was no place in the modern world for traditionalists like him, but he had a purpose here, today. He'd be damned if he'd shirk it. Or if he'd allow Mara to risk herself by helping him more than she already had.

He pushed her away a bit more roughly than he'd meant to.

"We'd better get some sleep," he said, although he didn't really expect to rest tonight.

Two days later, Mara stretched and rubbed her face contentedly on the pillow. She wasn't sure what had woken her—morning was still hours away—but she was content to just lie there in safety and peace. This wasn't a place or a situation in which she could ever say she was happy, but she felt . . . lighter than she had in days.

Seven days, to be exact. Since Connor had arrived.

They'd settled into a routine that almost felt comfortable. Her days were busy. With the other women quarantined in the basement, she handled meals for them and the men by herself. The few free moments she found during the day, she spent in her room—Connor's room—reading Wordsworth.

Connor usually left with Hard Case, or Baldy, as she preferred, and Benson after breakfast. He came back tired and unsatisfied in time for dinner. When she asked where he'd been, he'd grumbled something about "milk runs" and changed the topic. She suspected that meant they were only letting him participate in the busywork. They didn't trust him enough to let him in on the important operations.

Which meant he was no closer to breaking his case, or whatever his goal was. And she was no closer to getting out of there, or finding Angela.

Her eyes adjusted gradually to the dark, and she scanned the dark shapes in the room—the desk, the nightstand, with Wordsworth sitting open, the space on the floor where Connor had been sleeping. That was vacant now.

The click of the closing door had woken her, she realized. At least she thought that's what it had been. She rolled out of bed in the oversize T-shirt that fell to her knees and cracked the door to peek out.

No sign of him.

She should probably close the door and go back to bed, she realized. His business was his business. He'd made it clear he didn't intend to let her in on his plans.

Which was exactly why she wanted to follow him so badly.

Indecision held her in place for a moment, then she

made up her mind and rose to dress in the dark. If Connor was snooping into the group's business, he might dig up information on Angela. This might be Mara's best chance to find her friend.

Or maybe she was just desperate to know more about Connor. She was totally at his mercy now. It was only natural for her to be intrigued by him.

Besides, she wasn't out of this yet. She couldn't put her life—or Angela's—in the hands of a man who wouldn't even tell her who he really was or why he was here.

Her mind set, she slipped out of the room and closed the door silently behind her.

SIX

The best part of the old YMCA that was serving as home base for the Chicago congregation of Gargoyles while St. Michael's was being rebuilt was the atrium over what used to be the swimming area. The pool was long dry, but the stars shone through the glass ceiling, and with the windows cranked open, it was almost like being outside. The only exception was that Teryn could perform his rituals without having to worry about frostbite, as he had when he'd held the ceremonies on the roof of one of St. Michael's towers. The atrium provided access to nature, to the elements he needed, yet was much more comfortable. It was private enough that he wasn't likely to interrupted, especially at this hour of the night.

If only he'd had time to set up a new covey of pigeons, the place would have been perfect. As it was, it would more than do.

Teryn straightened his shoulders, breaking into a

smile at the sight of Rachel and Nathan walking into the poolside area. In Nathan's last incarnation, the body that had housed Nathan's soul at the time had fathered Teryn. Nathan was his *paytreán*. They shared a special bond. Having him back in the congregation during this time of crisis, after a long separation over Nathan's ideals, lightened a measure of the load that threatened to bow Teryn to the breaking point.

Now he had Rachel, too, and what a gift she was. Not only was she strong in spirit and body, but she was a first-generation daughter of one of the Old Ones, the original twenty-eight Gargoyles of Rouen. Female or not, the old magic ran strong in her. Her mind was untrained, but she'd made tremendous progress in shaping her natural gifts, gifts no daughter of later generations possessed.

He approached each day anticipating seeing what new lesson she had learned. What Gargoyle skills she had gained. Who knew how far she could go? Already she'd made great progress toward mastering the pagan rites—something most of his people had forgoten generations ago.

Wearing white robes with simple black cord belts identical to his, the three of them knelt on the throw rugs he'd placed on the points of a triangle within the ritual circle he'd already drawn. Each of them lowered themselves to the pillows, facing the center, and sat back on their heels. Candlelight flickered from fat wax pillars around the edge of the circle.

"Have the visions shown you any more about who is behind the darkness that plagues us?" Nathan asked.

One thousand years ago, a priest named Romanus told the men of Rouen he would end the reign of terror the dragon Gargouille held over their town if they would promise to convert from their pagan ways to Christianity in exchange. Desperate to rid their town of the death and destruction Gargouille caused, they agreed.

But Romanus tricked them. Instead of killing the dragon himself, he used their own magic, their pagan magic, to draw the souls of the beasts of the forest, the seas, and the sky into their bodies. He proclaimed that this new army would protect human life from now until the end of days, and that they should procreate and populate all the lands.

Despite Romanus's treachery, the people of Rouen kept their promise. They gave up pagan magic.

Until recently.

Nathan and Teryn had searched the ancient texts of their people to relearn the old ways. They'd studied for years and the deities had granted them many gifts, including the gift of foresight. But the visions were symbolic, not literal. They weren't always easy to interpret.

For some time, Teryn had been seeing the spread of some great evil from the east. It had crept closer at an alarming rate, finally splitting to the north and south until it surrounded the Chicago congregation on three sides. Yet he hadn't been able to sense who, or what, was behind the evil, or their intent.

"I've seen only that it grows stronger with each day," Teryn told his *paytreán*, "though I have noticed a tiny fracture in its power source. I'm hoping that's Connor's work, and that he's making progress."

"Then let's hope his work continues."

"It will. Though his path will not be easy, nor is the end of his journey certain. I have seen that much. But that's not why we're here today." He smiled at Rachel. "Today we welcome a new novice to the circle. She has completed her initiation, studied the texts, and made sufficient progress in the ways of the Old Ones to begin to seek her own visions."

Rachel inclined her head. "Thank you for being such a good instructor, wise one."

"We begin." Teryn unfolded the cloth next to the stone jugs of water and wine beside him, and held up each object inside the cloth in its turn: chalice, bowl, feather, and pouch of salt. He placed each in its place inside the circle.

Next he called on the four quarters: north, spirit of the earth; south, spirit of fire; and east, then west.

A breeze picked up through the open windows. The cement floor rippled like a living thing and the glass walls hummed with energy. Magic flowed the through the atrium, through Teryn and Rachel and Nathan. It crackled and sparked around them as if the air carried an electrical charge.

He let the awe of it, the sensation, pour through him, and then turned to Rachel. "What is it you wish to see?"

"My brother."

Rachel's parents had been killed when she was a child. She and her brother had been separated, adopted separately. She'd been searching for him ever since, and now Teryn and Nathan were committed to aid her search. Like Rachel, her brother carried the blood of an Old One. If he could be found, he would be a powerful ally against the evil that threatened their people.

Teryn poured the wine into the chalice and the water into the stone bowl, then picked up his last token—

a blackened bit of lapis lazuli. The stone was the single original piece of his ritual set that he'd recovered from the ruins of St. Michael's.

He placed the rock in the bowl of water. "Oh God and Goddess, lend us your eyes that we may see that which we seek."

Next he pulled his ceremonial dagger from its sheath at his waist, took Rachel's hand, and pressed the tip to her finger, opening a small wound. He held her hand over one of the bowls and squeezed a single drop of blood into the water. "Blood seeks blood. Let that which was lost be found."

"Let that which was lost be found," Rachel and Nathan repeated. They joined hands to strengthen the circle.

Ripples formed in the bowl of water, then it began to shake. The God and Goddess were generous tonight, for the vision began.

Mara crept down the stairs to the main floor of the farmhouse questioning her sanity, but determined to forge ahead. She would not be left cowering in the bedroom while Connor played hero. Not when her life—and Angela's—was at stake. He needed her, damn it, whether he wanted to admit it or not.

And she needed him, though she surely wasn't going to admit it any more than he was.

At the bottom of the stairs, she took a tentative step into the alcove, only to find herself snapped to her right by a firm hand on her wrist. Another hand clamped over her mouth, and her back pressed against the warmth of a hard male body.

"Shh," Connor whispered at her ear.

When she nodded, he pulled his hand from her mouth and turned her to face him.

"Are you trying to scare the life out of me?" she asked.

"What are you doing down here?"

"Looking for you. What are *you* doing down here?"

"Go back upstairs."

"No." She glanced behind him at the door to Jackson's office, then at the lock pick in his hand.

Even in the gang-infested slums of south L.A., two plus two always equaled four.

Mara leaned against the wall and cocked one hip out. "Planning to search the office? I'll wait out here and watch your back."

"My back is just fine," he hissed.

"All the same, I'll just hang out here." She motioned toward the closed door. "Go ahead. Go on in."

Crossing her arms over her chest, she waited. He dragged a hand through his hair as if he planned to pull it out by the roots.

"Unless of course you can't get the door unlocked," she whispered cheekily. "In which case I might be of some assistance."

A long moment passed with no response.

"Do you want my help or not?"

"I want you to go upstairs."

She lurched to a straight stance, grabbed the lock pick out of his hand, and clucked quietly in disgust. "Men. Jesus."

Bending down in front of the door, she popped the lock in under ten seconds. "Would it kill you to admit you need help once in a while?" She stood aside while he marched into the room without a glance her way. "I'll watch for any sign of life upstairs."

He grunted, but she couldn't tell if the sound was an affirmative or negative.

"Don't bother," he clarified. "They're all gone except for Dwyer, and he drank himself into a stupor hours ago."

"Gone where?"

"Out. Who knows? Some big mission." From the bitter tone in his voice, she guessed he was a little peeved at not being invited along on the big mission.

Mara was glad he hadn't gone. She didn't know what the goons were up to, but it couldn't be good. Besides, it gave her and Connor free rein to snoop. "Let's have at it, then."

Connor pointed at the filing cabinets on either side of the desk. "You take the left, I'll take the right."

She bit her lip, thinking. "If you find anything with the name Angela Cordoza on it, let me know."

"Who is she?"

"A friend," she said softly, swamped anew by the pain of Angela's loss.

"A friend who just happened to be kidnapped by the same people who took you?"

Mara's shoulders tensed. "Maybe she saw the same job ad."

He narrowed his eyes at her. "Or maybe she answered first, you found out what happened to her, and responded on some kind of kamikaze rescue mission."

He scowled, apparently reading the truth in her expression. "Of all the stupid—"

Her gaze snapped up to his. "Since when is helping a friend stupid?"

"Since it landed you in a cell in the basement of a house full of lunatics!" He raked a hand through his hair.

"Then exactly what are you doing here, Connor? And don't tell me you just like playing house with the goon squad. I know better."

He glared at her silently. His throat worked, but he offered no explanation, damn him.

Her eyes teared. She wanted to tell him about Angela. Her friend's funny laugh, the way she loved anagrams. The will to live that had saved her life after her abusive husband fractured her skill with a brick. The gumption she'd shown in escaping him and starting her life over.

But she'd be damned if she was going to spill her guts first. If Connor wanted to know her secrets, he could share a few of his own. She'd shown him nothing but loyalty, and still he didn't trust her. That fact added a new layer of hurt to the ache she'd suffered since Angela had disappeared from the women's shelter Mara ran.

Quickly she wiped her eyes and put a damper on the pain. Opening the file drawer, she got to work. Avoiding her gaze, Connor pulled a small penlight from his pocket and followed her lead.

Twenty minutes later, she had to concede defeat. Apparently goons were not big on record keeping. Connor had scribbled down a few addresses in Duluth from old FedEx shipping labels, but neither of them had found any reference to Angela. The list of names and dates Mara had picked up the other night, but hadn't had time to look all the way through, was nowhere to be found.

"We haven't checked the computer," she suggested. "Maybe there's something in his e-mail."

Connor booted up the machine, but it had been password protected since her last little break-in. Another dead end.

While Connor shut the PC down and put the office back in order exactly the way it had been when they'd come in, Mara stood at the window rubbing her neck and staring out into the night.

What next? If the goon squad didn't trust Connor enough to let him in on what was going on, and if there were no clues in the farmhouse, how would they ever end this ordeal? How would they escape?

The women couldn't be locked in the basement, pretending to be sick, forever. Time was running out, and with every tick of the clock, her chances of finding Angela grew slimmer.

Sighing, she started to turn from the window, but a movement outside caught her attention. There it was again, something near the end of the drive. Several somethings. Dark shapes moving swiftly toward the house.

"Connor—"

"Just a minute. I'm almost done."

She wanted to grab him, make him look. Call him, at least. But she couldn't move, couldn't speak. Her breath was locked in her chest. Even her heart felt as if it had quit beating.

The dark shapes had come close enough to distinguish. In the front, what appeared to be a grizzly bear lumbered across the snow. Four wide on either side of him, an assembly of all kinds of queer creatures followed on his flank: an ox, some kind of overgrown lizard with spiny ridges down its back, a big cat—panther, maybe—with hooves instead of clawed feet. Others she couldn't even name.

Overhead, a bird with the head and wings of a bald eagle and the body of a horse swooped low to the ground next to a misshapen vulture and a man-sized bat with a forked tail and a rhinoceros horn on its head.

One by one they came to a stop in front of the house, and then, in the blink of an eye, they were men.

Connor materialized beside Mara, followed her gaze out the window and then yanked her to the back of the room, but not before she made out Jackson, Benson, Hard Case, and Devlin kicking at the snow as they walked toward the front porch, laughing and jostling each other with friendly punches.

Mara knew she should move. There was some reason she shouldn't be here when the men—creatures—came through the door, but she couldn't remember what that reason was. Her legs felt like putty and her mind was mush.

Connor dragged her, numb and speechless, out of the office and locked the door behind them. Automatically she turned toward the stairs, but he pulled her back. "No time."

He took her hand in his and pulled her toward the kitchen just as the front door burst open. Devlin stepped inside and scowled. "What're you doing down here?"

"Getting something to eat," Connor answered as if the whole world hadn't just turned upside down.

"This time of night?" Jackson moved past Devlin and threw a casual glance at his office door.

Connor drew a long, heavy-lidded gaze over Mara's body. "Worked up an appetite while you were gone. You hungry? Mara's going to make eggs."

Hard Case pushed through. "I could eat."

Benson followed. The others went upstairs, except for Jackson, who grabbed his keys and mumbled something about an appointment in Duluth. Connor pulled out a chair at the dining room table and made small talk with his buddies.

Ten minutes later, Mara leaned on the kitchen counter cracking shells and dumping whites and yolks into a bowl by rote. Her mind wasn't in the task, but somehow she kept herself together. Kept moving. The fog that held her in a daze gradually cleared, leaving her more flummoxed than ever.

Monsters roamed the plains of Minnesota, and she stood in the kitchen making eggs.

SEVEN

As Nathan walked Rachel back up to their room with the first rays of dawn shining through the YMCA windows, Nathan laced his fingers with hers and pulled her close. "I'm sorry you didn't see everything you wanted to see, but you have to be patient. The deities deliver things in their own time, in their own way."

Rachel let go of his fingers to slide her hand up his arm until their elbows locked, and then leaned her head on his shoulder. "I tried not to get my hopes up tonight, but this . . . this was nothing like what I expected. I don't have a clue what to make of it."

"It will make sense in time. Visions often present information in metaphors."

"Riddles, you mean."

He stopped outside their door and tipped her head up to his with a finger on her chin. "You expected an address and phone number?"

"I don't know. I had hoped for something besides roiling clouds and lightning and gale-force winds. It felt . . . violent." If she were ever to be caught in the vortex of a cyclone, she imagined that was how it would feel. "But what does it mean?"

Nathan opened the door and guided her inside, where he wrapped his arms around her and pulled her flush against his body. "Think about the turbulence Levi must have felt growing up, realizing he was different but having no idea how he came to be that way, or why. I would imagine that could produce some anger in a young man. Some violence."

"God, I can't imagine what he must have gone through."

"The question is, how did he handle it? What kind of person did it make him?"

She pulled her head back to look at her husband. "What are you saying?"

"Just that he isn't the sweet-faced infant you last saw. He's a grown man, one who in all probability has led a very difficult life to this point. You need to prepare yourself for the possibility that he may not be the person you hope he is."

"He's my brother. That's all that matters."

But the seed of doubt had been planted long before tonight. Nathan and Teryn were both worried for Levi, for his very soul, growing up without the guidance of his own kind.

She was worried, too. About Levi and about the vision she'd seen tonight. For as she watched the storm clouds rumble and roil, she'd had the feeling that more than Mother Nature and Levi's emotions were responsible for the tumult.

She'd felt another presence behind the gray mists, stirring them as if to purposely obscure her view.

As if to prevent her from seeing it.

Whoever it had been, he'd been watching her.

Now, as Nathan lay her down on their bed, loosened the belt at her waist and removed her robe, worshipping each inch of skin he uncovered, she felt that presence watching still.

Morning had broken strong, cold and clear by the time Connor followed Mara into the room they shared. He'd no more than closed the door behind them before she whirled on him.

He was ready. He caught her arms by the wrists and held her, waiting for the fury, the fear, to erupt now that they were alone. It didn't take long.

"What the hell were those things? H-how did they do that?"

"Calm down."

"Jackson and Devlin and Hard Case. What are they? Aliens? Some kind of mutants?"

"Calm down."

"My God, they're like some science experiment gone horribly wrong. Pieces and parts of different species put together. Dr. Frankenstein meets Animal Planet."

"Take it easy." He reassured her with more soothing thoughts as well as words. Human minds didn't have the ability to send images, emotion, and intent the way Gargoyles did, but they could receive. They could be influenced.

On those few occasions when humans caught a glimpse of a Gargoyle in the form of the beast, *Les*

Gargouillen used that vulnerability to replace the images stored in their minds with other, less odious scenes. Memories couldn't always be erased entirely, but they could be muddied. People could be made to doubt what they'd seen, which led them to discount the vision as a nightmare, or to attribute it to stress, or fear, adrenaline, or even drugs or alcohol.

After all, who wants to admit, to themselves or anyone else, that they've seen an eagle with a horse's body fly by? Or a giant bat change into a man?

A spirit as indomitable as Mara's wouldn't be easy to misdirect, to confuse. She was as strong-willed as they came, and single-minded in her purpose when she focused on a goal, but Connor couldn't let her go on thinking she'd seen monsters. His mission was at stake.

"How did they do that?" she asked, wide-eyed but in control. The shock was fading and reality, acceptance even, was setting in. He didn't have much time. "Ch-change like that?"

He guided her toward the bed. "Come. Sit down."

"You saw them, didn't you? I know you saw."

Leaving her sitting on the edge of the mattress, twining her hands between her knees, he pulled the bottle of scotch out the desk drawer and poured a double shot. This time, she'd damn sure drink it whether she wanted to or not.

He needn't have worried about her refusing. She took the drink in two shaking hands and downed it in one swallow. A tremor shook her shoulders as she set the glass on the night table, but already she looked calmer.

Good. The more she relaxed, the easier this would be.

He pulled the chair from the desk up beside the bed and cradled both her hands in his to steady her. "What did you see?"

"Monsters. Monsters that change into men."

The images were clear in her mind, vivid in their detail. They wouldn't be easy to overwrite.

"Start from the beginning." Still holding her hands, he stroked her wrists with his thumbs. Her pulse pounded beneath his touch. "You were in Jackson's of- fice. Tell me what you saw."

As she described the scene outside the bay window, he built the image in his mind and focused it at her. Her real memories and his made-up ones wavered side by side as she spoke, then gradually began to merge like two identical transparencies laid one on top of the other.

"The moon was out. It shined on the snow and made everything bright. I could see almost all the way down the hill to the road. I was thinking how beautiful it was, and then . . ."

"Then what?"

This was where it got tricky. Where the two trans- parencies began to differ, and he had to blend them back to one. His.

Along with the mental pictures, he continued to send her feelings of calm. Peacefulness.

Her eyelids began to flag. Gently he eased her back to the bed and lifted her feet to the mattress, then leaned over her. One of his hands still gripped hers. The other smoothed her forehead and trailed gentle touches past her ear, down the line of her jaw.

For such a strong woman, her bone structure was incredibly fine. Almost delicate. He'd thought her attractive before. But now his senses flooded with a whole new awareness of her femininity. The softness of her skin. The sweetness of her scent. The strength of his desire to kiss her, to see if she tasted as sweet as she smelled, shook him.

Now was not the time. This was not the place.

He straightened, opening a few more inches between himself and temptation.

She lifted her head, as if seeking the touch he'd taken away, and then collapsed back onto the pillow. "I saw something move near the end of the driveway. Just shadows, at first. They were too far away to make out. Animals, I thought."

"Deer. A small herd moving across the field." Connor pressed the image, silhouettes of a small band of white tails against the snow, into her consciousness.

Her forehead furrowed. "I thought so at first. But then one of them stood on its hind legs."

"A buck showing off for his does."

Her head rolled from side to side. Her frown deepened. "No. It was heavier. Bigger."

Calm. He fed the emotion directly into her mind. *Peace.*

"A prize buck with a ten-point rack. He's lucky you aren't a hunter."

"No." Her head thrashed. "Maybe . . ."

He pushed deeper into her consciousness to plant the false memory. Her life, her essence surrounded him. He felt the innocence of her childhood, lost at far too young an age. The tough façade she'd built as a young girl growing up on mean streets. The will to survive an unjust incarceration. Her pride, at times bordering arrogance. Her stubbornness. Her passion to make a difference in the world. Her vow to control her own destiny. To never be a victim.

Yet here he was, forcing his will on her. Shame and disgust boiled into a toxic brew in his gut, but what choice did he have?

All he could do was try to make it easier for her. Try not to hurt her. *God, he didn't want to hurt her.*

He put his hands back on her face, then the column of her neck. He caressed her. Aroused her so that she would open her mind to him, let him in deeper.

She turned her cheek into his palm, rubbed against him.

He put an edge on the memory of deer crossing the moonlit field of snow and pushed it deep. Hard.

Her eyes opened. She whimpered.

Cradling her face, he lowered his head and captured the sound with his lips. His mouth locked over hers, tasted, tempted, then retreated with a brush of his cheek over hers. "Shhh. Just a bunch of deer."

She arched off the bed, her head rising, seeking the contact he'd taken away. Her hand curved around the back of his neck and pulled him down. Her mouth fused with his.

Delving into someone's mind always involved a degree of intimacy, but Connor felt as if he were falling. Sinking into her.

Blood rushed below his belt. Ancient magic stirred in his veins. The drive to procreate, to propagate his species, whipped him mercilessly.

He moved to the edge of the bed and his hands slipped down Mara's sides, past the outer curves of her breasts, tantalizing in their softness, to her waist. Pressing her down, he took over the kiss. He plunged and plundered. One arm curved around her back and drug her up to him. Her fingers slipped under the waistband of his jeans and pulled him close.

Control slipped from his grasp like a flag in a windstorm. He wasn't sure he could hold on. Complete his mission. He was too involved. Too attracted. Too damned *awed* by a woman who would put her life on the line to save a friend. When had he met a woman as strong, as loyal, as courageous as Mara Kincaide? Never. And he never would again. Didn't deserve to, if this is how he would treat her.

With one last, desperate reach for sanity, he yanked himself to his feet, away from the bed. Turning his back to her he raked one hand through his hair and tried to calm his heaving chest—and other affected parts of his anatomy.

When he'd regained some measure of composure, he turned around. She scrabbled up the bed, pressed her back to the headboard and drew her knees up to her chest. Her lips were full with that just-kissed look.

She touched them lightly with her fingertips. "Wh-what was that?"

"I believe it's called a kiss. And in a couple of minutes it would have been a hell of a lot more if we hadn't stopped."

"I mean about the deer."

Damn. *Way to go, Rihyad.* He'd gotten so turned on he hadn't been able to finish the job.

Maybe he never really wanted to.

"I was just trying to point out that it was dark. The shadows can play tricks on you—"

"You tried to convince me I don't know what I saw. You tried to confuse me."

"Mara—"

She massaged her temples. "It was like you were inside my head, whispering to me. Making me think I saw deer. What was that?" Her voice took on an edge of fear. "Some kind of hypnosis trick?"

He wished it were so simple. "The tricks are in your own mind—"

"Stop it!" She stood in a jerky movement and paced. "You lied to me, Connor. You said you don't rape women."

"It was just a kiss."

"Physically." She chewed her thumbnail as she walked, her gait gaining speed. "But mentally you were there, in my head. Penetrating my thoughts. Violating my memory. You were inside me in every way *except* for the physical."

He flinched at the truth in her accusations, and hoped she hadn't noticed. "Now you think I'm psychic?"

"Psychic? I don't know. Some kind of telepathic freak . . ."

She stopped and stared at him, her eyes round. Gold flecks swirled in their amber depths. She went so still, he couldn't see her breathing.

He waited, not sure what was happening.

"Freak . . ." she repeated, but in a much smaller voice. "My God, Connor. Are you like them?"

Connor stood motionless as seconds ticked by and the question hung in the air.

Walking away wasn't an option. That left him two choices: he could force her to the floor, pin her down and finish what he'd started, or he could tell her truth. Break the tenets he'd lived by for ten lifetimes. Unleash secrets that would change the world.

Except the world had already changed. His people were changing. He was the only dinosaur stuck in the old ways. Ways that might lead to extinction in the modern world.

Maybe Nathan Cross was right. It was time for a new order. Either Connor evolved for the better, like others in his congregation, or he evolved for the worse, like those of the group here in Minnesota.

Looking at it that way, he didn't see that he had a choice at all.

"No," he finally answered her. "I'm not *like* them. I don't kidnap women or children. I don't rape or steal or murder for pleasure."

He had to pause to swallow the bile that rose in his throat—and a wave of last-minute fear at what he was about to do.

"But I am one of their kind. I am a protector. One of an ancient race called *Les Gargouillen*." He pulled his spine straight, lifted his chin and looked her in the eye. "I am a Gargoyle."

EIGHT

Mara's knees wobbled. Her head went muzzy.

She reached out to the wall to steady herself. She'd never fainted in her life. She wasn't about to start now.

"A-a Gargoyle," she said, hating the breathy sound of her voice. She took a moment to gather her wits, then looked up at him. No fangs, no wings, no hooves. For that, at least, she was thankful. "Like one of those stone waterspout thingies on the sides of big buildings?"

"There was a time when humans revered us. They carved our images on their holiest cathedrals."

He didn't add that that time had passed. She guessed he didn't have to, since she didn't know of a single human who'd even heard of Gargoyles—living, breathing ones—much less revered them.

"Gargoyles." If this was a dream, she was ready to wake up.

When she blinked hard and didn't find herself in her cozy wrought-iron bed in her cozy little apartment, she cautiously pulled her hand off the wall. At least her knees didn't buckle.

"I'd like to go back to the basement now," she told him.

He smiled wanly. Sadly. "You wanted the truth, now you're afraid to hear it?"

"I'm afraid that when the men in the white coats show up to haul you off, they'll make a mistake and take me too."

"I'm not crazy."

"I guess that all depends on your point of view." From where she was standing, he looked like a card-carrying loon.

"You're the one who claims she saw men turn into monsters."

"Actually, the monsters turned into men." But he did have a point.

"Okay, so maybe we should just both admit to being a little nuts and leave it at that."

Was he giving her an easy out? She sighed, wishing she could take it, but she wouldn't be able to live with herself if she did. She'd spend the rest of her life wondering what had happened. What she'd really seen.

"Tempting as it is to take the road-less-painful and pretend I didn't see anything but deer out that window, I have to know the truth."

Know thine enemy, as the saying goes.

Connor took his place on the chair again and gestured toward the bed. She perched on the edge. On the corner. Practically as far away from him as she could get without leaving the room.

"A thousand years ago," he started, "what is now known as Europe was mostly a pagan land. But Christianity swept across the continent like a plague. Communities that had worshipped the God and Goddess—the earth, sea, air, and fire—for centuries, were pressured to convert, yet many held out. Held on to their ways."

"And the Gargoyles fit into this how?" she asked.

He raised an eyebrow as a teacher might to an impertinent student, and continued. "In the village of Rouen, in what is now France, the dragon Gargouille—"

"Gargoyles and dragons?" That nearly did her in. She wasn't sure she could listen to this. And yet she was fascinated.

Connor's eyes turned smoky gray. "Are you going to hear me out or not?"

She settled into a more comfortable position and folded her hands in her lap contritely.

Connor continued in a deep, storybook-reading voice. "Gargouille nearly ruined the village. He sank ships in the harbor, burned crops in the field, and stole infants from their cribs. The people who lived there began to load their wagons to move to new territory. The day before they left, Romanus showed up."

"Was he a good guy or a bad guy?"

"He was a priest. He promised to slay Gargouille if the townspeople would promise to convert to Christianity once the dragon was dead."

"Good guy."

"But Romanus tricked them."

Uh-oh, not so good.

"He called the twenty-eight healthy young men of the village to the hillside above Gargouille's den. They didn't notice until it was too late that they were standing in a ritual circle he had drawn. Romanus betrayed them. He used their own pagan magic to cast a spell on them.

"He called on the beasts of the air, the forest, and the sea, living and extinct, real and mythical. He stole the animals' souls and left their carcasses outside the circle. Then he merged those souls with those of the men."

Mara shuddered at the amalgamation of eagle and horse she'd seen. "In the process, a few of the body parts got mixed up, too, I guess."

"Hush." But Connor squirmed in his chair a bit, too. "He awakened the beasts within the men with a ritual chant and gave them two directives: to protect innocent humans and to procreate, so that the whole world would come to know the power of *Les Gargouillen*. Then he whipped the creatures into a frenzy and sent them after Gargouille."

"So the men themselves killed the dragon, not Romanus."

Connor nodded. "They ripped him apart with their beaks and teeth and claws, and burned his carcass. But they were still bound by their promise to Romanus. They gave up their pagan ways and built a Christian church, where the women of the town hung carved images of them in their honor.

"The species thrived for a while. We learned to control the beasts inside of us and awaken them only when they were needed, but as the years passed, the world changed. *Les Gargouillen* fell out of favor with both religious leadership and the governments of the time. Eventually they were forgotten altogether."

"Yet they still survived."

"And still carried out their mission. For a thousand

years, we've protected the humans who have forsaken us."

She couldn't fathom the irony and the sadness of that. She wasn't ready to face it yet. "So you're like . . . immortal."

He stretched his back and blew out a deep breath. "Not exactly. We die like anyone else. But if we've fulfilled our mission and propagated the species by producing a son, we reincarnate."

Something clicked in Mara's head. It took her a moment to put her finger on it, then she scooted up the bed and pulled the book of poetry from the nightstand. She flipped pages for a while, and then read:

> *Our birth is but a sleep and a forgetting:*
> *The Soul that rises with us, our life's Star,*
> *Hath had elsewhere its setting,*
> *And cometh from afar:*
> *Not in entire forgetfulness,*
> *And not in utter nakedness,*
> *But trailing clouds of glory do we come*
> *From God, who is our home*

Mara looked up at Connor, who smiled. "How did he know?"

"Truth like that only comes from firsthand experience."

"No." She closed the book and set it down quickly as if she were scared to touch it. "Wordsworth was . . . a Gargoyle?"

"We don't live in caves, Mara. We go to school and hold jobs and have lives."

"And protect people."

"When we can. We don't have much choice, really. The magic makes it almost a compulsion."

She frowned. "But these men—*Gargoyles*—here hurt people. How is that?"

"I'm not sure. Some of my congregation think that Romanus's spell is finally weakening, after a thousand years. Others think they may have gone insane. Reincarnating, having to start life over time after time, is tough on the psyche."

"What do you think?"

He hesitated, then spoke sincerely. "I think some beings are just evil. Even some Gargoyles."

She could buy that. She certainly believed it was true of humans. Why not Gargoyles, too?

A long silence passed between Mara and Connor. Mara didn't know what else to say.

"What are you thinking?" he finally asked.

"What am I supposed to think? It still sounds crazy." So crazy that no one could have made up a story like that. So crazy that it had to be true.

"You don't believe me?"

"I didn't say that."

He stood. "Would you like a demonstration?"

Mara flew backward across the bed and plastered her shoulder blades to the wall. "No!"

"If I were going to hurt you Mara, I would have done it long ago."

The softness in his voice eased her panic back a notch. The hurt in his eyes almost erased it completely. Almost. "I'm sorry," she said.

He fiddled with the shade on the desk lamp. "It's all right. After a thousand years, I've gotten used to that reaction."

She edged her way back down the bed and sat cross-legged. "Can you become anything you want?"

"No. A Gargoyle is given only one beast form when his soul is created. The form follows him from lifetime to lifetime."

"What are you? When you change, I mean."

"An ancient flying creature. To you I would most resemble a pterodactyl, I suppose."

"A dinosaur?"

He shrugged. "Fitting, huh?"

"Show me," she blurted out, hardly believing she'd uttered the words.

He let go of the lampshade and let his hands fall to his sides. His blue eyes blazed with intensity. "Are you sure?"

"Do it quick, before I change my mind."

She didn't have to ask again. Connor closed his eyes. He flexed his fingers and the muscles of his shoulders went slack. His lips moved. He spoke, but she wasn't sure she heard the words right. It sounded something like:

E Unri almasama
E Unri almasama

Jackson Firth bowed his head before the great Wizenot and waited for permission to speak. His palms sweated, and he could smell his own fear. The Great One was rumored to be in a foul mood this morning, and he had a reputation for taking his temper out on his underlings.

"You have a new soldier in your ranks," the Wizenot said.

Jackson raised his head and resisted the urge to wipe his palms on the thighs of his slacks. The Great One sat in an upholstered chair on a raised platform reminiscent of a royal throne of old. The room was overly warm and the air laden with cloying incense.

"Yes, Your Holiness," Jackson answered. "He comes from the Chicago congregation."

"Chi-caa-go." He said it like three separate words in a whining, nasal voice. A wolfhound sat at His Grace's right side, and the Wizenot absently stroked the dog's fur with long, gnarled fingers. An eight-foot oak staff with a brass top shaped like a falcon stood in a holder to the his left. "What brings this Chi-caa-go-an to our service?"

"He was excommunicated for his beliefs that *Les Gargouillen* should no longer serve the ungrateful humans, Your Holiness."

"Chi-caa-go is a source of great concern for me, Firth."

"For me as well, Your Grace. It is where we failed in our attempt to kidnap two young recruits. We have not been able to locate the congregation since."

"Do not fear. I have located them for you. In time, we will destroy them, but for now I want to know about this Rihyad. Do you trust him?"

Jackson swallowed hard. "I trust no one, Your Holiness." The Wizenot smiled, and Jackson prayed that meant the staff His Grace used to punish those who displeased him would stay in its stand and he would be leaving with both his kneecaps intact today. "But Rihyad has given us no reason to doubt him yet."

"Test him further. When I call, you will bring him

to me. We will learn once and for all where his loyalties lie."

With a wave of a spotted old hand that held the power of ages, Jackson was dismissed. He took his leave with a sigh of relief and a quick prayer of thanks.

His Holiness might be the most powerful Gargoyle in the world, but as far as Jackson was concerned, he was still a crazy old coot.

Mara drew a deep breath and gathered the courage to open her eyes. She had to look. She had to see what Connor really was. If she saw him, then she would be able to write him off as just another monster in a house of monsters. She could stop being grateful to him for saving her. She could stop caring what he thought or wanted or how he felt. She could stop caring about him, period.

Biting her lip, she slowly lifted her eyelids. And nearly screamed.

Where a moment ago Connor Rihyad had stood, a two-hundred-plus-pound bird—flying creature, rather—stretched its wings as far as it was able in the narrow room. It craned its long, thin neck around and watched her through eyes dark as obsidian.

Mara unfolded her legs and took one slow step toward the creature, then another, ready to bolt back to her corner at the slightest provocation. She circled him, tried to find something, anything, remotely human—remotely *Connor*—about the beast before her.

Finding nothing, she reached out and touched the

leathery skin at the base of his neck. A heart beat double time beneath the bony breast.

"Can you hear me?" she asked. "Can you understand?"

His head bobbed up and down once, and he made a clicking noise with his beak.

Curiosity dulled the edge of her fear. She stroked her fingertips over the joint of wing and back, traced the slender bones of his wing to its tip. "What's it like, flying without an airplane?"

Almost immediately the room seemed to shift beneath her feet. The walls faded to sky blue and wisps of clouds brushed by on either side of her.

He gave her this image, she realized, the same way he'd tried to make her see deer through the window. Only this time, he wasn't forcing it. The image floated by gently, there for her to see or to look past.

She chose to see. And to feel. The wind on her face. The sun on her back. The incredible freedom of gliding on a thermal draft, far above the travails of the earthbound.

As abruptly as the vision began, it disappeared. She was back in the stark little room, her feet planted firmly on the hardwood floor.

Only now she moved confidently around Connor, soaking in every detail, every texture. She touched his smooth beak, the bony ridge that bulged from the center of his forehead and sloped back to a point.

A million questions she wasn't ready to ask zinged through her mind. How did it feel to change from human to beast? Did it hurt? How far could he fly? How high and how fast? Had he been born with the ability to shape shift, or had it developed later?

For now, she would satisfy herself with the physical. The sight of deadly looking talons scraping the wood floor. The feel of veins bulging beneath leathery black skin. The twitch of a spiked tail.

Her hands were everywhere, assessing, measuring, memorizing, until his tail thumped more forcefully, and in the time it takes to skip one heartbeat, Connor became human again, and swiped her wrist into a bruising grip.

"Stop," he said. His eyes dilated and his nostrils flared. For a moment, he looked so angry that she thought he might strike her.

Carefully she eased her arm from his grip. "What's wrong?"

"You may only see the beast, but the man is still inside, hearing, thinking. Feeling."

Feeling. She understood. The way she'd been touching him. . . . He wasn't angry.

He was aroused.

Heat rushed up her neck to settle in her cheeks.

"Thanks to Romanus's damned curse, it's hard enough to keep our sex drives in check in human form. Once the beast is Awakened—" He shook his head. "A few billion years of primitive instinct is hard to shut off."

"I'm sorry."

"Forget it."

He rolled his head around his neck as if he had a kink, which she suspected he did. Only it wasn't in his neck.

"Are you convinced now?" he asked.

"Of what?"

"That I told you the truth."

Dragons and pagan magic. In her frenzy of exploration, she'd almost forgotten, but the story came crashing back.

She nodded.

"And? Where do we go from here?"

"I don't know."

Any sane woman would run screaming from the room, that much she did know. Yet some morbid fascination—or a death wish—held Mara in place. She'd always been one to ride the biggest roller coaster, face the meanest bully, tackle the toughest job—just to prove she could.

She'd always had a compulsive need to test herself, and Connor Rihyad was one helluva test. The question was, did she really want to pass this one?

"I need some time," she said. "I don't think it's really sunk in yet."

She'd thought that after she saw him in his other form, she would be sickened by him. She would be able to fear him, even hate him:

She'd thought she would be able to walk away from him.

But when she turned and hurried out of the room without looking back, it wasn't because she was repulsed by him.

It was because she wasn't.

NINE

Connor had just polished off his third cold beer when he heard Mara come up the basement steps after delivering supper to the women downstairs. From his place on the couch, he banked the empty bottle off the wall and sunk it into the plastic trash can in the corner with a satisfying clank.

"Hey!" Benson dropped his spindly legs off the coffee table and sat up. "You almost hit the TV."

Connor gave him the finger. "Up yours."

"Man, what is wrong with you?" Benson moved to a chair on the other side of the room.

It had taken them nearly eight hours, but his brothers-in-arms had finally noticed his foul mood. With each passing minute, it got fouler.

Mara hadn't said a word to him since she'd walked out on him this morning. She'd spent the better part of the day in the basement, supposedly "caring for" the sick women.

Only he knew she'd been hiding. From him.

He had no idea what she was thinking. How she felt.

What had he been thinking, Awakening the beast in front of her?

Nathan Cross was wrong, thinking that women could accept what they were. He only believed what he did because of Rachel, but she was different. She was one of them—as much as any female could be. Her father had been a Gargoyle. One of the Old Ones. The only other girl who knew about the Gargoyles was too young to know any better. They were unique cases. Exceptions.

No normal woman was going to accept them for what they were. Accept *him*. Even Mara Kincaide. Especially Mara Kincaide, with the past abuse she'd suffered. He'd been stupid to have thought she would. Stupid and naïve.

And now he was paying the price for it. He felt like he'd been sucker punched when she'd walked out on him. All the air had whooshed out of his chest.

Damn Nathan Cross.

Connor should have forced the altered memories on Mara. He should never have let her walk away with her head full of monsters.

It was a mistake he would correct. Tonight.

He yelled for another beer. Mara brought it out to him and left without a word.

Devlin snickered. "His little girlie friend there ain't looking too friendly tonight. Maybe she's not giving him any more action. That it, Con-man?"

Hard Case lifted his bald head from the *Soldier of Fortune* magazine he'd been reading. "Why should he be any different from the rest of us. Ain't none of us getting any action."

Benson sighed. "Not to mention the head hasn't been cleaned all week."

"Since when are you Mr. Clean?" Connor asked.

"Since we only got one girl to take care of this whole place. Those others are useless."

Devlin nodded. "I say we get rid of 'em. Get us a new batch."

Connor went very still. His day had just gone from bad to worse in a big way. He knew the women couldn't be quarantined forever, but he'd hoped the charade would last a few more days. Long enough for him to get the information he needed and call in the cavalry.

He needed a diversion, and he needed it fast. He figured Devlin could help him out with that. "Maybe if you'd done something besides sit around on your fat ass all day, you wouldn't be so worried about a bunch of sick women."

Devlin sneered. "I didn't see your ass out humping brick today, pretty boy."

"You would've if I didn't have to ask permission before I'm allowed to pick my nose. Man, I'm tired of you pansy faggot wusses. When are we going to get out and cause some real trouble?"

Devlin hefted his oversize frame out of the stuffed chair and stormed across the room, just as Connor had hoped he would. "You calling me a pansy faggot wuss?"

Connor stood toe to toe with him. Maybe a good fight was just what he needed. Work out a little frustration on old Devlin. "You denying it?"

Devlin cocked his fist just as the front door opened. Connor turned to see who was there, and Devlin clocked him. He hit the floor like a two-hundred-pound rock.

"Goddamn it, what's going on here?" Jackson put his arms under Connor's shoulders and lifted him to his feet.

Hard Case grinned. "Well, we were about to have a hell of a fight until you ruined it."

"A fight over what?"

Hard Case turned back to his magazine and flipped a page. "Ah, Rihyad's whining that he's not getting enough street action and Devlin's whining that he's not getting enough woman action."

Jackson strode through the living room toward his office, shaking his head. "Devlin's problem with the women can wait. As for Connor's issue, we'll take care of that tonight. We've got a job."

He stopped at his office door and turned back to face the men in the living room. "Mount up. We leave in an hour."

Forty-five minutes later, Mara slipped quietly into Connor's room and closed the door behind her. He stood near the closet, watching her with hooded eyes. He'd changed into black jeans and a black sweater. The color suited his mood.

"We need to talk," she said.

"I thought we got everything out in the open earlier."

"About the other women. I heard what Devlin said tonight."

He pulled on one dark boot and then the other. "He was just blowing off steam. They'll be okay for a few more days."

He didn't sound convinced. Mara knew she wasn't. "They're restless, too. They're happy the men are leaving them alone, but they want to know what's happening."

They bombarded her with questions every time she went downstairs. Unfortunately, she didn't have any answers.

"They just need to be patient."

"They are. But we need a plan."

"Yeah." He sighed and scrubbed his hands over his face. "I know."

She knew how he felt: frustrated, tired, edgy. The same feelings had churned in her gut all day. They'd led her to one conclusion. "It's time to get them out of here."

"I don't have that kind of magic, Mara. I can't just wave my hand and whisk them off to somewhere warm and sunny."

"But you have friends. A whole congregation of others like you. I know you have some way of communicating with them, or you couldn't have gotten the poison sumac. They can help."

"They can't just storm the house. It would be a bloodbath. You and the others might just get caught in the middle of it."

"Then help *me* get them out."

"You'd never make it. You saw what happened last time. It didn't take them ten minutes to chase everyone down."

"We could plan it for a night when most of you are gone, like tonight, and drug the guard. All you have to do is leave the door unlocked."

"Jackson always checks it before we leave."

"So we unscrew the hinges before you go."

"You've got it all worked out, don't you." He didn't sound like he admired her creative mind.

She took a deep breath and let her pulse settle before she told him the rest. "It's not just the others, Connor. It's time for me to leave, too."

He plopped down on the edge of the bed, his face twisted in a queer expression, as if he didn't know what to say.

She had no words for what she felt, either. She'd done all she could here. She'd asked the other women about Angela, she'd eavesdropped on the men for any clue as to where her friend had been taken. She'd searched Jackson's office to no avail. She wouldn't give up on finding Angela, but she had to try another tack. There was nothing else to do here, nowhere else to look.

And she was in way over her head here with men who could change into monsters at will.

She'd spent the better part of the day replaying the scene with Connor. For the life of her, she couldn't understand why the sight of him in beast form hadn't sent her into a screaming fit of hysteria. The fact that it hadn't, that she accepted the incomprehensible so easily, scared her far more than wings and talons and obsidian eyes.

She needed order in her world, predictability and control over her destiny. Connor represented the unknown, the unknowable. Staying with him, even for a few more days, would be like jumping blindfolded into an abyss. She wasn't ready to make the leap.

"What if I told you I can't let you leave, knowing what you know?" he asked.

She flinched as if she'd touched a hot wire when his words sank in. "I'd say you're not as different from Jackson and his gang as you claim to be."

This time he flinched.

"Who am I going to tell, Connor? The police? You think they're going to send the SWAT team out to hunt flying dinosaurs and giant lizards on my say-so?"

"Are you sure you want to remember?"

Truth be told, she didn't. The things she'd seen in the last few days would haunt her forever. She'd always wonder, when she met a man on the street, if he was really a man.

She'd always be looking for a dinosaur in the sky.

"I've never been one to run from the truth," she said.

"No." He got to his feet and stalked toward her like a big cat on the hunt. Her stopped mere inches from her face and towered over her. "Just from me."

Before she could point out that she wasn't running—hadn't, in fact, retreated an inch—his mouth closed over hers. Given his state of mind, she expected the kiss to be brutal and bruising. Instead it was shockingly sweet. Shockingly erotic.

He brushed her cheek with an evening growth of stubble. Sipped at one corner of her mouth and then the other. In between, his tongue played at the seam. His big hands skimmed up her ribs to her breasts, tracing their outer curves, then glided down to her hips to pull her against the growing bulge behind his fly.

Only when she moaned and rubbed herself against him did he deepen the kiss, tangling his tongue with hers. Heat flared between them. Mara's lungs burned and she had to pull back to grab a short, panting breath.

"What about this truth?" he asked against her cheek. His hands moved back up to her breasts, where his thumbs strummed her nipples into tight peaks. "Are you going to run from this?"

Without waiting for an answer, he slipped a hand between her legs and palmed her mound, pressing on her most sensitive spot with his fingertips. "What about this one? Feel like running now?"

"Bastard," she whispered as she nudged under his chin and nipped at his neck.

"Are you sure you want to leave?" Sparks of pleasure flashed through her body where his fingers pressed against her in rhythmic surges. "Don't you want to stay and find out what it's like to make love to a monster?"

The question hit her like a cold bucket of water. This time when she called him a bastard, she meant it. This whole setup hadn't been about passion, or even seduction.

It had been about punishment.

She thumped her palms flat on his chest and shoved him away. "Maybe you're right," she retorted. "Maybe I'll just run downstairs and see if Hard Case is up for a quick tumble in the sack before I leave. I have a real thing for lizards."

She could see by his reaction that her barb had hit its mark.

Out in the hall, booted feet clomped down the stairs. "Hey, Rihyad, let's go. We're burning moonlight."

Connor cut his gaze away and moved toward the door. "Too late," he said as he turned the knob. "Maybe tomorrow night."

When he was gone, and the lock had clicked shut behind him, Mara collapsed on the bed.

Well, hadn't that *just gone splendidly?*

Where had the plea for escape she'd rehearsed so many times today taken a wrong turn?

Probably about the time she accused him of being as reprehensible as Jackson and his goon squad, she figured. Certainly it was already well off track by the time she suggested she would rather have sex with Hard Case than sleep with Connor.

Her temper had often gotten her into trouble over the years, but lately she'd developed a real flair for letting it egg her into saying exactly the wrong thing at exactly the wrong time.

Now she had no idea where she stood with Connor. He hadn't exactly told her he wouldn't help.

But he hadn't told her would, either.

At least she was pretty sure he wouldn't actively work against her. He wouldn't rat her out to Jackson.

Unfortunately she was almost just as sure he had no intention of giving up on his attempts at seduction. He seemed driven to make her admit that his lust wasn't one-sided. That she was as hungry for him as he seemed to be for her.

She would chalk it up to male ego, except he didn't seem the type. This need of his seemed to be something more. When it wasn't met, it ignited a firestorm of emotion in him that was both powerful and angry. She had a feeling that if they ever did make love, and he unleashed the full force of that passionate fury on her, it would be an experience like none other. She wasn't sure either one of them would survive it.

Fortunately, she had no intention of finding out.

With or without Connor's help, she was getting out of this place, and soon.

Rolling to her belly, she punched the pillow on the bed and molded it into a comfortable shape.

No doubt, she was gone.

Just as soon as she figured out how.

TEN

Hidden behind the tinted windows of Jackson's Toyota SUV, Connor cradled a cup of tepid coffee with two hands and peered at the warehouse in front of him. Truck docks lined the exterior wall from one end to the other, some empty, some occupied by tractor trailer rigs with a variety of logos on their doors.

"What is this place?" he asked.

"A distribution center." Jackson drained his coffee cup, crushed the cardboard container, and put it in a plastic bag on the floorboard. "Semis come in and out of this place all night. Ours should be here any time now."

"Ours?" He didn't like that the rest of the team had been briefed on the plan hours ago, but he was just now getting the information. Waiting until the last minute to make sure he didn't have time to betray them, Connor figured. Just another sign they still didn't trust him. But at least they'd brought him along.

It was obvious from the fact that Jackson himself was here that this was not just another milk run.

Jackson smiled. "The target truck is coming from a company called Street Smart."

"What's it carrying?"

"Guns."

Connor's stomach plummeted. A bunch of renegade Gargoyles roaming the streets was bad enough. A bunch of renegade Gargoyles roaming the streets locked and loaded was a whole other level of disaster waiting to happen.

Mara's stubborn, prideful, beautiful face flashed in his mind.

Damn. He should have gotten her out of the farmhouse long ago. All of the women. At first he'd kept her there for the good of the mission. These last few days, though, pure, unadulterated selfishness blinded him to the reality that he'd held onto her for too long.

He just hoped that his selfishness didn't cost her her life.

Tomorrow he would contact Mikkel, tell him to get the women out by force. Connor's cover would be blown—no avoiding it. The mission would be a failure. His congregation would still be at risk from an enemy they knew little about.

None of that mattered. He wouldn't sacrifice six innocent women for his congregation's safety. His people wouldn't want him to.

Sighing, he let his head fall back against the rest and closed his eyes.

Guns. *Goddamn it.* His people weren't prepared to fight that way. No one in the Chicago congregation owned so much as a pea shooter. Teryn wouldn't allow it.

"Hey you." Jackson elbowed him. "Don't go to sleep on me. The party hasn't even started yet."

"I'm awake." He opened his eyes. "I was just thinking."

"'Bout what?"

"About a time when Gargoyles didn't need guns."

Did Jackson's fingers just tighten on the steering wheel, or had Connor imagined it?

"I know, it sucks," Jackson said. "But the days when we could defeat any enemy hand to hand are long gone. We have to change to survive."

Now he sounded like Nathan in a perverse kind of way.

"And we're breaking the ground on the new world order, huh?" Connor straightened his cramped legs as best he could. "Were you born into this congregation, Jackson, or did you join of your own free will like me?"

"None of us were born here. We were recruited."

"By who?"

"The great Wizenot."

"And where did he come from?" Connor strived to sound casual, thought he'd managed it, but Jackson still didn't answer, so he tried another angle. At this point, any information was good information. "Okay, then why did you join?"

"Because my previous life ended when I was shot by a man I'd just pulled out from under an overturned tractor. He was so scared of me, of what I was, that he didn't even give me a chance to try to explain, much less time to alter his memory."

Connor's chest pinched. He'd heard too many stories like that one. Good Gargoyles, good *men*, murdered by the very people they tried to help.

Jackson smoothed his mustache around the curve of his mouth with a thumb and forefinger. "The life before that, a woman being beaten to death put a butcher knife through my heart for breaking the arm of the husband who was attacking her." He shook his head. "I'm tired of dying for people who don't want my help. This time around, I want to do some living, you know?"

"Yeah, I do," Connor said quietly. He wished he didn't. Empathizing with Jackson made it that much harder to hate him.

Jackson picked up a handheld radio from the center console. "Outpost one, status check."

"Outpost one, condition green. Negative target." Devlin's voice boomed through the static.

"Outpost two, check in."

"Outpost two, condition green. Negative target."

Before Jackson could request status from the next sentry, Benson's voice crackled excitedly over the airwaves. "Post four. Positive target. Repeat, positive target."

Jackson pulled a black ski mask over his head, rolling the part that would cover his face later up on his forehead. "Time to rock and roll."

Connor followed suit and opened the door of the SUV with a sinking feeling. The other places they'd hit had been soft targets. There hadn't been any people around. This place hummed with activity, semis pulling in and out, forklifts beeping, workers shouting. And with a shipment of guns passing through, there were bound to be security guards lurking about.

He had a very bad feeling about this.

Connor and Jackson crossed the road under cover

of shadows and huddled behind a line of barren shrubbery across from the warehouse. Devlin, Dwyer, Hard Case, and Benson joined them, along with several others.

"Remember, we go in from the corners. There are security cameras everywhere, so keep the beasts in check." Jackson rubbed his gloved hands together and then drew a rectangle in the snow. He made dots at each of the front corners and in the middle of the back. "There are armed guards here, here, and here. Devlin, Hard Case, and Dwyer, you take them out. Your partners are your backup. Get their guns and squeeze everyone toward the middle. Don't be afraid to make a little noise. Fire off a few rounds to discourage any would-be heroes in the group. Get everyone down on their bellies and watch them. Everyone else, as soon as the building is secure, move in and get in that truck. We can't take everything, so go for the good stuff—automatics first, then semis. Don't bother with the revolvers. Understand?"

Jackson checked around the circle until everyone nodded, and then motioned them forward. "Rihyad, you're with me."

Connor pulled his ski mask over his face like the others and followed Jackson to the southeast corner of the building along with Dwyer and a younger guy named Pielsen. Jackson held up his radio and spoke quietly, but with authority. "On my mark . . . three, two, one, go."

Like snakes in tall grass, they slithered among pallets stacked with cardboard boxes and shrink-wrapped wooden crates. Dwyer and Pielsen stopped at the end of the row. Dwyer motioned for Connor and Jackson to wait, and then he and Pielsen swung around the corner in tandem to face the guard's chair.

The empty guard's chair.

Pielsen flashed a worried look back at Jackson, who pointed at his eyes and then into the warehouse in the "look for him" order. The two Gargoyles nodded at each other, then crept along the wall and out of sight.

From the other side of the warehouse, shouts echoed from the metal walls. Gunfire pinged off the ceiling.

Behind Jackson, a door flung open. Connor saw that someone had drawn the stick figure indicating a men's restroom in barely visible marker. A gray-haired security guard lunged onto the warehouse floor, reaching for his gun with his belt still unbuckled.

The guard ran right into Jackson. Together they slammed into a wooden crate, which splintered, and then they rolled to the floor, both struggling for the gun.

Connor lurched toward them just as the guard got one hand on a piece of wood from the broken crate and slammed it down into Jackson's shoulder.

Jackson howled and the guard rolled into a crouch, his weapon up and ready.

Connor slammed into him a moment before he pulled the trigger. The shot went wide and the pistol skidded across the cement floor. Connor scrabbled to it, but he couldn't hold onto the guard and pick up the gun. He opted for the gun. The guard spun around and took off down a corridor.

Rubbing his bleeding shoulder, Jackson pointed after him. "Get him!"

Connor raced in the direction the guard had gone. A bell clanged annoyingly, drowning out his footsteps. His errant guard had pulled a fire alarm. Pretty smart for an old guy. Probably a retired cop trying to supplement his pension. Where had he gone?

Connor turned a corner in the corridor in time to see a stairwell door click shut. He yanked it open and took the steps two at a time to the flat roof of the warehouse.

It was quieter up there. And a hell of a lot colder. His breath hung in the air like little thunderclouds. The pebbles on the roof crunched between the soles of his boots as he tried to get a fix on his prey.

Jackson had ordered them to stay in human form, and Connor wouldn't take the risk that there were cameras in place, even up here, but that didn't mean he couldn't rearrange a few of his internal systems to aid his search. He Awakened the beast just enough to heighten his sense of smell, and then sniffed the air.

There it was, to his left. The scent of fear.

He took the metal ladder to the top of one of the huge air-conditioning units and called down to his quarry. "Don't move."

He held the gun out before him for show. The guard raised both hands over his head.

Now that he had his prisoner, what was he going to do with him?

He couldn't let the man escape. His brethren would know he could have easily tracked him if he'd tried.

Neither could he kill an innocent man. They guy looked to be about sixty. He was probably someone's grandfather.

Connor hopped down from his perch. The others would come looking for him soon. He had to do something, and fast. Unpleasant as it was, he only had one option.

He stepped so close to the guard that he could see the beads of sweat trickling down the man's temple despite the cold. "Put your right hand down. Do it!"

When he complied, Connor took all the bullets except one from the gun and tossed them away, then turned the gun around so that he held it by the barrel with the muzzle pointed at himself. He took the man's right hand and wrapped it around the butt, covered by both of his own.

"Shoot me," he ordered.

"Wh-what?"

"Shoot me. Then leave the gun and run like hell. Get to a car fast. You can't escape these guys on foot. Don't tell anyone what happened up here tonight. Not the press, not your bosses—" He squinted at the man's brass name tag. "Charles P. Quincy. Don't tell anyone or I'll come after you. I will find you. You and your family. Now shoot me!"

He positioned the barrel off-center of his thigh, where he prayed the bullet wouldn't break bone or graze the femoral artery, then squeezed the stunned guard's hand for encouragement.

One thing about cops, retired or otherwise: They knew how to follow orders.

Charles P. Quincy put his forefinger through the trigger guard and fired.

ELEVEN

Mara hated not having a clock at her bedside.
They'd taken her watch when she was brought to the
farmhouse. Locked in a little room with no windows,
now she didn't even have the sun and the moon to help
gauge the passing of time.

Was it daylight yet? It seemed like Connor and the
others had been gone more than the span of a single
night. Intuition warned that something was wrong. She
did her best to ignore the feeling and occupied herself
by reading more of William Wordworth's poems.

> *I wandered lonely as a cloud*
> *That floats on high o'er vales and hills,*
> *When all at once I saw a crowd,*
> *A host, of golden daffodils;*
> *Beside the lake, beneath the trees,*
> *Fluttering and dancing in the breeze.*

The inherent contradiction of a Gargoyle poet intrigued her. How could a man with such a horrific nature create such beauty with words?

An electric current sizzled across her skin when she heard the door slam downstairs. Jackson and his crew poured in with their usual smattering of curses and catcalls.

Feet clomped up the stairwell in an uneven gait alongside thuds and scraping sounds, as if they were dragging something heavy.

A key turned in the doorknob and Mara swung her feet over the side of the bed, relieved that Connor had returned despite the tension between them.

But it wasn't Connor who opened the door.

Jackson pushed his way into the room. Behind him, Dwyer and Hard Case supported Connor with his arms across their shoulders. His head lolled and his legs dangled uselessly. A ragged hole pierced his jeans over his left thigh, and a river of crimson running from the wound to his knee was barely visible on the black denim.

"Put him on the bed," Jackson ordered. Mara moved quickly out of the way. The two men dumped Connor unceremoniously. He moaned and turned his head, but otherwise showed no signs of awareness.

Jackson looked at Dwyer and tipped his head toward the door. "Bring some towels and water."

Once his men were gone, Jackson turned to her, his expression flat. "Gunshot, a through-and-through. He lost a lot of blood, but its mostly stopped now."

"He should be in a hospital."

"Doctors have to report gunshot wounds. We can't afford to have the cops out here snooping around." He glanced at Connor's prone form and then back at her. "You're the best he's got."

Panic trilled through her. In her six years running a crisis shelter, she'd patched up a lot of abused women's scrapes and bruises when they didn't want to face the inevitable questions of the doctors and social workers at a hospital, but never anything as serious as a gunshot wound.

Unfortunately, she doubted Jackson cared about her qualifications—or lack thereof.

"I need antiseptic," she said. "Bandages. Antibiotics."

"I'll see what I can do tomorrow." He nodded toward the towels and mixing bowl of water Dwyer carried in and set on the desk. "This is the best I can do tonight."

He turned to leave.

Devlin leaned in the room, sneering. "If he dies, let us know so we can haul his rotten carcass out of here before he stinks up the place."

Blood rushed up Mara's neck and made her head buzz. She wanted to slap the crazy bastard, but she held herself in check. Getting into a fight with Devlin wouldn't help Connor right now.

God help me, she thought as Jackson stepped out the door and the lock snicked in place behind him. She wasn't sure anything could help Connor right now. Least of all, her.

Rachel Cross dreamed of angry black clouds boiling in the sky, thunder rumbling like cannon fire and wind whipping up silver-crested waves. The swells heaved her stomach into her throat with each upward thrust.

The deities had been generous in tonight's ceremony with Nathan and Teryn. They'd shown her the sea, and she knew now she'd find Levi on or near it, she just didn't know which coast.

Nathan told her again to be patient, but she was anxious to find her brother and reunite her family. Even in her dreams she searched for knowledge. Some clue that would help her narrow down his location.

Opening her mind, she let the storm wrap her in its violent cloak. The wind burned her eyes and the spray from the waves chilled her skin. Desperately she scanned the horizon for a point of land, some recognizable feature, but the weather limited the visibility. All she could see were rain and water and clouds.

But the cloud patterns were different in one direction. Instead of bubbling and mushrooming, they seemed to circle around one spot like some kind of vortex. An eye to another world.

Her blood ran cold, and not just from the chill. She sensed a presence on the other side of the eye. Evil. It drew her focus. She couldn't break her gaze away. She struggled. Mewled.

She tore free at last when three loud booms broke the eye's hold on her. The vortex winked closed. The vision vanished. Gasping, Rachel bolted upright in bed, Nathan at her side.

Three more knocks reverberated through the dark bedroom, and she realized someone was pounding on the door.

"Nathan. Come quickly." Teryn's voice.

Nathan clicked on the lamp beside the bed, threw on yesterday's jeans, and padded to the door in his bare feet. Rachel pulled the covers up to her armpits.

"I just got word from Mikkel," Teryn said without preamble when Nathan opened the door. "Connor's been shot."

The muscles in Nathan's back clenched. "Is he alive?"

"We think so. Christian saw them carry him into the farmhouse."

Nathan reached for his shirt and shoes. "I'm on my way."

Even before he pulled an overnight bag out of the closet, Rachel knew he hadn't meant he was on his way to Teryn's office.

Her husband was going to Minnesota.

Mara set the towels on the edge of the bed and moved the water to the nightstand before sitting next to Nathan on the mattress. If he was aware of her presence, he didn't show it.

She laid a palm across his forehead. His skin was cool and damp. Not a good sign. But his pulse seemed strong and his breathing was regular. Hopefully it would stay that way.

With shaking hands she got to work. First she lifted the hem of his sweater, then rolled him to one side and then the other until she was able to work it over his head. His clammy chest was smooth, nearly hairless, but a scar much like the one on his cheek, only bigger, deeper, ran the width of his abdomen. The thick ridge of puckered flesh was too jagged to have been left by a surgeon's scalpel, and she wondered what kind of injury could have done damage like that. Apparently, this wasn't Connor's first brush with death.

The pants were more difficult to remove than the shirt. She shimmied them down his hips inch by inch until he was left wearing only a pair of heather-gray boxer briefs that clung to his anatomy in a way that left little to her imagination.

His genitals weren't the part of his anatomy she was concerned with at the moment, though. Midway down his left thigh, raw flesh gaped through a hole a little bigger than a dime.

That wouldn't be the worst of it. Jackson had said it was a through-and-through, meaning there was an exit wound on the back of his leg. Growing up in Gangland, USA, she knew that bullets made a bigger hole going out than they did going in.

Sure enough, the wound in back was as big as a quarter and still weeping blood and clear fluid. The skin around the edges hung in flaccid strips where it had stretched before it had burst.

Mara tried to study the violation of his body clinically, to evaluate the damage without thinking about the pain, the suffering.

She tried, and failed. Her stomach turned and she had to take three slow, deep breaths to fight back the nausea before she could roll Connor to his right side and place a folded towel between his legs. She poured water over both bullet holes to flush any debris that might be caught in them, then dabbed the skin around the edges dry, careful not to touch the wounds themselves.

When she'd finished, she turned him onto his back again and reached for the bedspread to pull over him.

She jolted in surprise. His eyes were open and focused. On her.

"I'm sorry," he rasped.

"For what?"

"For not getting you out when I still could."

She tucked the covers in around his shoulders, her lips set in a firm line. "You'll have another chance."

He didn't argue, but he didn't agree, either. He swallowed painfully and licked his lips.

"Need some water?"

"Thanks," he said after he'd downed the drink she dipped out of the water bowl for him.

"How are you feeling?" It was probably a stupid question, but she didn't know what else to say.

"Okay for now. But it's going to get a lot worse before it gets better."

"Infection."

He nodded.

"Jackson said he would try to get antibiotics."

Connor scowled. "I wouldn't count on it."

"Can you contact your friends without going out for a jog?"

His eyes narrowed. She shrugged. "I've seen you out by the tree. You had to get the poison sumac from somewhere."

"No," he answered dryly. "Not without alerting Jackson and the others, too. But don't worry, my friends have been watching. They probably already know what's happened. They'll come for you the next time you're left here with just a few guards. After the disaster tonight, it may be a while before Jackson and the rest of them go out on another job, but eventually they'll have to. And when they do, my people will come for you."

"You might not have that long."

"I'm disposable."

Mara's mind rebelled at the thought. Her reaction must have shown on her face, because he shook his head. "I knew that when I took this job. My congregation can't make an all-out assault on the house. We can only spare a few men from Chicago. We can't afford to leave our children unprotected."

Mara blinked. "Children?"

She'd never really thought about Gargoyles as fathers. She wondered if Connor had a son, and knew if he did, that child would be surrounded by a circle of love and protection so fierce a rabid wolf couldn't get past it.

Connor shifted. His face furrowed as though he was in pain, and Mara placed a pillow beneath his knee to elevate his leg.

"Two months ago, two of Jackson's men came to Chicago, to my congregation. They set fire to our home and tried to steal two of our boys in the commotion. Nathan and I were able to stop them, but not before they almost killed me."

"The scar on your stomach?"

He swallowed and nodded. "Devlin's brother."

"What did they want with Gargoyle children?"

"To raise them up in their own images. That's what they wanted with you, too, I suspect."

"What do you mean?"

His eyelids sank to half mast. He was tiring, but he rallied enough to keep talking. "I don't think they're selling the women they take into slavery, Mara. I think they're keeping them for themselves to impregnate and bear them lots of little evil minions. They want power, and they need their membership to grow to get it."

Mara's eyes widened.

Connor chuckled weakly, ironically. "One of the tenets of our civilization, remember? Propagate the species. These guys have just put their own spin on it."

Connor continued as if he needed to get it all out while he still had the strength. "I had hoped to find out where they're keeping the women that came before you, and where their nursery is. But it's too late for that now. My brethren will come for you as soon as they get the opportunity. They'll deal with the guards left behind, then get you out of harm's way. You've got to tell the women to be ready. They'll have to move quickly."

Mara couldn't absorb everything Connor had told her. But she did latch on to a few key points. "But then you'll have sacrificed yourself for nothing. Your congregation will still be in danger. We won't know where the other women are. The babies."

Angela.

Thinking Jackson and his cronies were selling women for profit had been bad enough. Learning that they were using them to further their own evil cause—bringing babies into the world for the sole purpose of gaining power—that just made her plain mad. She couldn't even begin to contemplate the possibility of Connor losing his life to their despicable activities.

"We've still got time, then," she told him. Determination steeled her voice. "I'll find a way to get you some antibiotics. We'll figure out a way to let your friends know you're okay and the mission can continue."

"The women—"

"They can hold on a little longer." She would talk to them, but she was sure they would agree when they understood the stakes. They were a strong group, and they had each other to lean on.

His eyelids drifted shut.

She took his hand and squeezed, hoping he could still hear her. "We can do this if we stick together. We can beat these guys."

"I hope so." His words slurred as he sank slowly into oblivion.

"I know so."

"Tha's my girl." He smiled weakly, and then his breathing fell into the deep, slow rhythm of sleep or unconsciousness.

She couldn't tell which.

TWELVE

*By morning, Connor's condition had worsened ex-*actly as he had predicted. His cheeks flushed with a fever that was so far—thankfully—low grade and his eyes glazed with pain.

After a quick trip downstairs to make breakfast for the beasts and the women, she had hurried back to his side to pour some orange juice down his throat and shove into his mouth a couple of aspirin from a bottle she found at the back of one of the kitchen cabinets.

According to the label, the pain reliever had expired a year ago, but the outdated pills were all she had to give him for now. Jackson had been called to some important meeting in Duluth and wasn't expected back before nightfall.

Mara hoped he would remember his promise to bring supplies and medicine for Connor, but she wasn't counting on him. Just in case he didn't come through, she'd already put Plan B into motion.

First she'd stripped the linens from the men's bedrooms upstairs, washed them, and carried them back up in a basket. Then while the blankets and spreads were washing, she filled a bucket with soapy water and announced she was going to clean the bathrooms.

She got two grunts and a "whatever" in response, which was exactly what she'd hoped for. As long as she was in the house, and working to serve them, they didn't much care about the details.

There was a small bathroom at the end of the hall on the second floor. She set her supplies down where they'd be just visible from the hall, sloshed some suds on the tile floor, and turned on the faucet in the sink.

Then she grabbed the laundry basket and started tying sheets together. It was only ten or twelve feet from the window to the ground below. How hard could it be to climb?

She figured she needed fifteen minutes to get her feet on the ground, drop the note she'd written at the tree, and get back inside. As long as none of the men decided to come upstairs for their morning constitutional during that time, she would be home free.

Everything went according to plan until she made her dash across the hundred feet of open area between the equipment shed and the tree she needed to reach. Twenty-five feet from her goal, the door to the house crashed open. Devlin and Hard Case crashed across the porch and into the snow, rolling and punching and swearing. Dwyer followed them, egging them on, then saw her and yelled. "Hey, you! What the hell do you think you're doing out here?"

Devlin and Hard Case gave up their battle and

stormed after her. With one longing glance at the tree, she let them drag her back inside without protest.

In the living room, the men circled her like sharks building up to a feeding frenzy. "You think you can escape us?"

"No!" she said.

"What were you doing out there?"

"I-I just needed some air. I've been locked in this house for weeks."

Devlin snickered. "Yeah, right. You think just because Rihyad has been treating you like some kind of princess you can get away with anything you want. Well I got news for you, princess. Your boyfriend ain't here to look out for you now."

"Yes, he is."

Mara's head snapped up. Connor stood at the top of the stairs in nothing but a pair of sweatpants, holding onto the handrail as if it were the only thing keeping him upright, which it probably was.

Devlin's lips scrolled into a sneer. "Well, look at you. I thought you died hours ago."

"Sorry to disappoint you." He swayed almost imperceptibly. "Come on, Mara."

Devlin snatched her wrist and held her in place. "I'm not done with her yet."

"Wanna bet? Turn her loose."

"What are you going to do if I don't? Come down here and kick my ass?"

"If I have to."

"You wouldn't make it halfway across the room."

Benson piped up. "I got ten bucks says he would. Devlin would kick the shit out of him once he gets there, but I say he makes it across the room."

"I'll take that action," Hard Case said.

Mara's fingers had gone numb from Devlin's grip on her wrist. She tried to pull away, but he held tight.

Lunatics. They were lunatics every one of them, Connor included. Without Jackson here to keep the peace, they might all just kill each other.

"Better yet," Connor said, "I got five hundred that says I can take him in a real fight when the leg is healed, say in two weeks?"

"Woo-hoo." Dwyer pulled a pad and pencil out of the drawer in the coffee table. "Gentlemen, line up to place your bets."

"Aw, now you're just stalling," Devlin complained.

Connor tilted his chin in challenge. "What's the matter? You scared to take me on when I can actually fight back?"

Devlin kicked the corner of the coffee table, sending a stack of fortune-hunting magazines flying, and let Mara go. "One week. And you just make sure you don't die before then. You don't look so good."

Connor smiled grimly. "I'll do my best."

Mara hurried up the stairs to Connor, who hobbled toward their room leaning on the wall. When they were out of sight of the men, she slipped his arm over her shoulders to help.

"You all right?" he asked, his teeth gritted.

"Yes." Except that she hadn't gotten her message out to his friends. But studying his pale face and the way he was breathing in short pants, that was the least of her worries.

"You?" she asked.

"Hell, no."

He just barely made it to the bed before he collapsed.

* * *

Jackson stood stock still while white-hot flares of pain exploded behind his eyes, and his legs burned where the great Wizenot had rapped his staff against Jackson's shins in a home-run swing. Any show of pain, any reaction at all would only earn him another blow.

"Twice you've disappointed me, Jackson. Once in Chi-caa-go when you failed to bring me the children of the congregation there and now here in Minnesota, where you can't even pull off a simple robbery. And where are the women you took last month? Why haven't they been delivered to the infirmary yet? You've had plenty of time to impregnate them."

"They are sick, Your Grace."

"Sick? You fool. We'll see if they are sick. Bring them to me when next you come."

"Yes, Your Grace. I won't let you down. Anything else you want just tell me and it's yours." Apologies weren't welcome in the Wizenot's hall. They were considered a sign of weakness. Only promises of fealty held any sway with the Great One.

"I shall tell you when I have another task for you. But I warn you, if you fail me again, I shall not let your incompetence go so lightly."

"I will not fail you, Your Grace."

Thankfully, the silver-haired Wizenot returned his staff to its holder. "This Rihyad, did he betray you?"

"I don't see how he could have, Your Grace. I watched him closely up until the time we entered the building."

"Not closely enough, perhaps. Will he live?"

"I'm not sure, Great One. Perhaps if I get him some antibiotics."

The strange old man stared off for a moment, as if he could see something Jackson couldn't, then turned back with a calmer expression. "Your assistance is not necessary."

Crazy old coot. How did he know that?

The Wizenot scowled as if he'd heard Jackson's thoughts. "Bring him to me when he is healed. You are dismissed."

Gasping, Connor bowed off the pillow and startled Mara awake in the chair next to him where she'd dozed off.

She was on the edge of the bed at his side in a heartbeat, easing him back down. "What's wrong? What happened?"

His wide pupils slowly contracted to normal size. "I thought someone was there."

"Just me."

"No," he said and looked into space as if he could see past the walls. "Out there."

She pressed her hand to his forehead. His fever was up again. "Are you delirious?"

Connor had slipped in and out of fitful sleep all afternoon, but when he'd been awake, he'd been lucid. Until now.

"No. It's a Gargoyle thing. Second Sight. It's like a tunnel through space we can generate to see things somewhere we're not. Only it's a two-way street. If someone is looking at me, I can sense it and trace the tunnel back to them. And someone was definitely looking at me. He broke it off before I could get a good look at him."

Mara twined the edge of the bedspread between her fingers. "One of your friends, trying to find out if you're all right?"

He shook his head. "I would have recognized any of them. This was someone I don't know. Someone powerful."

"What does it mean?"

"I don't know. But I don't think it's good."

His head fell back to the pillow, his eyes closed. Blue circles marred the pale skin beneath his lashes. His cheeks had sunken to hollows.

"You need to drink some more juice while you're awake," she said, and gave him a reassuring squeeze on the shoulder before going downstairs to get it. He hadn't eaten more than a bite or two of his dinner, and he needed his strength.

The living room was empty except for the long-limbed Benson. Jackson's office door was open and the hazy light of his computer monitor cut through the dim alcove. The others were scattered around the house doing who-knows-what.

As long as there was no one around to hassle her, she decided to check on the women while she was down there. She flipped the deadbolt on the cellar door and closed it behind her, then stepped quietly down the stairs.

When she got to the bottom, Theresa giggled inside her cell. "Hello, Mara!" Then she whispered, "Is anyone in the kitchen?"

"No, why? And what are you so happy about?"

Jaina wrapped her hands around the bars on her door and smiled. "We've got a surprise for you."

Mara frowned. She'd had enough surprises for a

lifetime the last few weeks. Surprises were definitely overrated, in her book. "What?"

All five women looked down the aisle toward the storage area, and one of the most gorgeous men Mara had ever seen walked out of the shadows. His dark hair was shorter than Connor's and neatly combed. His strong jaw was clean shaven even this time of night, and his dark eyes held hers intently.

"Don't be afraid," he said. "I'm a friend of Connor's. My name is Nathan. Your friends tell me you're Mara."

She stuck out her hand stupidly and pumped it up and down when he took it. "How did you get in here?"

"The same way we got out last week," Jaina said brightly. "Through the window."

The window Dwyer had nailed shut after their escape attempt? She peered back into the darkness to see that the glass pane had been neatly removed and set aside so that it could, she assumed, be set back in place later.

Theresa giggled again. "And don't you know we nearly died when he climbed in?"

She blinked hard to clear her head. Someone had broken into their prison? "You took a huge risk coming in here. Why?"

Connor had said his friends wouldn't come until there were only a few guards in the house.

"You tried to make contact with us today."

"Yes." The infamous dangling-from-the-side-of-the-house-on-a-rope-made-of-sheets trick.

Nathan's face tightened. "Is it Connor? Did he send you? Is he all right?"

"Yes." She frowned. "I mean no. I mean, yes, I tried

to contact you for Connor. No, he didn't send me. I came on my own. And no, he's not all right."

"How badly is he hurt?"

"He was shot in the leg. I don't think the bullet did much damage, but the wound is infected. He needs antibiotics."

"I'll have a prescription called into an all-night pharmacy within the hour."

"How will I get them? I can't get to the tree."

"Don't try. I don't think I could stand to see you hanging out another window. You nearly stopped my heart today. I'll leave the meds on the outside of the kitchen windowsill before dawn. Just wait until no one is around tomorrow morning and grab them. After that, if you need anything else, close the shutters on that window halfway, and I'll meet you down here after dark. If it's urgent, like if Connor doesn't get better, and you think his life is in danger, close the shutters all the way and we'll hit the house. Shut this operation down."

"I thought Connor was disposable." She couldn't keep the ice from her voice. Didn't really try.

Nathan's eyes pinched. "Did he tell you that?"

"Yes."

He smiled grimly. "He would. He knows we would take casualties in a full assault on the house. He wouldn't want lives lost on his account. Especially now when we need every man."

To protect the children, she remembered. Damn Connor for lying to her.

"For the record," Nathan continued, "none of our members—or our members' friends—is disposable. We protect every one to our last breath. If you need us, we will come."

He grasped both her hands in his, and she felt power in his grip. Not physical strength, but something bigger. More meaningful. It sizzled through his body and leant strength to hers.

She raised her gaze to his and lowered her voice. "Were you by any chance watching Connor a little while ago? Through the . . . Second Sight?"

He looked taken aback. "Connor told you about Second Sight?"

She shrugged. "He said he thought someone was watching him earlier. Someone powerful. I just thought it might have been you."

"No." He dropped her hands. "I should go. I've kept you down here too long already. But remember this: You're not alone. And neither is Connor."

Then he was gone, and she was left standing there, still gawking.

Thirteen

*By the time Mara had been able to get the antibi-*otics the next morning, Connor's condition had deteriorated to the point that she worried the medicine had come too late. His fever spiked. His pulse was fast and thready and he wheezed as if he couldn't drag enough air into his lungs. He mumbled incoherently and fought battles to the death with the sheets and his pillow.

By midday, she was almost ready to close the kitchen shutters, but knowing the cost of that decision—and that it was a price Connor hadn't wanted his brethren to pay—she decided to give the antibiotics a few more hours to kick in.

In the meantime, she stayed by his side, sponging his fevered body with a damp cloth and murmuring in his ear. At first she'd just told him to hang on. To fight. But later she'd talked to him. Told him about herself, her childhood. Private things she'd never shared before.

The stress and lack of sleep over the last few days took its toll. Her shoulders sagged and she could hardly hold her eyes open. It took a concerted effort to muster the strength to wring out the hand towel she used to bathe him.

Finally, all she could do was sit back and listen to him breathe. As her mind relaxed, though, other sensations began to gradually take root in her mind. Colors flashed through her head, then pictures. Places she didn't recognize, people she didn't know.

She watched as a person might watch a movie on TV with the sound turned down—not quite following the plot, but fascinated by the photography and the settings.

How much time passed that way, she couldn't say. But eventually it dawned on her that she more than saw the events taking place in her mind. She felt the emotions of the person experiencing them.

Connor.

In his delirium he was sending images, much the way he had when he'd tried to alter her memory by projecting the scene of the deer in the field. Only she knew down deep that these weren't made-up images. These were his life.

His lives.

She rode a woolly pony across a Scottish moor with him. Broke her arm with him in a fall from an apple tree. She cried his tears of joy at the birth of a son and his tears of grief at the loss of a brother. Through it all she experienced the one unwavering constant in his life: his loyalty to his people and to those he called friend.

Years passed as scene after scene flew by. Decades. Centuries. The modern world came into focus and she felt his uncertainty. His longing for the old ways. The old world.

Then she came into view, and the film speed slowed until it seemed to click by one frame at a time. She felt the longing again, but not for the old world this time.

For her.

She felt his fear that she couldn't accept what he was. His certainty that she would reject him. And the tiny seed of hope he refused to acknowledge that somehow, some way, maybe she wouldn't.

The images passed by slower and slower as they reflected each day spent in the farmhouse, and finally stopped altogether at the current day.

The vision began to change in her mind. The edges softened, the light dimmed. The setting moved to a place she didn't recognize, an open-air villa on the side of a mountain overlooking a sea that could have been the Mediterranean.

She stood on a balcony, leaning on the rail and wearing a gauzy robe that fluttered in the breeze as she watched sailboats play on the water at dusk. A seagull called to its mate as it glided on the wind.

The scene was so peaceful, so relaxing, that a lethargy Mara couldn't deny pulled her chin toward her chest. She felt the towel slip from her hand and heard it plop softly on the floor.

The last thing she consciously remembered was hearing someone walk up behind her on the balcony—there was sound in this vision. He wrapped his arms around her and pulled her back against his chest.

Connor.

His body felt warm and strong and fully aroused against hers.

"Come inside, love. Back to bed." Connor palmed the column of her throat and tipped her head against his shoulder.

She smiled and skimmed a hand over his bare hip. "We've been in bed all day."

He hooked one eyebrow. "You see a problem with that?"

"None at all."

He turned her enough so that his mouth could close over hers. His tongue pierced the seam of her lips and she tasted both of them on him.

Rubbing her chest against his until her nipples peaked, she eased out of the kiss. "Let's go then," she said in her sultriest voice.

With a wicked grin, she slid her roaming hand inward from his hip, took hold of him by the handle and led him into the flat.

Two dozen candles flickered in the bedroom. The smell of warm vanilla and sex hung in the air. The bedsheets were twisted and tangled, the pillows on the floor.

"Quite a mess we've made," she said.

He answered by pulling her to the pillows. "Let's leave it this way."

Connor sat on the floor with his back propped against the side of the bed and his legs spread in a V before him. He tucked her back up to his chest and rolled the weight of her breasts in his palms. His thumbs strummed the already-puckered nipples into tighter peaks.

"*I love how you respond to me,*" *he murmured against her ear. The warm gust of his breath sent a shower of sparks tingling down that side of her neck.*

"*I love how you make me respond,*" *she said. Her voice had gone throaty and hoarse.*

As he played with her breasts, he nipped at the skin where her neck met her shoulder, but it was a bite designed to produce pleasure, not pain. His hands, his lips, his teeth all touched her with such exquisite tenderness, she thought she might cry from the sheer beauty of it.

Being raised in south L.A.—raising herself, really, since her drunk mother couldn't do it—Mara had grown up in a world of poverty, violence, and ugliness. For years, she'd railed against the way she'd been forced to live like an animal to survive. Now she realized that living that way had only prepared her to truly appreciate the other end of the spectrum: contentment, joy, and peace.

Who would have thought she could have found that with Connor, a man who lived with a beast of such primitive nature, such basic drives and motivations caged inside him.

Who would have thought that he'd enjoy poetry, or be capable of sharing his body so unselfishly, of bringing hers such pleasure.

When she'd first met him she hadn't understood him, she'd feared him even, but that time was long gone. Now he was her partner, her lover. Her love.

"*Bend your knees, darling.*" *He helped her by cupping the backs of her legs and pulling them up, then placing her feet on the floor outside the V of his legs.*

The position spread her wide, and her sex clenched in anticipation of what she knew came next.

His left hand splayed across her diaphragm to steady her. His right delved between her legs and stroked her from her clitoris to the stretch of skin just below her anus, spreading her dew.

Her head fell back to his chest. The flames on the candles flickered and blurred. Connor's fingers worked forward and back. Forward and back.

Her hips lifted. He cupped her mound and pushed her back down.

"Deeper, Connor. I need you deeper."

He obliged, entering her with two fingers in a heavy thrust. Her back arched in time with his rhythm. He began to move his own hips, too, rubbing his erection against the small of her back.

The dual friction, inside her and out, set her blood on fire. She grabbed his wrist, added her strength to his with each penetration.

"More, Connor. More."

The tension began to coil inside her, tighter and tighter.

He gave her another finger and moved faster. The heel of his hand rapped her pelvic bone with each stroke. His thumb and little finger pinched her nether lips around her clit, squeezing until she was ready to explode.

"I'm there." She grabbed his legs and held on, digging her nails into the hard muscles of his thighs. "I'm right there."

And then he stopped the thrusting suddenly and pressed down with the heel of his hand, squeezed harder with his thumb and little finger, and curled his fingertips against the sensitive spot at the front of her vagina.

Mara jolted awake so hard that she nearly fell out of her chair. For a moment, she didn't know where she was or how she'd gotten there, but she did know where she'd come from. She'd been watching the images of his past lives that Connor was unconsciously projecting. Then she'd fallen asleep. Her encounter with Connor in the Mediterranean might have been a dream, but her body still hummed and pulsed with the aftereffects of an orgasm that felt very, very real.

Leaning over the bed, she checked Connor. He lay on his side, scowling in his sleep. He flung one hand up on his pillow.

Thank heavens his skin felt cooler. The antibiotics had begun their work. His breathing sounded normal.

Unlike hers.

Against her will, her gaze traveled down the blanket to his hips, but in this position, it was impossible to see whether or not he was aroused.

Who knew if he even could get it up in his current condition?

A dream. It had only been a dream.

The question was . . . had it been her dream, or his?

Jackson stomped into the farmhouse, throwing his coat over a hanger in the entryway and tossing his gloves on the table. "Where's the woman?" he bellowed.

In the living room, Hard Case paused his current

Nintendo game and Dwyer looked up over his girlie magazine.

"Problem, boss?" Benson asked casually, dealing himself a hand of solitaire on the coffee table.

"Where's the damned woman?"

Figuring delaying the confrontation wouldn't make it any better, Mara stepped out of the kitchen where she'd been peeking out from the doorway. "Do you mean me?"

"Yes, you. How is Rihyad?"

She wiped her hands on her kitchen apron. "He's . . . ill."

Jackson scowled. He clomped across the living room, limping slightly, and pulled her into the kitchen, leaving a trail of footprints in melting snow on the carpet. "Is he gonna survive?"

"I'm not sure. I think so."

Jackson mumbled something like "damned well better," then gripped her elbow. "Get those girls up here."

A tremor passed just under her skin. "They shouldn't come up. If they're contagious—"

He jabbed a finger at her chest. "Get. Them. Up. Here."

The other men watched curiously from the doorway behind Jackson as he unlocked the cellar door. Mara's stomach clenched. Her pulse spiked.

What would they do when the women appeared, rashless and coughless?

She searched her mind desperately for some excuse to continue their quarantine, but finding none, led them from the cellar. The five women lined up like deserters before a firing squad.

Jackson paced down the row of them, his jaw growing tighter as he inspected them one by one.

"Sick, huh?" he seethed. "Contagious. You've made me look like a fool in front of the—"

He bit back whatever he was going to say. His complexion turned scarlet. He looked back at his men.

"Woo-hoo," Benson said, but without enthusiasm. "Celibacy is over."

"They could still be contagious," Mara said, and Jackson backhanded her for it.

Then he fisted his hand over the back of a chair. "Get them upstairs and get them pregnant. Tonight. Now."

The men cast sharp glances at each other.

"Sure, boss. I mean, why not." Dwyer cleared his throat. "They're healthy-enough looking, right guys?"

"Right," Benson said.

Hard Case rubbed his bald head. "Devlin, you got a thing for that young one, don't you? Why don't you go on and take her upstairs tonight. If you're feeling okay by morning, maybe I'll have a go at one of them tomorrow."

Devlin's face soured. "You think I'm gonna be the guinea pig? Maybe you ought to take one, and I'll see how *you're* feeling in the morning."

"They are not sick!" Jackson said.

"Then which one are you taking, boss?" Benson asked.

Jackson gritted his teeth. He scowled. He growled. But in the end, he left without a woman.

Mara decided she was going to grow gardens of poison sumac. She might make bouquets of it. She loved poison sumac.

"Get them back downstairs," he told her as he left, and handed Hard Case the keys to make sure they were locked up. "Then get back upstairs and make sure Rihyad doesn't die."

And that, Mara decided with a suppressed smile, was the first order Jackson had ever issued that she would actually be happy to obey.

Connor hadn't felt this bad since the first time he'd spent Mardi Gras in New Orleans. His tongue felt like twice its normal size. His head ached. His stomach was cramping and his muscles felt like Silly Putty.

Smelling something foul nearby, he cranked one eye open.

Mara stood beside the bed holding a bowl. She lifted a spoonful of something gray and lumpy, held it under her nose and sniffed. "Mmm. Oatmeal."

He reached for the barf bag on the bedside table and barely got it up to his mouth in time. She sighed and set the bowl on the night table.

The last couple of days came back to him slowly. The fever, the pain. The really bad oatmeal she had tried to force down his throat every time he woke up.

His stomach fell from his throat back to where it belonged in his abdomen, and Connor looked for something to do with the bag. Mara pinched the top between her thumb and finger, wrinkled her nose, and carried it out of the room. When she came back, she held a glass of water for him to gargle with and a clean cloth to wipe his face.

She peered at him as he cleaned up. "You look better today."

"I have the mother of all headaches."

"What about your leg?"

"The mother of all legaches, too."

She pulled down the cover and checked the wound. "When your stomach settles I'll get you some aspirin."

He shook his head, pushed the covers back, and gingerly swung his legs over the side of the bed. "What I need are some pants. Intermission is over. It's time to get back to work."

"It's too soon. You can hardly hobble to the bathroom by yourself."

He stood and limped toward the closet in his boxer briefs. Clucking in disgust, she hurried around him and retrieved his clothes. When she held the garments out to him, he braced her elbows and pinned her under a determined gaze. "The sooner I'm on my feet, the sooner I can start building my strength back up. We're running out of time, Mara."

"I know, I just—I'm tired."

"That's because you've been taking care of me twenty-four/seven."

He wished that was all it was, but he had a feeling it was more. If he hadn't felt so rotten these last few days, he would have enjoyed the quiet time in the room with her. But she'd been ill at ease, flitting around the room in constant motion and never holding eye contact more than half a second.

He would have written her behavior off as just another sign that she couldn't accept what he was, but she hadn't acted that way before he'd been shot. No, this was something different. The way she cut appraising glances at him when she thought he couldn't see and ran her fingers through her short hair every few minutes made him think this change in her had less to do with the fact that he was a monster, and more to do with the fact that he was a *man*.

"So where do we go from here?" she asked.

He brushed a fallen eyelash off of her cheek and grinned. "Downstairs."

FOURTEEN

Nathan checked his watch and brushed the snow off the shoulders of his cashmere coat as he strode through the halls of the YMCA. One simply did not arrive late to a meeting of the High Council of *Les Gargouillen*.

Unfortunately, no one told the airlines that. O'Hare International Airport was socked in, and everything was off schedule.

Several of the old cronies up front glared at him as he opened the door as quietly as he could and found Rachel near the back of the room. At least he didn't have to worry about locating an empty chair. As tradition dictated, council members and members of the congregation alike stood during the proceedings.

Business tended to get done a lot more quickly that way.

Before the attack on St. Michael's, council meetings tended to be formal affairs, rife with politics and pompousness. The council members wore ornate robes and stood before hand-carved lecterns. Rules of order had been strictly enforced.

Today, they were more like town halls. Everyone wore what had survived the fire and participated as they saw fit, offering opinions and ideas as the situation required.

Nathan hoped they never went back to the old way.

He leaned close to Rachel and couldn't resist taking a little taste of her ear before he whispered in it. "What's going on?"

She elbowed him discreetly, but smiled at the same time. "The elders have listened to reports on security for the children, reviewed bids to rebuild St. Michael's, and agreed that little Mark Zane will be allowed to keep his pet turtle in his dormitory room. I think it's your turn."

As if Teryn had heard Rachel's words, he swept a look around the semicircle of elders on either side of him, then lifted his gaze toward Nathan. "Nathan has just returned from Minnesota. What news do you bring?"

Nathan stepped closer to the elders. "Connor's condition has apparently stabilized. It's been three days and the woman he's working with hasn't signaled us to pull him out."

"God, another woman," someone in the crowd bemoaned. One of the traditionalists, no doubt. Their's was a congregation divided these days. Sometimes Nathan wondered, if they didn't have a common enemy to fight, would they be at each others' throats? "Rihyad is the last Gargoyle who I ever thought would take up with some female."

A chorus of murmurs and a few chuckles rippled through the room. He would bet Rachel wasn't laughing. Her position as the first woman ever admitted to a Gargoyle congregation was still a matter of great debate among the congregation.

"Calm down, everyone. Calm down," Teryn ordered.

The room quieted.

"What about the Minnesota congregation?" the Wizenot asked.

Nathan straightened his cuffs. "We've still only located this one cell, but we're certain there are more. Since the botched raid on a gun shipment, they've been quiet."

Teryn's voice's grew deadly serious. "Did they get any guns?"

"Mikkel observed them unloading several large boxes at the farmhouse. They may not have gotten everything they wanted, but we can only assume they're now armed."

No one murmured at that news, much less chuckled. Every man—and the one woman—in the room understood the deadly seriousness of the situation.

The elders asked him a few more questions, which Nathan answered to the best of his ability, then he assured them that Mikkel, Christian, Noble, and Rashid were all watching the Minnesotans very carefully, and they would inform the congregation in Chicago immediately of any new developments.

As the meeting ended, he wrapped his arms around his wife and gave her a proper hello. One based in action, not words. Lip action, to be specific.

"Mmm, I missed you," she said when he finally let her breathe.

"I was only gone three days."

"I missed you at least a week's worth."

He squeezed her tight, releasing her only when Teryn approached. He shook hands and clapped backs with his *saytreán*, the son of his soul.

"How is it up there, really?" Teryn asked.

"Cold."

"Like Chicago isn't?"

Nathan grew serious. "Whoever is leading the congregation there, he's done a good job of separating himself from the worker drones, and of keeping his forces spread out. I'm beginning to wonder if we'll ever be able to catch up with the head guy. And if we do, and we take him out, if we'll find all the little cells of his army before one of them rises up to take his place."

"We have to try."

Nathan cocked his head. "The woman did say one interesting thing, though. She said Connor told her he thought someone was watching him, someone powerful."

"That's odd," Rachel said. "I've had the same feeling lately."

Nathan's head snapped toward his wife so fast he felt his vertebrae pop. "What? When? Why didn't you tell me?"

"During the visions, and then . . . afterward. Mostly in my sleep, when I dream the visions again."

Teryn's brows pulled down. He exchanged a look with Nathan. "The visions continue in your sleep?"

"After we've broken the ritual circle?" Nathan added impatiently.

She nodded. "Is that important? I figured I was just obsessing about finding my brother and my mind was working overtime. As for the other, someone watching . . . I thought I was imagining it. But now that Connor has felt the same thing, I don't know."

Nathan dragged a hand across the back of his neck. The long hours of the trip and little sleep had were finally catching up to him. "You've felt this when I was near?"

She nodded.

He looked at Teryn. "It can't be the Second Sight, then. Rachel's mind might not be trained to sense it, but I would certainly have known."

"Then how else can someone be spying on me? And Connor?"

"Perhaps in the same way we've been looking for Levi. Through the ritual visions themselves."

Nathan's stomach turned over. "Someone else practicing the old religion?"

"We relearned our people's ways. It's possible someone else has, too."

He scowled. "The question is, who?"

"I don't know. But perhaps we can figure it out." Teryn took Rachel's elbow and turned her toward the door. Nathan followed. "Come, Rachel. Tell me about this feeling of being watched. What did you sense, exactly? What did you see?"

The next night after dinner and coffee, Connor made his first attempt at climbing the stairs to his room under his own power. By the time he reached the top, he was as winded as if he'd climbed Mt. Everest. Mara was inches behind him with her arms in the air ready to catch him if he fell, but he made it. Without help.

Exhausted, he settled in for the night but she fiddled around with the lamp on the desk. Sat and flipped pages in her book. Stood again and straightened the clothes hanging in the closet.

"Would you sit down?" he said. "You're making me tired just watching you."

"Sorry." She sat next to the bed and wrapped her arms around her legs.

He scooted to the far edge of the bed and patted the mattress. She shook her head.

"Is something wrong, Mara? You've been as nervous as a mouse in a cattery for days."

"No. Yes. I mean—" She chewed on her lip, a sure sign that she had something on her mind. "Have you ever been to the Mediterranean?"

"Many times. Why?"

"N-nothing. Just wondered."

He plumped a pillow and sat up straighter. "It sounds like something to me. Now you've got me curious."

"It's just . . . I'm feeling a little guilty about something, even though it wasn't my fault."

"You want me to hear your confession?" He winked at her. "Come tell Father Connor all your sins. Especially the really dirty ones."

She made a face at him. "When you were sick, you were sort of projecting memories. Like you tried to do with the deer, only these were real."

"I get it. What did I show you? Hopefully not the time I dyed my hair blue and tried to pierce my nose with a horseshoe nail."

She smiled. "No, nothing like that. These were scenes from your lives. All ten of them. Some of it was pretty intimate stuff."

He grinned and waggled his eyebrows. "Did you like what you saw?"

She flopped her hand up and smacked him on the arm. "Not that kind of intimate. Personal. I felt like a Peeping Tom."

She sucked that lip between her teeth again, and he waited for her to get to whatever was really bothering her.

"Then there was this part between you and I."

"On the Mediterranean."

She nodded.

"Only I know we've never been there together, so this wasn't a memory. It was more like a dream." She flicked a glance up at him. "Do you remember dreaming something like that?"

"Sorry, those days are pretty much a blur. Why don't you tell me about it. Maybe it'll ring a bell."

She blushed, and he began to understand.

"What, exactly," he asked, "were we doing on the Med?"

Her neck turned a deeper shade of red. "What healthy human beings do in villas that overlook the sea."

"I'm not a human being."

"You were that night."

"I see." He picked at the chenille bedspread, feeling a little warm, himself. "Was I any good?"

She looked up at him with eyes so round and luminous they could have been jewels. "Spectacular."

"Great." He hooked one corner of his mouth in a wry grin. "Now I've got a reputation to live up to."

She blew out a breath. "I don't know what's wrong with me, fixating on this."

"Come 'ere," he ordered softly, then added, "please."

She shifted onto her knees and faced the bed. He threaded his fingers through the choppy dark red hair behind her ear.

"Maybe what you need is a dose of the real thing to get the dream out of your mind."

"Connor—"

"Hear me out. We've been dancing around this since the day we met. Maybe it's time to put it to rest."

"You think we should sleep together so we can get it out of our systems?"

"Can you honestly say you won't always wonder what it would have been like if we don't? I know I will."

She frowned.

"What?" he asked, tracing the sorrowful bracket around her mouth with his thumb.

"What if it has the opposite effect? What if instead of getting it out of our systems, we become more obsessed than ever?"

He grinned. "Then we'll just have to keep trying until we get it right."

Very slowly, his gaze locked on hers. He reached out and pushed the top button on her blouse through its hole, then the next, and then another. All the while he distracted her by kissing her. Glancing blows that brushed her lips, the tip of her nose, her eyelids.

When the sides of her shirt hung free, he unsnapped the front closure of her bra and pulled the whole ensemble off her arms.

"Beautiful." He traced an index finger down her sternum, between her breasts. "Perfect."

Lacing his fingers with hers, he pulled her toward him. She let go of him long enough to rid herself of shoes, socks, pants, and panties, then stretched out beside him and took his hands again.

"Are you sure you're up to this?" she asked.

He pushed their joined hands down to his bulging groin. "I'm getting there."

Fifteen

Mara moaned when Connor's warm, wet mouth closed over her breast and then gasped when he pulled back a fraction of an inch and blew on the dewy tip. Instinctively she pulled his head back down and curled around him seeking warmth, seeking contact. Her hands fisted in his wavy hair, a silent plea for *more*.

In the Mediterranean, her dream-lover Connor had been infinitely tender, endlessly gentle, but a bit cool, perhaps. The real Connor was still tender, still gentle, but hot as a Miami summer.

With the real Connor there was sweat and there was hunger. There was consuming need that drove them both to touch, to taste, to explore. To please and be pleased.

Real sex wasn't a choreographed movement of body parts. It was a tangle of arms and legs. It was hair caught in the corners of the mouth and stubble burns in sensitive places.

Real sex was messy.

Mara tucked her head under Connor's chin and tickled the sensitive underside of his jaw with the tip of her tongue. In return he shimmied down her body and kissed the backs of both knees and the junctures where her thighs met her hips. Nothing but his breath touched the area in between.

Real sex meant both partners got to play and be played.

She led him back to the head of the bed with a finger hooked in the corner of his mouth. He closed his lips around her and suckled while he crawled.

When they were face to face again, she outlined the waistband of his underwear with her knuckles. "Have I ever told you how much of a turn-on I think boxer briefs are?"

"No."

"The only thing more exciting than seeing boxer briefs on a well-built man—" She hooked her fingers under the elastic and dragged the underwear down. "—is taking them off."

The veins on his neck bulged as his erection sprang alive in her hand, a whole new kind of beast within him.

"I can get into that," he said, but the words were half strangled as she closed her fist around him. "I can definitely get into that."

Mara had always let the man take the lead in her past liaisons, especially the first time. But with Connor she felt bold. Confident enough to forge ahead on her own. Maybe because she'd already seen the worst he had to offer—the Awakening—and faced down her fears.

She rolled until they lay on their sides facing each other, then she split his legs with one of hers and rolled her thigh up against his soft sac as she stroked his erection against her belly.

His eyes nearly rolled back. He grunted, and with an effort that seemed to rise from somewhere deep inside him, he put his arms around her and rolled to his back, bringing her down on top of him.

"You might have to handle the hard work here," he admitted.

She framed his face with her hands and lowered her head for a kiss as she raised herself over him. Their tongues darted and played, then locked together just as their bodies locked together.

A long sigh of contentment escaped Mara. She straightened and arched her back, pushed her hips down, taking him deeper. The sensation of him filling her, stretching her, the head of his penis bumping the top of her womb blocked out everything else. Light. Sound. Taste. There was only Connor and the long, slow ride to oblivion she took on him.

His hands on her hips helped guide her tempo. His upward thrusts helped counterpoint her downward strokes. She angled her body a little forward to increase the friction. He rolled his hips for maximum penetration.

The world centered down to a fine point, the point of contact. Hung there while the pressure mounted, mounted, then exploded out in blinding rings of sensation that reverberated through her until she thought they might break her apart, only to pass finally and leave her weak, spent, and sated.

She collapsed to his chest and listened to their heartbeats compete for drum line of the year.

"Well?" he asked.

"Forget the Mediterranean. Minnesota is beginning to look pretty damned good."

They laughed until a knock on the door cut them off. "Hey, Rihyad."

The knob turned and Jackson poked his head in. Mara dove behind Connor, and Connor tossed the bed-spread over them both.

"Did you ever hear of waiting for someone to say 'Enter'?"

"Sorry." He didn't look it. In fact, he looked amused. Bastard. "I just came by to ask Connor if he was feeling good enough to take a little trip tomorrow. Guess I don't have to ask."

He backed almost all the way out the door. "Be downstairs at eight A.M. We're going to Duluth. All of us."

Compared to the farmhouse where Connor had spent the last nine days, the Duluth estate of the Minnesota congregation of *Les Gargouillen* might as well have been Buckingham Palace. An electric gate, complete with armed guards, security cameras, and two giant stone gargoyles perched on the pillars of the bordering brick walls, opened onto a meandering blacktop drive, meticulously plowed and swept clear of snow. Fir trees, some thirty feet tall and nearly as wide at the base, dotted the sculptured grounds of the estate like ornaments, the midday sun glinting off icicles hanging from their boughs. A sculpture of a naked woman, her frozen gaze averted shyly to her feet and her arms crossed over her breasts and pubes, stood in the center of a marble fountain, shut off for the winter, in the center of the circular drive in front of the main house.

The residence itself looked more like a medieval castle than a twenty-first-century mansion. The exterior was composed of irregular-shaped stones in varying shades of tan and brown, high arched windows with glass panes that split down the middle and opened out, exposed twenty-inch beams, and a flat roof complete with parapet and battlements.

The rectangular center of the structure had to cover ten thousand square feet at the base, and stood four stories tall. In the center, a single open spire jutted up another twenty feet, probably some kind of watchtower. On either side of the main building, three-story wings lined by narrow, deep-set windows angled back and out, forming a V with a flattened point.

The only thing missing was the moat.

Jackson parked his black SUV in front of the door and Connor watched out the passenger-side window as the white cargo van carrying the women, including Mara, and two more SUVs with the rest of the men inside, pulled up behind.

A muscle ticked in Connor's jaw when five dark-haired men with bodybuilder physiques filed out of the double oak doors of the house and lined up in front of the vehicles. Dressed in nothing but identical thin black sweaters, neatly pressed black slacks, and dress shoes despite the bitter cold, they stood at parade rest, their expressions inscrutable and their gazes fixed straight ahead.

Muscle, Connor thought. Well-dressed, well-trained muscle, but muscle all the same.

He shifted his gaze over to Jackson. "What is this place?"

Jackson smoothed his mustache with his thumb and forefinger and answered simply, "Hell."

As Connor followed Jackson's lead and climbed out of the car, another man came out of the house, this one older, his appearance and carriage leaning toward brains instead of brawn. He wore a plain gray suit that fit to perfection and matched the shade of his hair and his eyes. The crisp white shirt and neatly knotted tie screamed conservatism, but a silver ponytail tied at mid–shoulder blade with a simple leather thong hinted at a streak of rebelliousness behind the uptight image. "Welcome, gentlemen. I am Thaddeus Cole. Should you need anything while you are here, you have only to call. Your rooms are ready inside. Please—" The major-domo gestured toward the house with the long elegant fingers of a piano player. "This way."

Jackson and the others started toward the doors. The five soldiers broke ranks to march the women, who'd piled out of the vans and now stood in a tight cluster at the curb, down a walkway to the left. Mara threw a worried look over her shoulder.

Connor stopped. "Where are they being taken?"

Thaddeus turned, studied Connor with open curiosity. "To the women's quarters, of course."

Jackson warned him discreetly by placing a hand low on Connor's arm, but the caution seemed unjustified. A hint of humor curled the corners of Thaddeus's mouth as his gaze slid back and forth between Connor and Mara, who was still looking back over her shoulder. "Don't worry. The women here are well cared for. And you will see her again soon."

Connor wavered a moment between his personal wishes and the requirements of the mission. Leaving Mara unprotected in the heart of the enemy's stronghold went against every instinct in his cursed nature. But success—and the survival of his congregation—depended on his ability to get in that house, gather what information he could, and get back to his people. Making a scene this close to the end of the game risked everything both he and Mara had worked for.

Giving Mara one last look that he hoped conveyed reassurance that she would not be abandoned, he made a point of visibly relaxing his shoulders, shrugging out of Jackson's touch, and marching toward the door.

Thaddeus smiled at Connor as he stepped over the threshold, then scowled at the motley bunch behind him. "Your rooms are ready on the third floor," he said, curling his lip as if he had a bad taste in his mouth. "Supper will be served in an hour. Don't forget that the Great One expects those who share his table to dress for the occasion."

With Jackson's comment about this place being Hell echoing in his mind, Connor went upstairs to get ready for dinner with the devil.

SIXTEEN

Mara braced herself for whatever new horrors awaited her in the dungeon of the imposing stone fortress that marked a new twist in the bizarre turn of fortune her life had taken these last few weeks. Visions of the rack, guillotines, and hanging from iron shackles against a damp stone wall while rats nibbled at her toes made her heart flutter and her mouth go dry.

The other women's imaginations were apparently working as diligently as hers. Jaina's normally healthy complexion had turned to alabaster, and if Theresa's eyes got any wider, they were going to fall out of her head.

But when the men guiding the gaggle of frightened women entered the plain wooden door on the side of the east wing, they turned up the narrow staircase instead of down. Far from the house of horrors she expected, the setting Mara found around her when she exited the narrow stairwell on the third floor rivaled the maternity ward of any modern hospital, only it was cozier.

The walls were painted warm colors, bright but not glaring. Potted plants seemed to be tucked in every nook and corner. Instead of the usual straight, sterile tile corridor, the hallway here was made of some cushioned synthetic material, like an indoor track, and meandered in an octagonal shape, ending up back where it started. On the outside of the ring were smaller octagons of patient rooms clustered around a carpeted common sitting area outfitted with overstuffed chairs, a couch, and a TV.

Most of the patient areas appeared empty, but women in various stages of pregnancy lounged in one or two, flipping through magazines or watching soap operas. Mara found it odd that the women didn't look up as the group passed. As if they didn't want to see. Didn't want to know.

Along the inside of the circle, examination and treatment rooms were interspersed with nursing stations manned by young men in yellow scrubs. At each point of the octagon, hallways bisected the center ring like spokes on a wheel, converging in the middle, at the hub.

Mara slowed and peered down one of the spokes, curious about what lay in the center, the spot that would logically be the most secure in the facility. As she passed the first two openings to the hub, she couldn't see much. Just more young men in scrubs working over what appeared to be small tables. Then, at the third, one of the men in yellow straightened up from his table with a bundle in his arms.

The hair raised on her forearms as the bundle

moved. Little fists flailed free of the snug blue blanket.
A round faced scrunched up below the little blue cap,
and the wail of an unhappy infant pierced the quiet
hum of white noise in the hallway.

An electric tingle zinged over Mara's skin. Connor
had told her they were raising their own army. Though
she hadn't questioned his assumptions at the time, it
hadn't seemed possible. Hadn't seem real.

Now reality was staring her in the face in the form
of an eight-pound ball of fury whose destiny had been
set for him from the moment he had been conceived.

He would be a soldier in a war against humanity.

The guard behind Mara nudged her forward and
she stumbled along on numb feet with the rest of the
women. Righteous indignation swelled in her throat
and her chest until she couldn't swallow, could hardly
breathe.

What gave them the right, Goddamn it? *What gave
them the right?*

Her resolve to put an end to these monsters' reign
of terror increased with every step. She wasn't alone
here. She had Connor.

She'd almost panicked when he'd let the guards
take her away. She hadn't understood why he didn't
fight to keep her with him, afraid that his cause, his
mission, was greater than any feelings he might have
for her.

Now she realized he was right. This cause was bigger than both of them. Bucking the system five minutes after arrival would have only drawn attention to
him. Attention would have made it more difficult for
him to gather the information he needed.

He hadn't forsaken her. Hadn't forgotten her. He

would come for her eventually, and in the meantime, while she looked for Angela, she would also gather as much information as she could to add to what he learned.

They would take these guys down. Hard.

So deep in thought was she as she worked out her plan to find Angela and learn what she could to help Connor that when she was shown into a room and had dropped her meager bag of belongings on a bed against the wall, she didn't even see the petite woman sitting on the windowsill.

"Hello."

Mara spun, ready to do battle, and then wondered how she'd missed the woman. She might not stand more than five-foot-two, but she was carrying a belly that looked like it could have held a linebacker. Fully grown. She had to be past due. Why on God's green Earth hadn't she been induced?

"You must be new," the woman said as she levered herself off the window seat and padded over to her. "I'm Colleen."

Mara marveled at the fact that the woman stayed upright, as front-heavy as she was. "Mara. Mara Kincaide."

Colleen eyed Mara's midsection, and for a moment, Mara almost felt inadequate. "Wow, they brought you in early. You're not even showing yet. How far along are you?"

Mara's hand automatically flew to her stomach. "Oh, I'm not—" She didn't want to alienate Colleen. Or to raise her suspicions. Mara would have an easier time getting information if she were just one of the girls.

She smiled and forced her tense muscles to relax. "I'm not sure, exactly."

"The doctor should be able to tell you tomorrow."

"Doctor?"

"They always give you a checkup on your first day. Just routine stuff. Blood pressure, blood sugar. You know." Colleen shrugged and then opened a folding closet door and shoved a few hangers aside. "There's plenty of room for your stuff. And you can have the bottom drawer in the bureau. I can't bend over far enough to reach that one anyway."

"Thanks."

A doctor's appointment. And what would he say when he found out Mara wasn't pregnant? At least not that she knew of.

Her palm returned to her abdomen. Her throat went dry.

No. She couldn't be. She hadn't even considered . . .

She and Connor had only been together one time. The odds were a thousand to one.

Only slightly more likely than being kidnapped by men who could change into monsters at will.

Suddenly lightheaded, she took one deep breath to regain her balance, then another. She hadn't thought about the possibility of being pregnant with Connor's child until now, much less the far-reaching ramifications of such a pregnancy. Even if she made it out of here and her baby wasn't born and raised in a world of hate, violence, and depravity, she wasn't sure she was ready to have a Gargoyle child.

The lightheadedness kicked in with full force, and she got so dizzy she had to sit heavily on the side of the bed.

"Are you okay?" Colleen asked.

She nodded. She had to pull herself together.

Pregnant or not, she had other things to worry about right now.

Like staying alive. Gathering information. Getting the hell out of here.

Her head cleared and Mara looked up to find Colleen giving her a sympathetic look. "Don't worry. That happens a lot in the first trimester. It'll get better later."

Oh, God.

Though Mara felt as if her mind had splintered, and some small fragments of her brain twisted and blew in the wind like glass chimes, she managed to turn most of her focus to Colleen. More specifically, to finding out what Colleen knew.

There would be time to think about the other thing later.

Much later.

Unpacking her two blouses, Mara looked over her shoulder at Colleen, who'd somehow lowered herself onto the edge of her bed without toppling over. With no need to fake the shakiness in her voice, Mara started the task of learning everything she could about the operation and the people here. "So what else do they do besides give you a checkup? I mean, how many of us are there? What's the routine?"

Dinner was a bust.

Connor stabbed the last spear of buttered baby asparagus and shoved it in his mouth without the slightest appreciation for the way it melted on his tongue. A four-star restaurant couldn't have topped the food. The table was elegantly set with real fourteen-karat gold-leafed china, Waterford crystal, and antique silver. The wine had flowed freely all night. And all of it had been a complete waste of time.

He glared at the empty captain's chair at the head of the table.

The devil never showed.

Connor needed a face, a name to take back to his people. He thought he'd get both tonight.

He should have known it wouldn't be so easy.

Across the table, Devlin tugged at the neck of his shirt. It was so tight—or Devlin's neck was so large—that a roll of fat spilled over the crisp crease in the collar. "May I be excused now?"

He sounded like a recalcitrant schoolboy.

Thaddeus, who'd stood silently at the serving table all night, gave him a cold look. "Coffee will be served shortly."

Great. Twenty more minutes of listening to the Swiss cuckoo clock on the wall tick. Was it against the rules to talk at the table?

To save his sanity, he decided to find out.

"So, Mr.— Uh, Thaddeus. Do you always eat like this around here, or is this a special occasion?"

No one ran him through with a sword—or a look—so he figured he hadn't committed a cardinal sin. Yet.

Thaddeus nodded at the servant who brought in the carafe of coffee and waited until all the cups had been filled. "The Wise One likes to be sure his guests feel welcome in his home."

Feel welcome, his ass. The dude was on a power trip, making them all dress like monkeys, putting a chair like a throne at the head of the table, not showing up. It was all about making sure the underlings knew their place.

Connor smiled pleasantly and dabbed his lips with his linen napkin. "I'm sorry he wasn't able to join us. Maybe we'll see him tomorrow. I'd like to thank him for the fine meal."

"I'll pass on your sentiments." Thaddeus's lips puckered. Connor suspected another part of the manservant's anatomy was puckered, as well.

So much for making conversation. All twelve men at the table gulped down their coffee and an after-dinner liqueur, then sighed in relief when they were finally released.

Connor caught up to Jackson in the hall outside the other man's room. He turned him with a hand on the shoulder. "What was that about?"

Jackson scowled. "Don't waste brain cells trying to figure things out. Just do what you're told."

"If I'd been *told* what I was supposed to do, I might consider it."

"We'll find out soon enough."

"We? You don't know what we're doing here, either?"

Jackson opened the door to his room, walked inside. Connor followed.

"Not specifically," Jackson said once the door was closed behind them.

"Your own Wizenot doesn't tell you what's going on?"

Jackson hung his jacket and loosened his tie. "This isn't Chicago, Rihyad."

Connor snorted for good measure. "Thank God. But you must have some idea why we're here."

For a moment, Jackson's tired face slackened. His shoulders sagged, and Connor thought he was going to talk. But before a word was uttered, Jackson's expression closed. His eyes shuttered. "We'll get our orders soon enough. Now get out of here and get some sleep."

Not given much in the way of a choice, Connor left. He strode down the hall toward his own room with his arms stiff at his sides to keep himself from putting a fist through the wall.

He hated this. Hated these people, playing their games. Most of all he hated playing alone.

Mara. How had she fared her first evening in Lunatic Castle? He was worried about her, and hell . . . he wanted her. He needed her to match his fury, match his rage. To be an outlet for all this energy building up inside him, and to provide her an outlet for her own.

The blood that had been running hot and thin in his veins began to thicken. To cool from full burn to seductive simmer.

He wouldn't try to find her tonight, not physically. He wouldn't risk it—risk her. But he could find her mind.

So what if one of the other *Gargouillen* sensed him using the Second Sight?

He hoped they enjoyed the show.

Mara lay on her back staring up at the ceiling, her book—the one personal possession she'd managed to sneak into her bag of clothes before leaving the farmhouse—spread open on her chest. She'd planned to read, but even the beauty of Wordsworth's poetry gave her no peace tonight. Not after the things Colleen had told her.

First, Mara had asked about Angela, and Colleen had told her she thought there might be a woman here by that name, but she couldn't be sure. Other than those in the same pod, the three rooms that clustered around a lounge area, they weren't allowed to interact much. When they were working, they weren't supposed to talk. Finding her friend would be difficult, if she were here at all.

The rest of what Colleen had to say was even more devastating.

"Those of us close to our due dates don't have to work, but everyone else gets an assignment every morning," she'd said. "When they come around, try to avoid nursery duty if you can."

"Why?" Mara asked naïvely. Taking care of babies sounded a lot better than scrubbing toilets.

Colleen's eyes misted. Rubbing her belly, she lowered her voice as if the baby inside might hear. "They don't even let you hold them. You just have to lean over the side and give them a bottle of formula."

"For God's sake, why?"

"They say it makes them soft, coddling them and cuddling them. These babies have to learn to be strong, they say. They have to be tough."

"But they're *babies*."

Colleen sniffed. Mara's heart twisted over the thought of babies—even Gargoyle babies—who would never know the comfort of loving arms.

"The worst part is at night," Colleen said in a tiny voice. "Even if you're not working in the nursery, the ward is quiet and you can hear them bawling. Pitiful, heart-wrenching screams. They cry and cry and no one goes and gets them." She choked on a sob. "No one rocks them back to sleep."

Mara put her book aside and flipped off the bedside lamp. There would be no reading tonight. Only crying in the dark until long after Colleen's breath had taken on the even rhythm of sleep.

Mara swiped a hand across her cheek. What if she didn't get out of here? What if she was pregnant, and her baby was raised that way?

God, no. No baby should be raised that way.

Gusts of misery blew through her, shaking her, rattling her like dry leaves in a tree. Her shoulders shook. She rolled to her side and put the pillow over her head so that the only thing she would hear tonight was her own heartbeat.

Then there were two heartbeats, pounding in synchronicity. She felt him, floating around her, inside her, looking for an entrance to her mind.

Relaxing, she closed her eyes and opened the door.

He was there—at least it felt like he was. He framed her face with his big palms, kissed her eyelids, licked away the tears as if soothing a hurt on her cheek.

He was using the Second Sight, she realized. Manipulating her mind by pushing in thoughts and feelings that weren't real.

Normally she would hate the deception, the falseness of an imaginary relationship, but tonight she didn't care. Tonight she needed him. She needed his warmth and his comfort. His strength.

His love.

He was a man of many contradictions, Connor Rihyad. Strength and gentleness. Primitive simplicity and modern sophistication. Loyalty and betrayal.

But in this one thing, his feelings for her, he was of one mind. He loved her. She felt it.

He may never say it. He may even walk away from it one day, given his people's ways.

But he loved her. She felt it.

Relaxing further into the sensation of his embrace, she let her mind drift on the patterns of thought he was sending her, and sensations became images.

Connor's chest pressed to hers. His knees nudged hers apart and his thick erection lay along her thigh. But instead of entering her, he crawled backward down her body, raining kisses along her collarbone, in the valley between her breasts, on her navel, and finally at the edge of the thatch of springy red curls between her legs.

When she realized what he was about to do, she drew her legs together, almost protested out loud, but these were Connor's images, Connor's dreams, not hers. She had no control. Helpless.

He wanted her helpless. The images and intentions formed and dissolved in her mind like shapes in a swirling mist. He picked up two red silk scarves and tied her wrists loosely to the bedposts, then returned to his position with his shoulders between her legs.

He bent her knees, pulled apart her folds with his thumbs and entered her with his tongue. She grabbed her bonds to keep herself from floating to the ceiling.

His mouth moved against her with the same rhythm his body had—had it really only been twenty-four hours ago?

So much had changed since then. So many frightening new possibilities had appeared on the horizon.

None of those mattered tonight, though. Tonight was for dreaming.

The thrusting, sucking, and nibbling stole her breath. The rasp of his cheeks against her inner thighs left her gasping. Her back arched. Her muscles tightened and her skin tingled. With the movement of her hips, she silently urged him on. Urged him to take her higher. Harder.

Connor was more than willing to comply. She felt the power gathering inside, pulsing through her molten core. Her arms and legs began to tremble, then shake. The flat surface of her abdomen quivered. With one final invasion, Connor triggered the earthquake.

Tremors rumbled out from her epicenter. Her world shifted on its axis. Fissures opened in her mind and swallowed all her problems, all her fears, in a giant wave of ecstasy.

When the aftershocks faded and the dust began to settle slowly to the ground like dust motes on a stream of sunshine, she realized he was still there, still holding her tight, his body curved protectively around hers. And he was humming in her ears.

If any babies cried that night, she didn't hear them.

SEVENTEEN

Mara peeked around the corner of her pod's lounge area. Colleen had gone for a walk. That's why the hallways were padded, Mara had found out. So the women could use them as an exercise track without stressing their joints. For their sons' sakes the Gargoyles wanted these women healthy and as happy as possible under the circumstances.

Until they delivered. Mara didn't want to think about what happened to them after that.

She pushed the thought down deep, where she could deal with it later, and checked the hall again. The guard near the stairwell still had his head buried in the morning paper. The nurse's station was empty.

It was now or never.

She hadn't been assigned a work detail this morning because of her doctor's appointment, which had, thankfully, turned out to be a non-event. The doc had drawn a little blood, checked her vital signs, asked her if she'd ever used drugs, had a family history of diabetes or the like, embarrassed her with questions about her sexual activity and when she'd had her last period, then sent her on her way.

She'd decided it was best to pretend she believed herself to be in the early stages of pregnancy, though she still doubted that was likely. This place existed to produce babies. She didn't want to be seen as a wasted asset. Heaven forbid they sent someone else to her to try to correct the situation.

Since she wasn't likely to get another day off, she decided to do some snooping. First up, she wanted to get to the computer at the nursing station and see if she could find a patient record on Angela. She might even be able to get total record counts, and find out how many unlucky women and babies had passed through this place, though she wished she didn't have to know. One was too many.

Holding her breath, she crept across the hall and ducked behind the empty nurse's desk. She waited a moment, heard nothing, and let out a careful, quiet breath in relief.

On her hands and knees she crawled to the computer and eased the keyboard drawer out, then squatted where she could type and see the monitor, but not be seen by the guard.

The screensaver was on, but not password protected. Guess they didn't believe in patient confidentiality around here. The software wasn't difficult to figure out, but it was going to take a while, typing one gently-pressed letter at a time so she wouldn't be heard.

Her nerves were tattered by the time she had up the list of Cs: Campbell, Centerman, Cooper, Cordoz—

The stairwell door slammed shut. Murmured voices echoed down the hall, followed by the soft squish of footsteps on the padded floor.

Biting her lip, she closed the patient program and pushed the keyboard drawer in place as sharply as she dared. With nowhere else to go, she squeezed as close to the desk as possible, her only hope that the visitor would pass by without noticing her.

Her heart kicked when the footsteps stopped right in front of the desk, then started around. A pair of black boots came into view first as she raised her eyes, then dark jeans and a belt with a small sterling silver buckle. A strong torso clad in black knit. Broad shoulders—

Connor!

She fell backward onto her butt.

He extended a hand to help her up. "It's all right, you're clear."

She popped her head up cautiously. "What are you doing here? Where is the guard?"

"I came looking for you, and bribed him to take a break since I'm not supposed to be up here. What are you doing?"

"Looking up Angela's record on the computer. I found her, but I didn't have time to read it—"

"Are you crazy? What if you get caught?"

"I'd be done and gone by now if you hadn't come along."

He dragged a hand through his hair and glanced up and down the corridor. "All right. Hurry up and get what you need. I'll keep an eye out."

She could type faster this time, and knew the program, so she had what she needed in under thirty seconds. Angela was here, sixteen weeks pregnant, and four pods down from hers.

Connor practically dragged her across the hall to her room. His mouth closed over hers before she could get a word out.

His hands on her shoulders were hard, but his lips were gentle. They coaxed and cradled. Accused and gave absolution.

When he finally lifted his head, his pupils were wide dark discs surrounded by a rim of blue. "What happened to you last night?"

Heat flowed to her cheeks as she remembered. "You should know. You were responsible."

"Before that."

She shook her head, confused. "Nothing."

"I thought someone had hurt you. You were in pain."

She raised a hand to lay alongside his face, realizing what he'd felt. "I was aching. And you soothed it."

"I don't understand."

Neither did she. How did anyone comprehend what was happening here? "This place. What they're doing to these women. It hurts."

"We're going to get them out."

"They'll need a lot of help afterward."

"Then you'll help them."

She supposed she would. It was what she did—she ran a shelter for women in crisis. It was how she'd met Angela six years ago.

But they were both getting ahead of themselves.

She pulled out of his embrace because the temptation to lose herself in it again was too great. "How about you. Have you found out anything?"

He scowled. "Only that the grand Wizenot doesn't

show up for his own fancy meals. He skipped the big dinner last night, and breakfast this morning, too."

"Any idea why they brought us here?"

"I think it's kind of standard procedure for the women. They farm them out to cells around the area like Jackson's then bring them back once they're pregnant and work on getting a new bunch. But I don't know what the hell is going on with Jackson and the rest of us."

She could tell that weighed on him. He wasn't the kind of man to sit back and wait to see what happened.

She wasn't that kind of woman, either. "I hate being here, seeing this."

He pulled her forward and planted a kiss in the center of her forehead. "Something's got to break soon. It won't be much longer."

"What are you going to do next?"

He smiled. "If the Wizenot won't come to me, I'll go to the Wizenot. How about you?"

"According to the records, Angela works mostly in the laundry. I'll try to get a work assignment there tomorrow."

His expression turned serious. "Be careful. If she lets on that she knows you, you're going to have a lot of explaining to do. You want to keep a low profile around here."

She poked a finger in his chest. "Hey, spending the day washing your dirty underwear. It doesn't get much lower than that."

Connor's step felt lighter as he left Mara, knowing she was all right—better than he had a right to expect, under the circumstances. Sleep had eluded him last night after he'd felt her suffering. He hadn't been sure she could hold herself together, but once again, he'd underestimated her. She not only held herself together, she was making more progress in her end of the mission than he was in his—an imbalance he intended to correct before nightfall.

He found Jackson in the weight room doing ten-pound curls and straddled the bench next to him without a word, just watching.

As expected, Jackson had soon had enough silent scrutiny. "What?" He curled his lip as he drew the weight in his left hand up and into his bicep.

"What the fuck is going on?" Connor asked.

"I'm trying to get in a little workout."

"We pack up and move the whole damn group up here to Frankenstein's castle on a moment's notice, and here we are sitting on our butts doing nothing again. What's going on?"

"Have you ever been happy just to take a day off?"

"No."

Jackson set his weights in their holders, wiped his face with a towel, and lay down on the bench press. Connor moved into position to spot.

"We're waiting on intelligence," Jackson said, flexing his fingers on the bar.

"Could be a long wait for some of us."

Jackson didn't laugh, but amusement flickered in his eyes. He puffed out his chest, lifted the bar off the poles, and began to pump up and down, breathing with each stroke.

Connor cupped his hands an inch below the bar. "Intelligence on what?"

"Our next target."

"Which is?"

No answer.

Connor grabbed the bar and pushed it down until it rested a hair above Jackson's Adam's apple. Jackson tried to push it back up, but leverage was against him.

"You still don't trust me," Connor said.

"This isn't helping you earn it." Jackson's brow began to sweat in earnest.

Connor pushed the 250-pound weight a fraction lower.

"I don't know what the target is, either. No one does but the Wizenot."

Connor lifted the weight bar, set it back on its stand. "Then how do I get an audience with him?"

Jackson sat up and mopped his forehead again. "You don't. When the Great One wants to talk to you, you'll be called."

"Are you sure this Great One even exists? No one I've talked to has ever seen the man."

"He exists. And he's not a man you want to trifle with, Rihyad." Jackson got a bottle of water from a bucket on the floor and drank thirstily as he turned to walk away. "Not everything here is what it seems."

Now what the hell was *that* supposed to mean?

The great Wizenot of Minnesota—of the world!— sat in the center of a ritual circle, his loyal dog Wulf lying by his side, and surrounded by the tools of his trade: a wilted rose, a chalice of soured wine, a stone jug of putrid water, a black-and-white striped candle now burning black, and statues of the God and Goddess knocked facedown on the floor.

He raised his arms, palms up, and a breeze flapped the hem of his black robe. "Oh Lord of Darkness, oh Master of Night. I call upon your weighty might. Rid the world of veils o'er Earth and mind; show me she who seeks to find."

Wulf whined as the Wizenot plucked a spot of hair, then groaned and rested his head on his paws when his master dropped the hairs into the chalice of wine.

The red liquid swirled slowly, thickening and growing darker in shade until it reached the color and consistency of blood.

He dipped his forefinger in the chalice and painted red lines across his forehead, his cheeks, his chin, and his wrists, then did the same to Wulf before raising the vessel to his lips and drinking the foul contents.

The dregs of the wine once again swirled in the bottom of the cup. The Wizenot stared at the pattern of crimson and gold, his physical sight blurring while his mental sight came into focus as the vision began.

Ah, yes. There she was, she who seeks her brother.

She lay in bed with her husband's arms banded tight around her middle. How sickeningly sweet.

He looked past the physical plane to her mind. She was strong in the old magic, this one, for with only a little help from him, her visions continued in her sleep, long after the ritual circle in which she requested them had been closed.

In minutes, the sea and wind whipped her and a bolt of lightning charged the air as it speared through the thunderheads above her.

With each seeing, the vision became a little clearer.

A little more detailed. This time, the Wise One heard the groan of a boat being tossed about and the shouts of men over the roar of the sea.

He kept his distance from that vision for now. The woman's mind was untrained but sharp. She had sensed his presence last time, and he didn't want to give himself away again. Leaving the wail of the wind and weather for her, he drew back his viewpoint, taking in the stars above the atrium roof, the skyline, the room in which she sat with two other men, her husband, and the weakling Wizenot of Chicago.

The path of her travels was still fresh, and he traced it back to the room she'd come from, and the office in which she'd had tea with this same pair that afternoon.

Only when he was satisfied he knew the location of her quarters did he press closer to her vision of the sea.

He watched as the bow of the boat dipped precariously beneath the black water, then shot straight up like a dolphin doing a tail dance in the surf. The deck tilted. Ocean spray stung his face, as it did hers. He tasted salt on his lips, as she did, and heard the same sailors' curses she heard.

He felt her struggle to pull back, to move off the deck of the ship for a wider angle. Her will vibrated in the air with almost as much ferocity as the storm. She fought her way back to the broader view, working for every inch. He felt the ache of her muscles, the burn of her lungs, but she overcame.

Inches opened up between her consciousness and the boat being battered by the waves, then feet, then yards.

The next time the bow of the boat lifted up on the

crest of a swell, he saw it. Painted in peeling white on the black hull: THE WHITE WHALE.

He smiled.

Very good. Another clue to the brother she had lost. The son of Damien Paré, one of the Old Ones, the original townsmen of Rouen who had been converted to Gargoyles so many years—so many lifetimes—ago.

Laughing, he blew out the candle and the vision vanished.

Yes. Very good.

It was almost time.

EIGHTEEN

Hours after Rachel had broken her ritual circle
with Nathan and Teryn, the sound of unhealthy, morbid laughter jerked Rachel out of sleep. Her head
snapped back, thudded on something solid, and it took
her a moment to place it as Nathan's chest. By then
she was sitting up and shaking. She could still feel the
freezing weight of seawater-soaked clothes and feel
the deck rolling beneath her feet, leaving her nause-
ated.

Nathan sat behind her and pulled her close again.
"Are you okay?"

"Another dream."

"The same one?" He rubbed warmth into her
shoulders.

She nodded. "How can the visions continue even
after we broke the circle? Why do I keep seeing it?"

"I don't know," he soothed. "You shouldn't. The visions should end once the ritual circle is broken. Teryn is studying the old texts that survived the fire, looking for answers."

She turned to face her husband, remembering more of the dream. "I saw more this time. I heard men shouting about running lines and turning her into the waves before she capsized."

"Sounds like they were are caught in one hell of a storm."

"Or they're going to be. I still haven't figured out if it's past, present, or future that I'm seeing."

"I'd rule out present since you've seen it several days in a row."

The tastes and smells of the dream welled up in her senses. The pitch of her voice changed as she remembered more. "I saw the name on the boat, Nathan." She grabbed his arms. "*The White Whale*. We can trace it. We can find Levi."

He didn't hesitate. He swung his legs out of bed and reached for a pair of sweats. "I'll get on the Internet and see if I can find any registrations."

But she pulled him back before he left, her excitement suddenly turned to cold fear. "He saw it, too, Nathan. Whoever is watching me. He was there. He knows the name of my brother's boat."

Goddamn mother-effing son-of-a-bitch!

Connor squirmed in his ladder-back chair at the lunch table. The veins in his neck bulged dangerously under the shirt and tie he'd had to borrow from the loaner collection the major-domo Thaddeus kept for guests. He clenched the handle of the elegant antique silver soupspoon so tightly, he thought the soft metal might bend in his hand.

He glared at the ornately carved oak captain's chair at the end of the table.

The *empty*, ornately carved oak captain's chair.

This asshole Wizenot had a real flair for head games, getting them all gussied up for another supposed audience over lunch, only to send Thaddeus with his regrets after the first course had been served.

*God*damn *mother-effing son-of-a-bitch!*

He tried to take a bite of the sweet potato soup in front of him, but he'd worked himself into such a state that his stomach wouldn't let him eat. All he needed was one look at the guy. A name. A face to put on his dartboard back home. Then he could grab Mara and leave.

He was beginning to wonder if the Wizenot was really even here at all. Maybe the man was paranoid enough to keep misleading his own people in order to keep his location secret.

Probably not a bad idea, since his people consisted of murderers and thieves.

He lifted another spoonful of soup, then set it back in the bowl uneaten.

How long did he hang on here, hoping to catch a glimpse of the man behind the curtain? This great wizard everyone seemed so in awe of.

The answer came more easily than he expected.

Not long.

Tonight, tomorrow night at the latest, he had to

leave. He needed to take the information he did have back to his people. They had an estate full of soldiers to deal with. A house full of women and children to rescue.

If he couldn't deliver the death blow to the Minnesota congregation, he would at least deal it a critical setback. He'd buy some time to hunt down the man responsible for the misery of so many.

The server's door at the end of the room swung open, and Mara came in with a pitcher of ice water in one hand and a carafe of coffee in the other. She'd changed into a poorly fitting plain black dress covered by a white apron. More borrowed getups to please the elusive Wizenot.

He bet she hated it.

She looked tired as she glided around the table, quietly filling glasses and cups, but her back was straight, strong. She held her head high.

It relaxed him a little bit to see her holding up, hanging in. If she could hang on to her hope and her dignity in this place, he should at least be able to keep his frustration in check. Watching her, he decided that if he hit another brick wall in his task this afternoon, he would help her with hers.

He'd help her find this woman, Angela.

Mara reached his place at the table and leaned over his left shoulder to top off his water glass. As she did so, the carafe in her right hand caught on the back of his chair and tipped, spilling coffee down the front of his borrowed suit coat.

He nearly toppled the chair—and Mara—jumping up to yank off the jacket before the steaming hot liquid soaked through to his skin. A trickle seared his collarbone before he could divest himself of the garment, and a few drops stung the back of his hand, but other than that, he avoided disaster. Narrowly.

"Oh, I'm so sorry!" She set the half-empty carafe on the table, scooped up his napkin, and dabbed at the stain on his shoulder. Jackson was already mopping the table with his own linen before the spill dribbled over the edge of the table and onto his lap.

Thaddeus watched the whole exchange from his place by the serving table without moving.

"I'm so sorry," Mara repeated, sounding so upset that it took Connor a moment to realize the whole accident had been staged. "Are you burned?"

"I'm fine," he said in a clipped tone, wondering if that was the answer she wanted. "No harm done."

What was she up to?

"Your poor jacket." She took the soaked wool off his hands. "It'll be ruined if this stain sets. Let me take it down to the laundry for you. Maybe we can salvage it."

Ah, so that was the game. Didn't get the work assignment she wanted and needed an excuse to get into the laundry area, where Angela was supposed to be, eh?

He gave her a hard look that had nothing to do with having coffee spilled on him. She was playing a dangerous game with dangerous people, and if she wasn't careful, *she* was going to be the one who got burned. "See that you do."

He trailed his hand down her arm as she turned to leave. "And deliver it to my room in person tonight."

The men behind him guffawed and elbowed one another.

Something—anticipation, or just surprise?—flickered in Mara's eyes and her mouth rounded into an unspoken O. A heated look passed between them, and then the moment was gone and she hurried out of the dining room, jacket in hand, without a backward glance.

Staring at the few men who were still chuckling, he settled back into his seat. A new server instantly appeared to bring him a fresh napkin and clear the soggy ones from the table.

With a new appetite, Connor picked up his spoon and lifted a mouthful of sweet potato soup. Prospects for his day—and his night—were looking better all the time.

By providing him the perfect opening to get her out of the women's ward and into his room, where they could make an easier escape, Mara had sealed his decision about leaving. He regretted that he wouldn't get to look the Wizenot in the eye, so that he could know the face of evil, but he had what he needed.

In his wanderings he'd learned much. Enough for his people to put together a plan of attack.

He had troop strength and location. He had most of the security features in the building. He had the sentry locations and the times they changed shifts. He had the weapons store.

And now he had Mara.

Even sour-faced Thaddeus, who had watched the exchange with more interest than Connor found comfortable from the corner of the room, hadn't challenged his authority to bring her into his room.

* * *

The guard at the door only gave Mara a cursory look as she showed up at the laundry area with Connor's stained jacket. The change in the air hit her like a slap when she walked in. The room was uncomfortably hot, and the air was heavy with steam. The scents of bleach and industrial detergent were enough to make her head reel.

Suddenly she was glad she hadn't gotten the assignment she'd requested here when this morning's work details were handed out.

Nerves churned in her gut. This was it. Everything she'd worked for, everything she'd risked had been for this moment. To find her friend.

She took a few slow steps forward. The facility was huge. This first area seemed to be for bed linens. Rolling carts piled with sheets, pillowcases, and blankets lined one wall. Commercial washers with glass viewers on the doors hummed and swished.

A short woman with dark hair unloaded one of the washers into a cart and rolled it over to an oversize dryer. She had dark hair and an olive complexion like Angela, but it wasn't her.

Mara moved on to the second area. This one appeared to be for washable clothes. Three women sorted whites and darks at a table, staring at her curiously as she passed. None of them was Angela.

Her heart pounding, she started toward the third area. Through the doorway she could see the specialty equipment for the finer clothes—steam presses and dry-cleaning chambers. But the half of the room she could see was empty save for a guard posted at the door that led back into the main part of the house.

What if Mara was wrong? What if Angela wasn't

there? What if there was another Angela Cordoza? What if the computer records were wrong, and she'd died or been moved?

What if her friend was beyond help, and everything Mara had done, everything she'd suffered, was for nothing?

She put that fire out right away. Everything she'd done counted for something. This was bigger than just Angela now. All these women needed help. All the babies upstairs.

Angela or no Angela, Mara was going to make sure they got out.

Or die trying.

With the three women folding clothes watching her openly, Mara walked across the room to an angle where she could see the other half of the room.

There, standing over a steam press, was her friend.

Tears of joy sprang to her eyes, clogged her throat. Her chest felt as if someone had inflated a balloon inside it.

Angela's round face wasn't as round as Mara had last seen it, and her stomach was a little more round than it had been, showing the first signs of her pregnancy. Her eyes weren't as bright and the ever-present smile Mara remembered was missing.

But as far as she could see, Angela was healthy and whole. The rest would come back in time.

The urge—the *need*—to run into the room and throw her arms around her friend had her feet twitching, but Mara held her ground. Angela would be surprised, and there was no telling what she might blurt out. With a guard standing so close by, that could be dangerous. Plus there was still the no-talking-while-working rule.

For now, it was enough for Mara just to stand and absorb the sight of the woman she'd wanted so badly to find. And a delicious sight it was.

They'd met over five years ago, when Mara's women's shelter had only been open a few months, and she was having a hard time dealing with the building upkeep, the paperwork, and the women's needs all at the same time without any help.

Angela had been a client, beaten by her husband, but she'd seen the need and pitched in right away. Said hard work made her feel less like a charity case.

Angela had never been a charity case. She'd been a blessing.

Angela eventually left the shelter and reestablished her life sans husband. Mara developed a routine for dealing with the needs of the shelter. But the two of them had stayed firm friends since that time.

A few months ago, the insurance company where Angela worked closed its Minneapolis office. Angela had talked about moving away, starting over someplace warmer. Mara had encouraged her, not wanting to lose her friend, but understanding how healthy fresh starts could be.

Lives were like garden soil in that way. They needed to be turned over once in a while to stay rich and fertile.

When Angela had disappeared, Mara had felt guilty. After a cursory investigation, the police concluded she'd left of her own free will. Mara knew that wasn't true. She never would have dropped out of sight without leaving contact information.

But Mara had a longstanding distrust of the "the system." When her concerns were disregarded, she took matters into her own hands and traced Angela's final days in the twin cities—including answering a job ad she'd found circled in the Sunday newspaper she found in Angela's house.

And here she was.

It had been a long, hard road, but they were together again.

She willed Angela to look up from her task. She wanted her to get a glimpse. To know she wasn't alone anymore.

She might not be able to talk to her, but Mara felt sure she could send her friend a look that would tell her friend everything would be okay.

She was still waiting for that glance when Connor came through the door behind her and stood at her shoulder.

"Is that her?" he whispered.

She nodded.

Gently he took her hand, as if he understood that she might never leave without someone to make her, and led her through the laundry area door and into the main hallway outside.

Underneath the LAUNDRY *sign, Connor tipped* Mara's head up and studied her. Her eyes shone with both tears and happiness. A measure of the color she'd lost over the last two weeks had returned to her face. Her smile lightened his heart.

"She looked okay," he said.

She nodded.

"You made the right decision not going to her."

"The guard . . . What are you doing down here, Connor? You said I was supposed to come tonight."

"I wanted to tell you to bring anything you want to take from this place with you tonight. We're getting out of here." He couldn't resist lowering his head and nuzzling her ear. "And I wanted to see you. I couldn't wait."

She pulled her head back, out of his reach. "How are we going to get out?"

He checked over his shoulder to make sure no one was watching, then folded his arms like chicken wings and flapped.

The color that had spotted her cheeks just moments ago drained from her face. "You forgot one little detail: I don't have wings."

"I can carry you."

"You can't."

"I promise you, I can."

She looked hesitant. "What about Angela?"

"We'll come back for her, and all the others. With the whole Chicago congregation to back us up."

She pulled her lip between her teeth. "It'll be a war zone. You can't leave women and children to be in the middle of that."

"I can't smuggle out two dozen or so women and God knows how many infants, either." He steadied her with hands on both her shoulders. "I know it's risky. But if you were in their place, and your choice was either to go on living like this, or to take that risk, which would you chose?"

"You know which."

"I bet all of them would, too. We'll do our best to keep every one of them safe. I promise."

The tears in her eyes weren't tears of joy anymore. "Maybe I should stay. Get them ready."

Connor's heart kicked. "No. You're leaving with—"

Mara straightened, pulling out of his grasp just as Connor heard the footsteps behind him. Jackson was coming toward them, shaking his blond head. He threw a pointed look at the sign on the door, then at Mara. "Now how did I know I'd find you down here?"

"Guess you're just quick like that. What do you want?" Connor said.

Jackson held his hands up shoulder high, palms out. "Fine. You want to snap at me? I won't give you the good news."

"What news?"

"Your wish has finally come true. The Wizenot wants to see you."

NINETEEN

*Connor followed Jackson upstairs with the enthu-*siasm of a hungry predator who's finally caught the scent of his prey. Maybe he would have a name and face for this Wizenot before he left, after all. He'd know who to look for when he came back so that he could personally kick the man's ass for the suffering he had caused.

Raw energy bubbled and boiled inside him to the point that he could hardly stop moving when they reached the Wizenot's office. At least, he assumed it was the Wizenot's office. The Wizenot's personal gofer, Thaddeus, sat at a small secretary's desk outside the massive oak door, a large, scruffy dog on the floor beside him.

Connor flexed his fists, shuffled his feet, forced himself not to pace while they waited for Thaddeus to acknowledge them. He forced himself not to stalk.

Finally, Thaddeus straightened the single sheet of

white paper on his desk and looked up. He touched a button on his phone and two of the black-clad bodyguards that seemed to be everywhere in this place entered through a side door and took positions behind Connor and Jackson. Blocking the exit.

Some of Connor's enthusiasm faded, replaced by wariness.

Thaddeus gestured toward two chairs in front of him. "Welcome, gentlemen. Won't you sit?"

"We came to see the Wizenot." Not his servant. The implication was clear.

"I'm sorry," Thaddeus said smoothly. "He's tied up on another matter right now. He's asked me to convey his regrets. And his instructions."

Connor swore. "More head games?"

Thaddeus cocked his head, his expression sincere, as if he truly didn't understand. The son of a bitch. "Head games? The Wizenot has many responsibilities, as I'm sure you can imagine. He simply can't be bothered with every detail."

Ah, now *Thaddeus's* implication was clear. Connor was a detail. A triviality not worthy of the Great One's attention.

The man would regret not paying more attention to him one day. One day soon.

Jackson took a seat. Connor stood his ground.

"I was told the Great One had a mission for us," Jackson said.

"Indeed." Thaddeus leaned back in his chair and picked up a pen, tapped it on the tabletop, purposely drawing out the suspense—and his moment of control—Connor was sure. "Actually it's a second chance at a mission that failed before."

"Another shipment of guns?"

"No, this merchandise is much more valuable." He threw a smug look up at Connor and held his gaze, no doubt anxious to see Connor's reaction when he dropped whatever bomb he was holding.

"We're going after the children in Chicago again," he finally said. "And this time, we intend to get them."

Jackson shifted in his chair. "I thought they were in hiding."

His gaze still locked on Connor's, Thaddeus said, "We found them."

A thunderstorm of loathing roiled inside Connor, but he let none of it reach his face. He couldn't afford to react at all. Not here. Not now.

Connor made sure he could keep his voice even before he spoke. "They weren't as vulnerable as you thought last time. Now they'll be even more on guard. How do you expect us to get in?"

"You'll force your way in, if you have to. Jackson, you will be in command and all the men of your house will be with you, along with three other houses who are on the way here and will join you for a full tactical briefing within the hour."

An all-out attack? Did Thaddeus know how many lives would be lost—on both sides—in a battle like that?

Of course he did.

He also knew that four houses—forty Gargoyles or more—would overwhelm the small Chicago congregation. Connor's people didn't stand a chance.

"I don't care what it takes," Thaddeus added. "Kill every one of the adults if you have to. In fact, I prefer if you do. I want those children."

"You mean the Wizenot wants those children."

Thaddeus acknowledged Connor's correction with a minute tilt of his head. "Of course."

Then Thaddeus leaned forward and steepled his hands. "Just so we're clear, Rihyad. Eric and Paulo back there—" He nodded toward the burly guards at the door. "They will be with you every minute from now until you return. *If* you return. If you attempt to warn your former congregation, or help them in any way during the attack, they will kill you."

"I thought I'd proven my loyalty, Thaddeus. Is this another test?"

"Consider it a final exam." Thaddeus smiled. "Oh, and one more thing. In case you're considering trying to escape Eric and Paulo, you might want to rethink that."

He nodded toward the men. They opened the door to the hallway and a third guard dragged Mara through.

Thaddeus's smile widened as Connor couldn't help but flinch.

"Your little friend, and the child she may carry, will be with me while you're gone." Thaddeus's eyes gleamed as if he had a fever. He was enjoying this, the bastard. "Betray me, and they die."

Connor had never before known hatred as he knew it at that moment. It roared and seethed inside him, threatening to tear him apart from the inside out. Threatening to tear Thaddeus apart.

If Mara were pregnant, and if she were carrying a son, that child guaranteed Connor a chance to live again if he were killed. To reincarnate. Without a son, if Connor died, his soul was gone forever.

Not a bad option, as far as he was concerned, if he

had to watch his congregation be slaughtered and Mara murdered.

"Now that we understand each other . . ." Thaddeus leaned back in his chair, his eyes returning to normal intensity and his voice less menacing. Almost friendly. "Tell me Connor. Is it true the Chicagoans have allowed a woman to join their congregation?"

Connor would have just as soon spit in Thaddeus's face as give him any information, but he couldn't afford to be uncooperative with Mara's life at stake.

Besides, he wasn't sure he had enough breath to spit. Thaddeus's surprises had robbed him of air.

"The Wizenot there caters to a few liberals in his congregation. Not all agree with his decisions."

"How about you? Do you agree?"

Connor wasn't sure what his opinion had to do with anything, but he answered honestly. "No."

"Is that why you left them?"

"In part."

Thaddeus tapped his pen again. "Then your alliance with young Mara here is only for the sake of producing a child? Once your son is born, you'll take the child and have nothing more to do with her?"

Now Connor understood. More head games, this time aimed at Mara. Why bring a woman into the room unless you can torture her a little while she's there?

Or maybe he was trying to turn Mara against him. Planned to pump her for information about him while he was gone.

This game got more dangerous with every turn.

The truth was, he hadn't allowed himself to think

about what he and Mara would do once this was over, assuming they survived. Hadn't allowed himself to think that far ahead.

Maybe he hadn't wanted to think about it. About leaving her.

He still had trouble believing women could be integrated into *Les Gargouillen*. He was still a traditionalist.

He was also a realist. He knew that walking away from Mara would be one of the hardest things he'd ever done, if it came to that.

He wasn't sure what the right answer was for the future of his people. Some things were just bigger than one man could decide. Even if that man was a Gargoyle.

He met Thaddeus's gaze directly and avoided Mara's, hoping she would know the truth inside him regardless of the words.

"If I wanted to change the way I've lived for ten lifetimes now, I would have stayed in Chicago."

With that, he and Jackson were dismissed to prepare for their briefing, and Mara was pulled away to God knows where.

Under any other circumstances, Connor would have been happy to be back in Chicago, but this was like a nightmare—one that didn't end at daybreak.

Already the first pink and orange rays of sunlight glowed over the top of the old YMCA that housed the Chicago congregation of *Les Gargouillen*. The Y was actually an amalgamation of five separate buildings, two classroom units, a dining hall, a gymnasium, and administrative offices, patched together haphazardly as the facility grew and evolved over two decades. It sat in the middle of a district of subsidized housing projects and light industrial businesses. The streets were mostly empty this time of the morning.

A snow began to fall. The wind whipped the flakes along the curb and Connor's thoughts swirled with them, moving fast but mostly going in circles.

Did he warn his people, or not?

Yes, Eric and Paulo, who sat in the back of the SUV parked on the corner across from the YMCA, would kill him. But that wasn't what stopped him.

The problem was that Thaddeus would kill Mara.

How did he choose between her and his people?

On the one hand, he could argue that there were dozens of people in the Y. Many lives could be saved if he warned them, whereas only one would be lost. Mara's.

The needs of the many outweighed the needs of one.

On the other hand, Mara was human, and those inside the Y were Gargoyle. Except for Rachel, who was human. Sort of.

The directive of his people was to protect humans, even at the expense of their own lives, if need be.

So he should let an entire congregation die to ensure one woman's—one human's—survival?

It was a dilemma without an answer. And while he sat out there safe and warm in his SUV agonizing over it, teams from Minnesota were positioning themselves around each of the buildings, ready to make entry. They went in as men, not in beast form. It was easier to carry the guns that way.

Eric and Paulo wore radio headsets so they could monitor progress of the invasion—the massacre—and they'd forced Connor to wear one, too.

They couldn't pass play-by-play images of the carnage to Connor through the use the Second Sight without the Gargoyles inside sensing it, and warning them of the intruders' presence, but that didn't mean they wanted him to miss out on the fun.

The countdown began: three, two, one. Entry.

Connor listened to the shuffle of feet and the quiet *whoosh* of dozens of men's quiet breaths through his earpiece. With each second that passed, his own breath became more difficult to draw. His heart squeezed painfully.

Warn them, or not warn them? Save them, or kill them?

He squeezed his eyes shut and tried not to listen, but every sound, every whisper seemed amplified in the earpiece, which was why it hurt so much when a roar so loud it could have come from the belly of the Earth screamed through it.

Glass shattered and men moaned. The SUV vibrated as if an earthquake passed beneath its wheels, then went still.

Jackson's voice sounded frantic when he called out. "Team one, what the hell was that? Team one? Team one, report!"

Only static answered.

"Team two, where are you?"

"In the east corridor, outside the dining hall."

"What the hell happened down there? Where is team one?"

"Some kind of explosion. We're checking now, but we think team one is . . . gone."

"Team two, back out of there. Get over to the children's quarters—"

This time, Connor saw the explosion as well as heard it. Glass and clouds of dust blew out the windows on the side of the building facing the street his car was parked on. Debris rained down on the roof.

"Team leader, this is team five. What the hell is going on? We're coming back."

"Negative. Get to the children's quarters. Complete your assignment. Repeat, complete your assignment!"

Eric growled. "What the hell is going on in there?"

Paulo shook his head. "Sounds like World War Three."

"Damn. How did we get stuck with baby-sitter duty?" They both glared at Connor.

The concussion of a third explosion shook the SUV.

"It's rigged!" someone yelled over the radio. "The place is booby-trapped!"

"Help!" another voice called. "Help! The wall collapsed. We can't get out!"

Voices, too many to determine how many, talked over each other, all calling for help.

Eric and Paulo looked at each other, their hands on the door handles. "Let's go," Eric said.

"I'm with you," Paulo answered.

Eric shot Connor a warning glare. "You. With us. You try anything, I'm not even going to tell you before I kill you."

Heads down, they ran across the street and into the building. Dust clouded the air inside. It was hard to see, hard to breathe. Connor pulled the neck of his sweater up over his mouth as a filter.

"This way." Paulo headed toward the stairs that led to the children's wing. At the stairwell door, they nearly ran down Jackson. His team crowded close behind.

"The children's rooms are empty," Jackson said. "The whole damn thing was a setup. Team three is trapped on the second floor."

"Let's go." Eric reached for the door, choking on the dust. "We've got to get them and get out of here."

"Go," Jackson said, and the group stormed up the stairs. Connor brought up the rear except for Jackson, who was behind him.

And then not behind him.

Connor paused halfway up the staircase. That was strange.

He glanced up. Eric and Paulo had reached the top of the stairs. In their fervor to rescue their comrades, they neglected to check the door for a booby trap before opening it.

The concussion of the explosion almost blew out Connor's eardrums. A tongue of fire speared down the stairs. He dropped and tumbled down the steps while splinters of wood, metal, and body parts flew overhead.

Something gouged his shoulder. The corner of a step bruised his hip. Then he hit the bottom and the breath was knocked out of him.

He lay still a moment, waiting for the bells to stop pealing in his ears.

When he could breathe again, he stood and wiped the blood and other matter from his face. At the top of the stairs, a blackened door hung from one hinge. Two bodies lay beneath it.

He looked up, then down the hall, the way Jackson had gone. He didn't have to worry about Eric and Paulo any longer, so he followed Jackson.

A few minutes later, he caught up. A dark shape,

hard to identify in the dust-clouded air, turned a corner down the hall toward the administrative offices.

Really strange. The mission had been the children, and they weren't here. So where was Jackson going?

The hallways twisted and turned, but Jackson negotiated the maze as if he knew exactly where he was going. At one point, he stopped and huddled against the wall.

Connor frowned, trying to see through the smoke until he realized what Jackson was doing—talking on his cell phone.

Stranger and stranger.

Jackson flipped the phone shut and continued on his way, sticking close to the wall. His steps grew lighter, slower, and Connor figured he'd just about reached his goal.

It wasn't hard to figure out where he was going. This hallway only led one place: Teryn's quarters.

Jackson lifted his foot and kicked in the door.

TWENTY

Mara watched Thaddeus the way a mouse without a bolt hole might watch a cat on the prowl. He worked at his desk, ignoring her, but she didn't fool herself that he wasn't aware of her. He hadn't let her out of his sight since dawn.

She wondered where Connor was, and if the raid had begun. What would he do? She couldn't imagine the untenable position he was in, knowing that his friends, his family, were going to be attacked. Killed.

Surely he would find a way to stop it. Surely he wouldn't let them die to save her. She hoped he wouldn't.

Thaddeus stood from his desk outside the Wizenot's office, stretched, and sauntered toward her.

She resisted the urge to run away from him. There was no escape, nowhere to run to.

The two guards he'd posted outside the door in the hall would make sure of that.

"So," he said, looking down on her, "it will have begun by now. What do you think he'll do?"

Surely he would warn them. She hoped he would. Then he and his congregation could come back here and free the women and children. End this diabolical scheme of kidnap and slavery.

Even if she didn't live to see it.

She lifted her chin. "He will do exactly what you asked of him. Your suspicion of him is unfounded."

"Is it?" He brushed her cheek with the back of his hand, and she flinched. "You defend the man who is your captor? Who raped you, impregnated you, and admits he intends to take your child and leave you. Or worse."

Why did he keep insisting she was pregnant? He couldn't possibly know. It was too soon for anyone to know. Even her.

"I am a survivor," she said. "Resisting him would only have gotten me killed, or locked in a cage. As long as I carry his child, he will protect me."

"And afterward?"

Her stomach churned. "Afterward is nine months away. I can't know what will happen then."

He squatted before her, resting his fingers on her thigh. "What if I said I would protect you? For nine months and beyond."

"I'd say you wanted something."

He laughed. "Indeed. Tell me about Rihyad. Is he really as loyal to me as he claims?"

Mara dug her fingers into her palms to keep herself from jumping up from the chair and running. He wanted her to rat out Connor. To sell her soul.

"For as long as it serves him," she said. She

wouldn't sell herself. But she didn't want to oversell Connor, either. Painting too noble of a picture would give him away as surely as the truth.

He smiled. "You are a prize, Mara Kincaide. I can see why he chose you." His fingers crept up her thigh toward the juncture of her hip. His thumb rubbed little circles on her flesh. "I'm just not sure why you would choose him, when I can give you so much more. Is he that good?"

His eyelids lowered seductively.

Mara had trouble swallowing. Every muscle in her body tensed, protesting his touch. "No," she gritted out. "You're that bad."

His hand went still on her leg. His eyes snapped wide open to reveal gray irises as cold as snow clouds.

He stood and moved to the other side of the room. "That's too bad, then, because I'm going to kill him when he returns, whether he's betrayed me or not. I don't trust him, and I won't have anyone in my congregation that I don't trust."

"*Your* congregation?"

His nostrils flared a moment. Then his expression went passive. He inclined his head toward the door to the Wizenot's office. The door behind which Thaddeus's boss was supposedly hard at work.

"The Great One's congregation, of course. I am but his humble servant."

Something bothered Mara about his sudden change from Master-of-the-Universe mode to complete subservience. She decided to pull the tiger's tail a little more, see if she could figure out what he might be hiding.

"Must be a pain being at someone else's beck and

call night and day," she said. "Are you really just his office drone, or do you render your services in his bedroom as well?"

He crossed the room to her chair in two strides, his fist raised.

Mara ducked under his arm, turned so that she could see him and backed away. She flicked a glance toward the door to the hall, but knew she'd never get past the guards. That left only one alternative.

The door to the Wizenot's office.

Hell, at least she'd get to see the elusive leader of the creeps before she died.

Taking a deep breath, she darted toward the door, yanked it open, and stepped inside the revered Wizenot's domain.

The empty Wizenot's domain. Empty except for a large, scraggly dog sitting on the side of a raised platform dominated by the gaudiest throne-chair Mara had ever seen. The dog thumped its tail once, stood, and walked to Thaddeus, where it nosed at his hand to be petted.

Realization struck Mara like a thunderbolt. "You're not a servant at all, are you? You're him. You're the so-called great Wizenot."

Jackson crashed through the door to Teryn's office. Connor charged in on his heels. Behind his desk, Teryn jumped to his feet. Rachel, who stood in front of the bookcase, leaped back.

At the window, Nathan turned calmly toward the commotion. "Good morning. We've been waiting for you."

Connor charged in on Jackson's heels and nearly ran the man down when he skidded to stop, staring at Nathan.

"You," Jackson said, looking Nathan up and down as if to be sure he wasn't an apparition. "You're not dead."

His gaze whipped around to Connor. "You betrayed us."

"No," Connor said. "You betrayed all of our people. Everything we stand for."

Jackson stared at the face of a grandfather clock on the wall, his gaze going hazy. Time and space wavered.

Sensing the tunnel of Second Sight beginning to form, Connor lunged toward the wall, grabbed an antique broadsword from its display brackets, and ran it through Jackson's midsection.

Clutching his middle, Jackson sank to his knees, still looking up at Connor. Blood seeped between his fingers.

"I'll see you in the next life," he said, then fell to the floor. His eyes stared up at the ceiling, unblinking, unseeing.

Connor dropped the sword from his shaking hands. God, he'd never killed one of his own kind before. Not for real.

"He was going to use the Second Sight," Connor explained to no one in particular. "He was going to contact his leader."

Teryn stepped around the desk, stood over the body. "You had no choice. They came here to kill us."

Connor blinked to clear his mind. "The children. They're safe? They're not here?"

Nathan reassured him. "They're safe. We moved them."

"How did you know?" Understanding dawned slowly. The truth left his mouth bitter. "You moved them right after I left, didn't you? You didn't trust me."

"We had no way to know what they might do to get information out of you if your cover was blown."

Connor's fists clenched at his sides. "I did not lead them here."

"We know," Teryn said.

"Then how—?"

"I did it." Rachel spoke up for the first time. "Accidentally."

Nathan moved to his wife's side, wrapped an arm around her waist and pulled her close. "We think someone was watching her somehow. She didn't realize it until recently. When she did, and told me and Teryn, we knew they'd be coming."

"And you set this trap." Connor frowned. "But if someone was watching Rachel through the Second Sight, you should have sensed it, Nathan."

"It wasn't the Second Sight. Whoever it was used . . . some other power to observe her."

"And what he saw through her eyes led him to this place. But if he saw through her eyes, wouldn't he have known the children weren't here?"

Teryn and Nathan exchanged glances. "We don't think he really wanted the children this time," Teryn said.

Nathan pulled Rachel closer. His touch was gentle, but his eyes were ferocious. "He was after my wife."

"But why—?" Connor didn't have to finish the question. "She is a daughter of an Old One. The magic is strong in her."

Nathan's dark eyes went hard as stone. "She'd

make a fine broodmare for his stable. Produce powerful soldiers."

Connor shook his head in disbelief at the lengths to
which Thaddeus and his evil boss would go in their ef-
forts to become the most powerful beings in the world.
"They sent their own men in to die as a diversion. The
real mission was Jackson's attempt to take Rachel."

Teryn sighed. "It appears so. But this will be the
last time they attempt to harm anyone in my congregation. You're back now. You must tell us what you know
so that we can mount an offensive of our own."

Connor quickly filled Teryn in on what he knew, including the location of the Duluth estate.

"We'll call a meeting of the Council as soon as possible to finalize our plans." Sirens sounded in the distance, growing closer. "Right now, I'm afraid we have
to get out of here before we're asked many questions
for which we have no answers."

Rachel, Nathan, and Teryn skirted around the body
toward the door.

"You go," Connor said. "I have to rejoin my
brethren."

Teryn's brow furrowed. "You've given us what we
need. Your place is back with us now."

Connor shook his head. "He has Mara. He'll kill
her if I don't come back."

The bastard may already have killed her, for all he
knew. But Connor had to find out for sure. He had to
go back to Duluth.

"You'll be on your own until we can get there,"
Nathan warned. "The Wizenots in the Detroit, St.
Louis, and Denver congregations have agreed to send
men, but they won't be here for another day."

Connor nodded curtly and gave a small salute before leaving. "I understand."

The odds would be against him, but he'd beaten the odds before. He just hoped his luck held out.

For Mara's sake, and for his.

Connor circled the sky above the Duluth estate of Les Gargouillen of Minnesota, announcing his presence with a piercing shriek. Two guards in front of the house lifted rifles and tracked his flight. Diving and banking, he shrieked again, this time in challenge.

The side of the house gave him cover, and he glided just below the roofline, positioning himself so he could come over the top and dive at them, or circle around and strike from behind.

A cold draft beneath his wings lifted him, pushed him forward. He rode it like a runaway train on a downhill rail, picking up speed with every meter. His heart raced with the wind. A savage blood pulsed in his veins.

The bastards below might have guns, but he was a Gargoyle fully Awakened. He had the power of the beast.

Over the top, he decided. He would shoot straight up over the roof, then tuck his legs and wings in tight to his body to decrease wind resistance, dive, and break their necks before they could bring their cumbersome human weapons to bear.

As he topped the roof he scanned for more guards and found none. The two men on the ground stood back to back, swiveling as one, searching. But they would not see him in time.

He nosed down and dove. The wind roared around him, buffeted him, pulled at his wings, his skin, his bones, trying to disrupt the streamlined shape streaking toward its prey like a bullet. But he held fast, kept his eyes on the targets. He extended his talons an inch, then six.

"Stop!" Thaddeus's voice made Connor jerk off course. His shoulder hit one of the guards, who fell into the second. Both dropped their weapons, and Connor climbed again, craning his neck around to see the house.

Thaddeus stood on a small porch outside a fourth-story window. He held Mara in front of him as a shield, his arm wrapped around her throat. One twist, and he could snap her neck.

Connor beat the air with his great wings and screeched a warning. If Thaddeus hurt her, he was a dead man. Right here, right now.

The guards retrieved their rifles and scrambled to their feet, muzzles pointed skyward.

"Do not shoot," Thaddeus ordered, then looked up at Connor. "Let him land. Bring him to me."

Connor did them one better. He swooped toward the small porch, stretched his claws out at the last moment to land on the balustrade, then changed back to human form and hopped onto the porch in one smooth movement. "Why bother with them? You want me, I'm here."

Thaddeus edged his head back a bit, but never flinched. He swung around, dragging Mara in front of him, so that Connor had to move toward the door to keep them in view. "Inside."

Connor stepped through the glass door into a room that could only be the Wizenot's office. The only piece of furniture was a high-backed chair with wide arms and a heavily cushioned seat set on a raised platform. A fucking throne.

Thaddeus flexed his hold around Mara's neck. "I didn't think you'd have the balls to come back here, Rihyad."

"You thought wrong." He glanced around the empty throne room. "So where is the lord of misery and mayhem?"

"He is the lord of misery and mayhem," Mara blurted out. "He's the Wizen-whatever."

"The Wizenot." Connor nearly gagged at Thaddeus's superior smile. "I guess I should have seen that one coming."

"Don't fret over it. Some of the others have been here for years and haven't figured it out. I find I get a much truer picture of what's going on when people think I'm just a lowly subordinate."

"You mean when you spy on them."

Thaddeus raised one eyebrow. "Call it what you like. A man in my position needs a front man he can trust to monitor the troops, make sure they aren't plotting something unexpected."

"Like a coup?" Connor could see how that might happen here.

Thaddeus inclined his head. "The problem is, I don't trust anyone but myself, so creating the Thaddeus persona was . . . a stroke of genius, as I see it."

"You need to get your eyes checked. Jackson knew, didn't he? He tried to warn me that things weren't what they seemed."

"Yes, Jackson and a few other key lieutenants knew.

What happened to dear Jackson, anyway? I understand he isn't coming back with the rest of the troops."

While Connor had provided his own means of travel back to Duluth, few of the rest of the troops— those who had survived—had that option. They had taken more conventional transportation, cars, and wouldn't be back to the estate for another four or five hours by Connor's estimation. There were some advantages to having wings.

"You sent your troops into an ambush," Connor said. "But then you already knew that, didn't you? You don't care about their lives. They were just a diversion for the real mission. Jackson's mission."

Thaddeus's eyes narrowed. Connor stalked slowly toward him. "If you wanted the Cross woman, you should have asked someone who can get the job done to get her for you."

"You?"

Connor nodded, easing ever closer to Mara. "Jackson failed. I would not have been so careless."

"He is dead?"

"Yes." Connor stopped directly in front of Thaddeus and Mara. He could see the fear in her wide, dark pupils, but he couldn't afford to offer her reassurance now. Life or death for both of them hung on the next few moments. "I killed him," he admitted.

Thaddeus's arm tightened on Mara's throat. Her right hand flew up to his forearm and tugged, but she couldn't pull herself free. "I told you what would happen if you warned them, or interfered. Now you're both going to die—"

"He betrayed you."

Thaddeus's sentence died off. Mara pulled on his arm with both hands now, still to no effect.

"I killed him because they captured him. They threatened him and he begged for his life. He would have told them everything if I hadn't ended it. As it was, he told them enough."

"What did he tell them?"

"About this place. That it was your men who tried to take their children and burned their church. About the army you're raising."

Thaddeus hissed. "May his soul burn in hell! I should never have trusted the weakling."

"They'll mount an attack, and soon."

"Let them come. I'll crush them. Every one of them." Thaddeus spun Mara away from him.

Connor caught her as she stumbled, her hands on her throat. He had her in his arms. The door to the porch was still open. He could have made it. He could have scooped her up, changed form on the balcony and carried her away before Thaddeus or the guards below could stop him.

But it was too late. He couldn't leave.

Thaddeus didn't know the Chicagoans had formed alliances. He thought only the original congregation would attack. A group that size would hardly be enough to make a dent in his defenses.

He had another think coming. And soon.

Mara was right. It was going to be a bloodbath.

He couldn't leave the other women and the children in the middle of a war zone. He couldn't walk away and leave his brethren and those of the congregations joining them to die in a battle the likes of which humans had never seen, and would never see.

If he stayed, he could get the women—including Mara—and the babies to safety. He could help his brethren by weakening the estate's security from the inside.

He could see to it that a man with so little regard for life did not escape with his own.

"By killing Jackson, I am the rightful successor to his position." Gently Connor eased Mara aside. She watched him with round eyes as he bent to one knee and bowed his head and struggled not to choke on the words. "Great One, where he failed his mission, *I* will not. I live . . . only to serve."

Serve Thaddeus Cole up on a platter, that was.

TWENTY-ONE

Mara had to jog to keep up with Connor as he made his way down the long hall toward his room. Thaddeus had given him fifteen minutes to shower and meet him and the other lieutenants downstairs to plan their defenses. At the rate he was going, he was going to have a good thirteen and a half of those minutes to spare.

More than the need to hurry drove his long strides. He left a wake of tension in his path, and the stiff bunch and release of his shoulders as he walked reminded her of a volcano about to blow.

She had a thousand questions about what had happened in Chicago. About what had just happened in Thaddeus's office. But Connor didn't look like a man who wanted to talk. He looked like a man who wanted to kill.

She just hoped he still wanted to kill the right people.

What had all that "I live to serve" stuff been about?

She trusted him. She knew he wouldn't turn on his people, or on her. She *knew* that.

And still . . . he'd been damned convincing.

When they reached his room, he shoved the door open so hard it banged on the wall behind it, then he dragged her in and kicked it shut with one foot. He turned her, planting her back against the wall. He pinned her in place like a butterfly on a board with his chest pressing against hers, his hands planted outside her arms, his legs planted outside her thighs. His erection nestled against her hip.

"Connor—?"

His mouth cut off the rest of her query. His lips came down strong and demanding on hers. His tongue invaded. He gave her no chance to speak, no chance to breathe, but more opportunity to feel than she'd gathered in a lifetime.

Feel his moist breath warm her cheek. His beard stubble scrape her jaw. His hands mold and shape her breasts through her shirt and bra until the nipples stood in tight peaks.

"God, Mara," he murmured against her ear, licking, probing, tasting.

There was an urgency in his touch. A fever in his kiss she'd never experienced before. It brought a rush of blood to the pool between her legs and a heavy ache to her breasts.

Both his hands returned to her face, held her still for his mouth to forage. His fingers trembled on her cheeks, and she raised her hand to cover them and still them, awed by the strength of this need, this wild yearning that coursed through him into her.

She arched her back, grinding her pelvis against his, and pushed her hands between them to the button on his jeans.

His chest heaving, he jerked away from her. The rush of cool air where his warm body had been made her shiver.

She wanted to throw herself back in his arms, but sensed it wouldn't do any good. The moment had passed. Whatever demon had plagued him had been exorcised. At least temporarily.

He dragged one hand through the roots of his hair. "God, Mara. I was afraid he would kill you before I got back."

"You shouldn't have come back. You had the information your people needed. You were free."

"I wouldn't leave you here. With him."

"And now he'll kill you for it as soon as he finds out. How long do you think you'll be able to fool him with that 'loyal servant' crap?"

Tears filled her eyes as the enormity of what he'd done sank in. He'd come back for her. The idiot.

He framed her face with his big palms again, but this time with earnestness, not passion. "Listen to me. There's going to be a battle."

"There're too many of them—"

"A really big battle. A lot of innocent people are going to die if we don't get busy. I need your help."

She sniffed. "Help how?"

"I need you to get the women organized. Gather whatever you'll need for them and the babies—food, water, blankets, medicines, diapers, formula, candles. We need to move everybody out of harm's way until the fighting is over."

"Out of harm's way, where?"

"To the wine cellar."

"The basement." Her stomach cramped, memories of her days locked in the dark at the farmhouse trying to rise. Of eight years wasted in a state penitentiary before that. "No."

"Listen to me. It's safe down there. As soon as it's over, I'll come and get you."

"No! I want to be with you!"

He pulled her into his arms and rocked her. "I know. But I'll come for you. I promise."

"What about Thaddeus?"

"He'll agree it's for the best. He has a vested interest in keeping his future soldiers safe!"

She pulled back until she could look into his blue eyes. "And while we're hiding in the basement, what are you going to do?"

"I'm going to help Thaddeus plan his defense so that I know every guard placement, every weapons cache." He smiled and smoothed her hair. "And then I'm going to kill the son of a bitch."

Colleen listed to the left as Mara helped her down the hallway to pod one, where the women were gathering for their trip to the wine cellar. The women assigned to kitchen and housecleaning work for the day had already been brought in by the guards. Now they were collecting all those who hadn't been assigned to work details.

"You okay?" Mara asked, tightening her hold on Colleen's hip. At least she thought it was a hip. Colleen was so swollen with child that it was hard to find any recognizable anatomy between the woman's breasts and her knees.

Colleen braced the small of her back with one hand. "Sure. Nothing a good epidural and twelve or fourteen hours in labor and delivery wouldn't cure."

"You just keep a cork in it, you hear? We've got enough going on right now without having to birth a baby."

Colleen looked at her cockeyed. "What *is* going on, exactly?"

Mara didn't know what to say to that. She didn't want to give the women false hopes of liberation. They were still a long way from being free. She especially didn't want any nervous chatter among the women to tip the guards off that they were expecting rescue. It wouldn't take them long to trace down the source of that information, and that would spell disaster for all of them, including Connor.

In the end she settled for a half-truth. Or at least a quarter-truth. "There's a storm brewing."

A firestorm, she added silently. With all of them, and Connor, right in the center of it.

"Must be a bad one if they're going to all this trouble."

"Really bad," Mara said.

A keening wail swelled from the doorway of a room ahead, so intense and sorrowful that Mara drew back.

"That's Caren," Colleen said. The sorrow in her voice said that Caren's story wasn't a happy one. As if the crying hadn't.

Mara took a few steps forward and peered through the open door. Inside the room, a woman with dirty blond hair thrashed among a tangle of sheets in a hospital bed, a mid-term pregnancy burgeoning beneath her thin gown. Her wrists and ankles were cuffed to the side rails with thick leather straps.

Mara's breath caught. "My God, what are they doing to her?"

Colleen's eyes shone with sympathetic tears. "She keeps trying to kill herself . . . and her baby. So they keep her restrained."

The woman turned her head toward the door. The suffering in her hazel eyes could only be likened to that of an animal caught for days in a metal trap, knowing death would be the only release.

Mara eased her hands a few inches away from Colleen, and hovered there in case she needed to catch her. "Can you make it to the lounge on your own?"

"Sure. What are you going to do?"

"We have to get everyone downstairs."

Colleen looked at Caren, her eyes still sad. "You're going to need some help."

"I'll be okay. You go. Get off your feet."

Colleen didn't look convinced, but she waddled down the hall as ordered.

Mara poured water into a glass with a straw on the table beside Caren's bed and held it up to the woman's mouth, but Caren wouldn't drink.

She dipped a washcloth in the water and cooled the woman's forehead, talking soothingly, saying nothing, just random comforts, until Caren's gaze quit jumping around the room and her hands stopped twitching.

"There. That's better isn't it?"

"Please—?"

"Much better. I'm going to take off the restraints. Legs first, okay?" She unbuckled the straps. The skin beneath was chafed raw.

Biting her lip to force back her outrage, Mara moved to her wrists. Slowly she pulled the first leather band away.

Caren gasped. Mara jerked back. Caren's free hand flew to her face, her hair, her dirty gown.

Breathing slowly to calm her pulse, Mara leaned over the bed again. This time she talked as she worked. "We're going to get you out of here. Get you cleaned up and take you downstairs with everyone else. We'll get you some food and you can sit up and we'll talk. It'll be like a slumber party."

She slid the final strip of leather away, and Caren arched straight off the bed. Her eyes went wild, the whites showing. Her hands came up, fingers bent like claws, raking the air, raking anything she could reach, including Mara.

Mara backed up against the wall.

Caren grabbed the water pitcher and threw it at her. She wailed and cried and ground her teeth. She flailed with her fists and swung her legs out of bed, then stumbled across the room toward the door.

And into the arms of two guards. She swiped her nails across the face of one of them, leaving a trail of blood on his cheek. The other she tried to kick, but he got hold of her ankle, and the two men took her to the ground, wrapped her up in a wrestler's hold that effectively immobilized her, left just her hands and feet twitching as if she were having a seizure.

"Don't hurt her," Mara yelled. "God, don't hurt her."

One of the medical staff came in with a hypodermic in his hand and injected something into Caren's upper arm. Within seconds the screaming stopped, and then the twitching ceased.

The guards picked Caren up by the arms and legs and carried her toward the lounge where the others waited.

Mara slid down the wall, her legs unable to hold her.

God, please. She had to get these women free.

Connor worried about the weapons. Nearly all of Thaddeus's forces carried guns. But he couldn't think of a way to disarm them of the firearms they had, or hide, disable, or destroy the cache in the house before the coming battle.

He would have to trust his people. They would fight as Gargoyles, not humans. They would attack at night, he was sure of that. Either just after dusk or in the hours before dawn. Instead of guns they would fight with horns and claws and fangs. The ferocity of the beast Awakened was more powerful than any manmade weapons. Add to that the stealth and cunning of the animal form, and Thaddeus's pitiful soldiers wouldn't have a chance.

Still, Connor would give his people what help he could to be sure.

He went still in the dark closet where he stood with a penlight in his mouth, rewiring the fuse box as footsteps pounded past outside. He was just about done. Three down, two to go. He was no master electrician, but if he'd done this right, with a single flick of a switch in the kitchen, the entire security system should short out. Motion sensors, outdoor lights, alarms—all would be out of commission, making it easier for his brethren to breach the estate undetected. A second switch, this one in the main hall, would take out the interior lights. Without light, the soldiers' guns wouldn't be of much use. At least they'd be fighting on even terms.

He stripped the last copper wire with his teeth, twisted it onto the end of a second strand, and tucked it back into the fuse.

Once the women and children were safe in the cellar, and he'd done all he could to aid his brethren's cause, his own hunt would begin.

Thaddeus would be his.

TWENTY-TWO

Mara's stomach rumbled. She hadn't eaten all day. Her legs felt like rubber from walking up and down the steps four or six or ten or however many times it had been, getting the women and infants settled. The guards were bringing up the last group of women to collect clean clothes and toiletries before relocating to the cellar: the laundry crew.

She paused in the hallway just out of sight of the pod where they were to gather. The hand she laid on her stomach when she heard the stairwell door open wasn't to calm the rumbling. It was to settle the butterflies.

This was it. The moment everything had been for. The reason this crazy journey had begun. She was going to see Angela.

This time, she was actually going to get to talk to her. To hug her. To cry with her.

Used to following orders, the women stumbled to

their rooms without question. As soon as the guards had taken up their posts by the door to wait, Mara slipped into Angela's room. She stood with her back against the door, hands behind her, biting her lip and just . . . soaking up the sight of her friend.

"I'll be ready in a minute," Angie said, opening the top drawer of her dresser and pulling out a toothbrush and comb. "I just need to get—"

Angie turned, saw Mara, and the comb and toothbrush fell to the floor. She stood, her jaw slack, wide eyes disbelieving.

"Hi, Angie," Mara said quietly.

"No." Angela's hands covered her mouth. "No, dear lord. No. It can't be."

Mara held out her arms. Tears streamed down her cheeks. "Aren't you going to give me a hug?"

Angela hit her like a linebacker, nearly taking them both down. "Oh my god. What are you *doing* here? Oh my god!"

Mara laughed through her tears. "It's good to see you, too."

Angela set her back at arm's length, her face as fierce as it was tear-stained. "Did they get you, too? Did they hurt you? Tell me they didn't hurt you."

"I'm okay." Her gaze fell to the signs of Angela's pregnancy. "But you—"

Angela waved her hand dismissively. "Don't you worry about me. I've had babies before."

Angela had gotten pregnant as a teenager. Her family had forced her into giving the child up for adoption. Just one of the tough breaks in her life. But those breaks had made her strong, too.

"I'm a survivor," Angela continued. "There ain't nothing they can do to me that I can't get through."

Mara wiped the tears from her cheeks. Lord, how she needed to hear her friend's can-do attitude right now. Angela was right. She was a survivor. And with her at Mara's side, Mara just might survive, too.

Angela threw a worried glance at the door. "They told us we have to hurry. Now you tell me what's going on. What're you doing here, and tell me quick."

Mara started with how the police didn't seem interested when Angela disappeared and ended with how she'd followed the same employment ad her friend had—with the same results.

"Child," Angela clucked. She was less than four years older than Mara, but she liked to play the role of wise old woman. "Are you insane?"

Mara shrugged. "I knew there was something wrong with that ad, that company. I thought it was the only way to find you."

Angela's face turned somber. "Did one of them knock you up, too? Seems to be the way around here. All they want us for is babies. It's the craziest thing."

Mara drew a deep breath. She didn't know what to tell her friend—and not tell her—about Connor. She trusted Angela implicitly, but she didn't know if what she said would make sense. Especially the turning into a monster part.

It took some doing, but she found a way to tell the truth without giving away much else. She laid her hand on her stomach again. "I—I'm not sure."

"Well." She patted Mara on the shoulder and then pulled her into another hug. "It's not the end of the world if you are. Bringing a new life into the world, it's an awesome thing. Not that little baby's fault how it got put there. We'd better get going before them guards come to roust us."

She picked up her dropped things, hooked Mara's arm by the elbow, and headed toward the door. "We gotta find some way to get out of here soon, though. Gotta get these babies someplace safe where they can be raised around decent folk."

Mara nodded, but in her mind she wondered just how they would do that. How many decent folk would want a baby around once it starting sprouting horns and flying out of its crib?

One thing at a time, she told herself. One thing at a time.

"We'll get out of here," she told Angela as they stepped into the hall. She made up her mind to tell her everything—except a few details about Connor—as soon as they got downstairs where they wouldn't be overheard. She needed Angela on her side. She needed a confidant.

She needed a friend.

"We *will* get out of here," she repeated.

It was nearly midnight before Connor finished his last round of the guard stations at the gates, on the roof, inside strategic windows in each wing. The feeling was a strange one, talking to them, giving them final instructions. Knowing many of them would be dead in a few hours.

He didn't relish the taking of life, especially Gargoyle lives when his species was struggling to survive,

their population dwindling every year. The horrors
these men had perpetuated on innocent women, children, and other humans certainly justified his actions.
Validated their deaths.

But that didn't make it any easier to watch.

The knowledge of what would come, and come
soon, sickened him. He headed back to his room to try
to cleanse the guilt away under a steaming shower.

His room was dark and quiet when he entered, just
as he'd left it, but something was . . . off. There. A
slight rustle. The soft sough of a breath.

A scent in the air.

Slowly he closed the door behind him. Without
turning on the light he shrugged out of his leather
jacket and tossed the coat on the dresser. Next he di-
vested himself of boots, belt, and sweater as he headed
into the bathroom to warm up the water.

A dark shape moved behind him, captured him
next to the vanity, her arms encircling his waist. She
was naked, and the feel of her warm skin against his
back warmed his cold blood.

He pulled her closer and lifted one hand to kiss her
knuckles. "How did you get our of the cellar?" he
asked Mara.

She purred between his shoulder blades. "I told them
the new lieutenant would be displeased if I weren't here
to warm his bed when he came in from the cold."

"You told the truth, then." He turned in her embrace, looped his arms around her back and dragged
her close. She'd already made use of the shower, he
noticed. He smelled his plain soap and masculine
shampoo barely concealing her feminine scent, and
immediately felt the urge to get her dirty all over again.

Or clean all over again.

He stripped off his pants, opened the glass shower door, and tugged her inside with him. Water cascaded over him and onto her as he kissed her slowly. Leisurely.

"What's happening outside?" she asked as he bent her head to one side to lave a sensitive spot beneath her ear.

"Nothing. Everyone is ready. All we can do now is wait."

"How long?"

"Until they come."

He tried to distract her from conversation, stroking and teasing her, but she pulled back.

"What's going to happen to the women, Connor? Even if they get out of here—"

"They will get out of here."

She smoothed her hand down his chest. His heart leaped beneath her fingertips.

"What's going to happen to them then? Most of them are pregnant. They'll want to go to the police."

He poured a glob of shampoo in his hand and massaged it in her hair, not because the hair needed washing, but because touching her that way felt so good. "My people will take care of any of our congregation who might be . . . killed." It hurt to say. "There will be no trace back to Chicago. As for the Minnesotans left behind, nothing in their remains will raise questions."

She looked up at him for an explanation.

"The beasts within us are created by magic, not DNA. When we die, we revert completely to our human form. Even if an autopsy is performed, they won't find anything out of the ordinary. If the women report that they were kidnapped and raped, I imagine officials will close the case as some sort of white slavery ring."

"And the babies?"

He shrugged. "If they're female, it won't be an issue. The mothers can keep them, or give them up for adoption if the memories are too painful. If they're males—"

He sighed and worked his fingertips deeper into her scalp.

"What if they're males?"

"We make it as easy as we can on the mothers, Mara. Faking accidents, illness. The women will grieve, but they'll come to accept their losses."

He felt her stiffen.

"These children can't be raised in normal human society," he scathed. You know that. We care for them. We love them. They're not abused or neglected or turned into criminals."

"They're kidnapped. How is what you're doing different than what Thaddeus and his bunch are doing?"

Now he went stiff. "Can you really compare me to them?"

"From where I'm standing, the difference is only a matter of degrees."

Connor hit the shower door with his palm and stepped out, dripping wet, yanking a towel off the bar as he passed. He heard the water shut off behind him, and her light footsteps slapping across the tile.

Her fingers danced along the top of his shoulder. "I'm not saying you're *like* them, Connor. Just that losing a baby isn't any easier for a woman because she's given a nice death certificate instead of having it ripped from her arms."

"We didn't choose what we are. We never had that chance."

"But you do choose how you live." She took the towel from him and dried his back. Gradually the numbness he'd felt at her accusations faded and warmth returned.

"What if I am pregnant? Will you take my baby and send me away?"

"Are you?" he snapped over his shoulder.

"I don't know. I'm just asking. I want to be prepared."

He turned away from her again. "It's different with you. You know about us."

"You didn't answer my question."

He didn't have an answer. God help him, he'd lived ten lives believing in the ways of his people. It wasn't easy to change.

He turned to face her, pulled the towel from her hands. They stood in front of the bathroom vanity, warm, wet, breathing hard. Her hair stood up in adorable spikes. His tangled around his ears and curled on the nape of his neck. Her breasts stood out, firm and proud, pink-tipped and begging for his touch, his mouth.

Her red lips parted as if she sensed his intention.

"This is your answer," he said, and he kissed her, long and slow, then took a breast in each hand, lifted and kneaded, tweaked the tips between his thumb and forefinger, bringing them to pert attention.

"And this is your answer." Arching her back, he lowered his mouth to her chest, circling the areole with his tongue, suckling her ripe peak until her breath escaped her in a moan.

"And this is your answer." He slipped one hand down her rib cage, over the curve of her hip and inward, to the sweet spot between her legs. Her moisture flowed over his fingers, and he spread it, massaging gently, then easing inside.

He felt her surrender. The melting in his arms. She gave herself over to him, moved with him, her heavy-lidded gaze glazed. Lost.

In him.

He hoped she was pregnant. Not because a baby, if it was a boy, would secure his reincarnation, but because his child, inside her, would bond her to him. Bond him to her.

A baby might be all they'd have when this was over and she went back to her life without slavery rings and monsters.

It might be all he had left of her.

He turned her in his arms, laid her limp body chest-down over the vanity. She lifted her head to watch him in the mirror, and the reflection of him watching her watching him, brought even more blood pounding to his groin. He stretched and lifted, aching for her. For release. For freedom.

With one hand on her hip to brace her and the other linked with hers, he pushed inside her in one smooth stroke.

She was velvet heat and iron grip. Smooth and slick. He glided in easily, struggled to pull out as she contracted around him.

He locked his gaze on hers in the mirror, a battle of wills between them. Closer together, then drifting apart. Moving as one, then fighting for independence.

The beast roared within him, awake and hungry. He fed it with another stroke. Then another. He plunged and plundered. She offered up her treasures, drawing him deeper, luring him so far inside that he might never find his way out.

Her breath came in uneven pants. She broke eye contact, her head sagging, and shoved herself back against him each time he moved into her. A tremor began in her thighs, worked up through her belly to her shoulders and out her arms.

She came apart, crying out, clenching his hand in hers and finally going limp in his arms.

He leaned over her, still inside, still hard, and kissed the back of her neck.

Breathing hard, with eyes glittering, she bumped him back until he had to pull out, then pushed him against the wall and sank down on her knees in front of him.

Fire wrapped like a blanket around him when she took him in her mouth. Every breath scorched his lungs. Every heartbeat fanned the flames.

His fingers tunneled through her short hair, grasping for purchase, showing her the rhythm he liked. His hips moved with the swaying of her body until she brought him to his flashpoint and the world exploded in a fireball of white light and heat.

He sagged against the wall until his vision cleared and his legs would hold him, then scooped her up and carried her to his bed to start it all again.

TWENTY-THREE

Rachel pulled back the tangled sheets, climbed out of bed, and belted a robe around her waist. Dawn was still two hours away, and yet Nathan was up and dressing at the closet. She kissed his bare shoulder, the salty-clean smell and taste of his skin still fresh in her mind. Still imprinted on her body.

"So soon?" she asked.

"It's a ten-hour drive, at least. We have to be there before nightfall."

She pulled him into her arms. "I hate this."

"I know," he answered simply.

She drew a strengthening breath and straightened. "There's something you should know before you go. I was going to save it until we could celebrate properly, but I think now is the time to tell you."

He pulled a leather coat from the closet. "Tell me what?"

"We're going to have a baby."

He froze with one arm in his coat, one arm out, then let it fall to the floor altogether and wrapped her up in a bear hug. "Oh, Rachel."

He held her a little too tight, a little too long for mere happiness.

"Hey, this is a good thing, right? We need to get you that son."

And she needed to know she'd have something to hold on to, just in case . . .

No. She refused to think that way. He would be back.

"Damn, I wish I didn't have to leave."

She slid out of his embrace. "Me too. But this is bigger than both our wishes."

From what Nathan and Teryn had told her, nothing like this had ever happened before. Gargoyles had never gone against Gargoyles. No one seemed quite sure what would happen, but everyone agreed it would be bad. Bloody.

He tucked a curl behind her ear. "When I get back, we'll have that celebration."

She smiled bravely. At least she hoped it looked brave. It felt pretty pathetic, actually. "Sure."

"I love you." He laid a palm on her stomach. "You, too."

She cocked her head to the side. "I'm pretty sure he said he loves you, too."

With nothing else to say, and the others waiting, he picked up his coat and left.

Rachel sat in the rocking chair, thinking that one day soon she'd be sitting here nursing a fussy baby, and hoped his daddy was there to help. She thought about going back to bed, but was afraid of the dreams, and the stranger who watched them from afar, so instead she sat. And she rocked. And waited.

It was going to be a long day and night.

"It's gotten colder." Mara pulled a scarf tight around her throat and handed Connor a mug of steaming coffee.

He stood at a parapet on the roof, looking out over the estate. Taking the cup in both hands to warm his fingers, he sipped.

The snow had begun to fall about two o'clock. Now, as the sun neared the horizon, the wind kicked up, whipping the delicate flakes into projectiles that stung the eyes and burned the cheeks. The temperature had dropped about ten degrees and a bank of clouds had rolled in that would block the light of what little moon was due to rise that night.

He smiled to himself and took another sip of coffee. "It'll get colder yet when the sun goes down."

She checked over both shoulders to be sure no one was near. "This is it then?"

He nodded. "Just after dusk, or maybe a few hours before sunrise. But I'm betting for dusk. It gives them plenty of time before the sun comes up and exposes them."

"I can't believe this is really happening. There's really going to be a battle. It's like something out of *Lord of the Rings.*"

"Mmm." He grinned at her over the rim of his mug. "Tolkien was a great writer, but not a Gargoyle, in case you were wondering. How are the women?"

"Restless, but otherwise holding up okay. How about you?"

"Ready to have it over with."

She snubbed her toe in the dusting of new snow on the rooftop. "Connor, just in case we don't see each other again, I wanted to say—"

"We're both going to get through this. We're getting out of here. Together," he said gruffly.

"I know, but . . . just in case. For what it's worth . . . I wanted to tell you that, well . . ."

He lifted her chin with a knuckle. Her amber eyes sparkled and he was the fly caught in their depths. "I love you, too."

She pulled that edible lower lip of hers between her teeth and suckled, the way he wanted to suckle it. He almost gave in to the urge, when a movement in the trees out front caught his eye.

A stag stepped out from behind the cone of one of the massive fir trees. He was as large as a bull elk, with at least a twelve-point rack and liquid, intelligent eyes that Connor would have recognized anywhere.

They belonged to Noble Grant, one of his brethren, and once a Friday night poker partner of Connor's.

He drained his coffee and handed the mug back to Mara. "Go on back downstairs, now. Try to keep everyone calm."

Her gaze jumped to the sky, then the walls of the estate, then the front lawn. But the stag was gone, faded into the wild to prepare.

"I love you," Mara said.

He dug up a final smile. "I'll see you at first light, if not sooner."

* * *

*Thaddeus sat in a ritual circle with his totems be-*fore him: a wilted rose, a dead mouse, fouled wine, and putrid water. But God and Goddess granted only visions of fog this evening. An impenetrable gray wall.

Damn the Chicago woman. She and her little wizard friend must have found a way to block him. That or they weren't invoking the old magic, which he doubted.

He'd hoped to gain divine insight into what the Chicagoans were up to. The attack would begin soon, he knew. But how would they come, and how many? Were they armed, or would they Awaken their beasts and fight in the traditional, if outdated, Gargoyle manner?

Despite hours in the circle, though, the visions had shown him nothing, so he turned his inner eye closer to home, to his own compound, and asked the deities to grant him one more favor.

At last, the fog began to clear. He saw Lake Superior in her winter glory, the waves crashing on the shore and leaving majestic ice castles on the rocks. He saw the twin lighthouses that stood guard at the entry to the Duluth shipping channel, and finally the fields and rolling hills of his own estate.

But there, something rattling in the trees.

And there, tracks in the snow.

Lots of tracks.

Dozens of eyes gleamed through the boughs and over branches.

Thaddeus frowned. His fists clenched until his nails drew blood from his palms.

This wasn't right. There were too many of them.

Far too many.

TWENTY-FOUR

The first cries of the dying echoed from the estate wall across the frozen landscape barely an hour after sunset. The guards on the roof immediately swung their rifles over the low battlement and fired into the darkness.

Connor stalked from station to station, man to man. "Hold your fire. For all you know, you're shooting your own men."

Not to mention Connor's brethren.

"Hold your fire until you can see the enemy!" he ordered. By then it would be too late, he hoped.

The heavy *whumpf whumpf* of wings sounded overhead. Connor and the guards closest to him craned their heads back, but all Connor could see was clouds. Roiling mist and shadows. The fog had an unearthly feel tonight. An eeriness about it.

Connor wondered if Mother Nature provided the much-needed cover, or if Teryn was responsible. He'd long suspected his leader of dabbling in the old magic. There had been a time when, if Connor had had proof Teryn had broken his vow to give up the old religion, he would have used the old man's indiscretion to unseat him from power in the congregation. Now he was only thankful for the lives the mist might save, regardless of its origin. In fact, if Teryn was responsible, Connor would have to see if the Wizenot could muster up seventy degrees and sunshine the next time he went out for a round of golf.

A second later all thoughts of sunny days fled as the guard at the far corner of the roof screamed. A dark shape knocked the gun from his hand and lifted him by the collar.

While the other guards fumbled to take aim and Connor's heart tripped at the risk Nathan was taking, the large griffin simply flew a few feet away and released its prisoner to plummet four stories to his death, then banked into the clouds again and was gone before a shot was fired his way.

"Retreat!" One of the younger men yelled. "Retreat inside!"

Connor grabbed the young man's gun and held the muzzle beneath his jaw. "Hold your ground," he ordered, then lifted the gun to point at them in general. "I'll shoot the first coward who runs!"

Speed was his people's ally. Outside they could attack and disappear, come back from another direction and disappear again. Inside they would be sitting ducks.

Connor marched up and down the line again, barking orders. One by one the wide-eyed men turned back to their posts, except for one, who Awakened the beast.

In the form of a lizard, he crawled over the edge of the parapet and down the wall of the house.

Let the coward go, Connor thought. *One less to fight.*

The battle began to wage in earnest now. Gunfire cracked from the sentry stations on the ground. Muzzle flashes lit the cold night like summer lightning.

Connor wondered how the women were doing. If they understood what was happening outside. The crusade that was being fought for their lives and their freedom. Hell, freedom for all of them, Gargoyle and human alike. Freedom from having to worry about their children being stolen.

Mara's point had hit home last night. He'd come here, risked his life, because someone had tried to steal the children from his congregation, St. Michael's. Yet he and his kind had done the same to women for centuries. They'd taken their sons without remorse, and left the grieving mothers behind.

Someone shouted a warning from behind Connor. He ducked reflexively. A giant hawk whooshed by his ear, raking Connor's shoulder with its talons before grabbing a black-clad soldier at the rooftop entrance to the building and dragging him off screaming into the dark sky.

That had been too close. He'd do well to remember that his brethren from Chicago weren't the only ones fighting out here tonight. The Denver, St. Louis, and Detroit congregations didn't know him. He was sure Nathan had told them they had a man undercover in here, but the other Gargoyles might not recognize him in the dark and the heat of battle.

The good guys seemed to be making inroads into

the estate. The woods were full of movement and the few guards posted outside the house were gone, either dead or deserted.

It was time for him to get off the roof and move on to his portion of this mission, the final breakdown of command and control of the Minnesota congregation. Hopefully, without a leader, the soldiers would put up less organized resistance and would eventually give up the fight altogether.

It was time to find Thaddeus.

In the cellar, the women sat clustered in small groups, some talking, some sleeping, others rocking infants. The babies had been fussy, and their crying annoyed the two guards who had been left with the women to the point that they'd finally relented on the rules, and let the women hold and comfort the babies back to sleep.

Mara moved from group to group, checking on everyone. She bent over Colleen, who was lying on a blanket with her knees drawn up and one hand under her head as a pillow. She found another blanket and lifted Colleen's head to place it beneath. "You okay?"

Colleen smiled, but she looked tired. Was that a sheen of sweat on her brow?

"I'm fine. Just can't get comfortable."

"Here, have some water."

Colleen drank thirstily, then handed the glass back to Mara. "What's going on out there?"

The sound of gunfire was distant, but unmistakable.

"I'm not sure." She didn't know who was winning and who was losing. Who was alive and who was dead.

And it was slowly killing her not knowing if Connor was okay. Not knowing if they were really going to get out of here by morning, or if the good guys would lose, and they were destined to continue suffering.

She patted Colleen's hand. "You just try to get some rest."

Caren sat with her back to the wall a few feet down. The guards had bound her wrists with the plastic handcuffs that cops sometimes used. Her eyes were open, but vacant. She hadn't moved in hours. Mara wasn't even sure she'd blinked.

She scooted up next to the woman and poured a fresh paper cup of water. "Caren, honey. You need to drink something."

She held the cup up to Caren's lips, but the water dribbled to the floor.

"Please, Caren. You need some water. For your baby."

There was some flicker of life then. Just a shadow in her eyes. "My baby," she mumbled. "They're going to take it anyway. Might as well kill it as give it to them."

"Don't say that. We're going to get out of here. You've got to believe that."

"Nobody gets out of here. 'Cept in a casket."

She leaned in close to Caren's ear. "You hear that fight going on out there? That's people trying to help us. Trying to get us out. You just have to hold on a little longer. And drink some water."

Caren turned her head in little jerks and stops, as if the muscles were weak from lack of use. "Getting out of here?"

"Yes. Soon."

Caren reached for the water, and Mara gasped at
the raw rings of flesh around her wrists. She called the
guard. "You have to take these off."

He shook his head. "No way. Not her, crazy bitch."

"She could get an infection in this damp basement."

He turned to walk away.

"If it gets in her blood, it could hurt the baby."

That stopped him. These men were serious about
growing their little army of evil.

"All right," he said after he'd looked at her bleeding
wrists. "Just for a minute. I'll see if I can find something softer to tie her up with."

He pulled a knife out of his pocket, flipped open the
blade, and cut through the plastic straps just as the
lights went out.

The women gasped collectively.

Mara reached for Caren to keep her quiet, and
found only air next to her.

Rachel sat cross-legged on the floor across from
Teryn. His hands rested, palms up, on his knees. His
eyes were closed and his breathing even and shallow,
but he wasn't sleeping.

"Can you see anything?" she asked.

"No." He was perfectly still except for his lips. "It's
taking all my concentration to hold the weather pattern to shield our people. I can't bring the vision."

"I'm sorry. I shouldn't distract you."

His mouth curved up in a slow smile. "You are not
a distraction. Perhaps you should try."

"Bringing the vision? I can't do that by myself. I
need your help, or Nathan's."

"You're getting stronger every day. Have you felt the intruder watching you again?"

"No. I did what you said and pictured myself in a closed room with no windows. He couldn't see in."

"Good. Then picture yourself in that closed room, and draw the vision. Find Nathan and see that he is okay. We'll both feel better."

She did as Teryn suggested, carefully setting out her ritual items in the prescribed order, then calling the four quarters and making her request. Red wine rippled in her gold chalice, and in the waves, images began to appear.

Breathless, she drew them nearer.

TWENTY-FIVE

❧

Mara heard the guard who'd just cut off Caren's plastic handcuffs gasp, a wheezy, surprised kind of sound. Then a body fell at her feet.

She felt around in the dark. "Caren? Caren!"

Her eyes hadn't adjusted to the dark yet, but her hands found an arm, much too muscular to be Caren's, and moved across the chest. Something warm and sticky coated her fingers. It took a moment for it to register as blood. The handle of his knife protruded from his chest just left of center.

The second guard yelled, "Hey, what's going on over there? Billy?"

Mara scrabbled back from the body. "Caren?" She whispered this time, not wanting to alarm the second guard any more than he already was.

The sound of heavy footsteps approaching told her she needed to do something fast.

"Billy? Where'd you go?"

Angela materialized beside Mara. "What is it? What's happening?"

"I can't find Caren," she hissed. "I think she killed the guard."

Angela knelt beside the body on the floor. "Uh-oh."

"Yeah. Now what?"

Angela rose and nodded toward the approaching guard. "Can't let that one find this one. Get his attention."

Then she was gone.

"Angela. Damn it, Angela, what do you mean get his—?"

Guard number two was too close for comfort. Mara ran up to him and grabbed his sleeve, led him back. "Over here! I think your friend is having a seizure or something."

The guard bent over Billy. Angela raised up over him, holding the neck of a wine bottle in two hands. It hit his head with a satisfying thunk before breaking. He fell next to his buddy.

Hearing the commotion, the other women began to gather.

"What's happened?"

"What's wrong with the guards?"

"What's going on outside?"

A baby wailed.

Angela took charge. "Calm down, everybody. Just take it easy."

"But what's happening?"

"That sounds like gunfire!"

"What happened to the lights?"

Angela straightened to her full five-foot-two

height, put two fingers in her mouth, and let loose with an earsplitting whistle. "I said CALM DOWN!"

The rapid-fire questions quieted to murmurs.

Mara felt around the floor until she found one of the dead guards' bodies. Wrinkling her nose, she unclipped a small flashlight from his belt and shone it on Angela.

"All right, that's better," Angie said. "Now, what's happened here is our guards have had a little accident."

"What kind of accident?" someone asked.

Angela propped her hands on her wide hips and glared.

"Sorry," the woman said meekly.

"Now, what's going on outside is another story. There're some nice people trying to help us out. Get us out of here."

Breaths swooshed and women squealed. Quietly.

A tall figure stepped up to the circle. "Then why aren't we out there helping them?" Caren asked, as Mara turned the light on her. For the first time since Mara had met her, she appeared to be *all there*. Her back was straight, her shoulders were square, and her voice rang clear and strong.

Angela looked up at her. "Now that's a good question."

Mara got a bad feeling. "We've got babies to take care of. Most of you are pregnant."

"We're pregnant, not helpless," Angela huffed.

"Half of you can't even climb the stairs by yourselves."

"Okay," Caren argued. "That half'll stay behind and take care of the babies. The rest of us go fight."

Mara was all for getting out of the cellar and getting involved in the action. She didn't do well sitting around waiting for someone else to come rescue her. She preferred to hold fate in her own two hands.

But with a bunch of pregnant women?

And what if one of them saw the men in their . . . alternate state. How would she explain that?

The same way it had been explained to her, she guessed, if it came to that. Sans the demonstration, perhaps.

These women had been kidnapped, abused, held captive. They deserved to take a part in their own liberation.

Besides, Connor and his friends might need them.

"All right," she said. "Those of us who can, fight."

A cheer went up from the crowd. Mara, Angela, Caren, the four women from the farmhouse before Duluth, and a willowy woman named Beth headed for the stairs, armed with bricks and crowbars and broken bottles—whatever weapons they could find or forge.

With the lights cut and most of his men engaged in mortal combat on the roof, Connor ducked through the fire door into the building and stopped at the top of the stairs, listening. The dark passageway was quiet, but that didn't mean it was safe. At this point in the battle, he could run into forces from either side and find himself dead before he could identify himself.

When several seconds had passed with no sign of life from inside, he crept down the steps. Every footfall sounded like a cannon shot to him. Each breath like a gust of wind through the trees.

He moved slowly, carefully. Measuring every step.

He hated fighting indoors, where his winged form was more of a disadvantage than an advantage.

At the bottom of the steps he turned right and worked his way along the wall where he wouldn't cast shadows if a stray flashlight beam crossed the corridor or enough moonlight cut through the clouds to illuminate a room.

Near the building's central hallway, he heard voices. Two guards commiserated outside Thaddeus's outer office.

"I know the old man told us to stay here, but listen. It's a war zone out there. We're getting our butts kicked."

"You're talking about desertion. You know what he'll do to you if he catches you?"

"I don't care, man. Can't be worse than what them other Gargoyles are doing. I saw one guy ripped in half by some kind of big cat, dude."

"Go, then. See if I care."

"You sayin' you're staying?"

Connor had had enough. He couldn't wait all night for these two weasels to make up their minds. He took a brisk step out of the shadows, ignoring the weapons they drew. "You two, what are you still doing here? We're retreating to the great hall on the first floor."

He figured they'd like that option. Retreat sounded pretty good to a couple of cowards about now.

Still, they put up at least a token argument. They exchanged a look. "But Thaddeus . . . We were ordered to stand guard here, sir."

"And now I'm ordering you to get downstairs. Get a move on. Now. I'll get Thaddeus."

Wearing expressions of great relief, the pair of guards hightailed it to the stairwell.

Connor collected himself a moment, then gently eased the door open.

The outer office was empty. Thaddeus's small desk had been cleared, his chair neatly pushed in. Connor stepped through the room toward the closed entrance to the inner sanctum.

Was Thaddeus—or whatever his name really was—even here? Or had the guards been a ruse to make an intruder think he was here? Had he already run, leaving his men behind to die?

Connor spun and checked for a trap behind him, but the doorway was empty, the hall quiet.

He started again toward the rough-hewn double oak doors that led to the Wizenot's throne room.

Before he could touch the knob, the heavy doors swung open. Thaddeus sat in the big chair, a staff of some sort in a holder on one arm, a scruffy dog on the floor near the other.

"Welcome, Connor," he said, and Connor knew from his tone of voice that he was anything but welcome. "I've been expecting you."

Instinctively, Connor realized he was only going to get one shot at this. Maybe he'd already hesitated too long.

Somehow Thaddeus knew he'd been betrayed.

The ritual chant played in fast-forward in his head:

E Unri almasama
E Unri almasama
Calli, Calli, Callio
Somara altwunia paximi

In less than a heartbeat, the beast Awakened. Connor spread his wings, extended his talons, and put his head down to rush the Wizenot, but a blow akin to an unseen battering ram planted in the center of his chest sent him reeling backward. Ribs splintered. Blood leaked into his lungs.

He lay on the floor, thrown back into human form, and gasped for breath.

Thaddeus stood over him. "You could have been a part of the most powerful movement on Earth—the liberation of *Les Gargouillen*. But you chose to betray me instead."

"*Les Gargouillen*," he said, coughing up blood on every word, "are already free. You enslave them, making them your soldiers."

"I give them power."

"You give them hedonism and greed. You infect them with a poison that turns them on each other. You kill everything that is *Les Gargouillen*."

"I am the Great One. The one who will lead our people into a new age!"

"You are a miserable blight on our people. You will be exterminated tonight."

Thaddeus's face reddened.

Connor struggled to his hands and knees, only to find himself knocked flat, his wrists and ankles pinned by invisible restraints.

His tormentor pointed a finger and Connor felt it like a blade at his throat.

How the hell did he *do* that?

"You cannot defeat me."

"Hell. Can't . . ." He didn't have breath for more.

Thaddeus's mouth widened in a twisted smile. "Do

you not recognize me now, Connor Rihyad, fourth-generation descendant of the soul of Pierre Moriet of Rouen?"

Connor's gaze flew up. His eyes were the only parts of himself he could move. "Who are you?"

A wind gusted through the room even though the door to the balcony remained closed. Static electricity crackled in the air, making the short hairs on Connor's neck and arms stand.

The leather thong tying back Thaddeus's neat ponytail fell to the floor. His smooth hair turned coarse and dry. The ends lashed his face and whipped around his head.

His skin aged decades in mere seconds. His shoulders slumped and his long, elegant fingers gnarled. He reached back for the staff next to his chair and leaned on it as if it were the only thing holding him up.

Then, wobbling as if his aged knees were about to buckle, he tipped his head up and lifted his gnarled hands from his sides. Blue lightning shot from his palms and illuminated the room in an unearthly glow.

The walls began to rumble and the floor shook.

"I am Romanus," he said, practically yelling to make himself heard above the wind.

"I am your creator!"

TWENTY-SIX

Mara led her ragtag group of female warriors through the house, not quite sure what their mission was, but knowing they had to do something. In her hand she gripped the knife she'd pulled from the dead guard's chest. The others carried makeshift weapons they'd found in the cellar.

God help them if they actually had to use them.

The ground floor was mostly clear. Outside they heard sounds of combat, but chose to stay inside, where they knew their way around, for now.

Occasionally a voice or a scream would break the silent trek, but mostly silence greeted them at every turn. They made it through the dining hall and kitchen, where Caren and Angela traded crowbars for butcher knives.

"What now?" Angela asked.

Mara had no idea. She just knew she wanted to find Connor. Needed to see him whole and healthy.

Near the Wizenot. That's where he would be.

"Upstairs," she said.

They took the servants' stairs, figuring they would be less likely to run into trouble. But even there were signs of violence. A pool of blood puddled on the landing. They stepped around it, focused on their goal.

Whatever that might be.

On the third floor, they heard shouts above them. Stomping feet and pounding and wild, animalistic sounds.

Uh-oh.

Mara paused. "Maybe we should go the other way."

Caren pushed past her. "This is what we came for."

"To get killed?"

"To help!"

The others followed Caren. Mara brought up the rear. She was deathly afraid that helping in a fight between two Gargoyles was much more than any of these women had bargained for.

As they reached the bottom of the staircase to the fourth floor, the sounds of combat increased, and Mara's worst fears were realized. The door at the top of the stairs opened. On the landing, a glorious creature, half lion and half eagle, reared above a snarling hyena with horns.

The women drew back with a collective gasp. Jaina dropped her butcher knife and slumped into Mara's arms.

The vision came swift and powerful, like a rising river. It swept Rachel away. She saw Gargoyles of all shapes locked in battle to the death. She saw blood on the steps, bodies in the snow. Babies crying in the dark.

Some of the images merged with scenes from her own past. Her parents' murder, the fire in her home, the attack on St. Michael's. But Rachel was able to ease those aside and concentrate on what was happening in Minnesota.

She searched for Nathan. Her mind knew his so well, it should have been easy to detect. But amid the chaos and confusion, the swing of emotions from victory to grief to fear to death, she couldn't lock on.

She forced herself to take a deep breath and search methodically. The basement. The roof. The floors, one by one.

When she neared the fourth floor, her skin began to tingle, then to burn almost uncomfortably. The air smelled of ozone and a change in pressure made her ears pop.

She frowned. "Teryn?"

"Yes, Rachel. I feel it."

"What is it?"

His forehead furrowed in concentration. "I don't know. It's big. It's powerful." A sweat broke on his brow. "It's evil."

The floor beneath her began to vibrate. An eerie blue light lit the room. The walls sucked in and out as if they were elastic. Only it wasn't her floor, or her walls. It was the house in Minnesota, literally being shaken off its foundation. Pressurized until it was ready to explode.

With people still inside.

Nathan, her mind screamed frantically. *Get out! Get out!*

She tried to hold the house together by sheer will and magic, the same as the destructive force trying to tear it down. "Teryn. There are still people inside. We have to—" She gasped for a breath. "Hold it up."

She felt her mentor's tenuous hold on the weather pattern let go and he grasped both her forearms in his hands. His mind joined with hers. They were one thought. One force braced against the ferocious wind. Against death.

Her muscles began to shake, cramp. Sweat soaked her robe, plastered it to her skin. "Don't let go. Don't let go."

But the energy in the house continued to build until it threatened to rip them apart.

Mara held the unconscious Jaina in her arms. The other women stared at the top of the staircase, wide-eyed and mute.

The women weren't the only ones surprised. The lion-thing turned its round avian eyes on the rag-tag group and cocked its beak in surprise.

The hyena took advantage of his distraction and lunged for the lion's leg, digging in its fangs until blood trickled from the corners of its mouth.

The eagle screeched, a painful sound, then dug its beak into the hyena's neck and back. When the hyena drew back, the eagle-lion swiped at it with one rear paw—a paw with lethal claws, ripping through the hyena's torso and sending it slamming against the wall, where it left a streak of red as it slumped to the floor and turned into a man.

A man Mara recognized as one of the Minnesota congregation.

The lion-thing studied them quietly from the top of the stairs. His dark eyes held equal measures of intelligence and savagery.

"You—" Mara knew what these men were, and she was still having trouble processing what she'd seen. What must the other women be thinking? If their brains were working at all . . . "You're from Chicago? One of Connor's friends?"

Before she could swallow, a man stood where the griffin had been, his feet spread, clothes rumpled and cheeks flushed with exertion. "You know me, Mara."

She found her breath. "Nathan Cross."

He nodded.

Jaina stirred in Mara's arms. She set the woman back on her feet.

"Whaaaaat?" Jaina mumbled, looking upward.

"It's all right," Mara said. "He's one of the good guys."

Theresa's voice was high-pitched. Near panic. "You. I remember you. You came to the farmhouse."

Beth, who hadn't met Nathan previously, tightened her grip on the butcher knife she held. "If you're one of the good guys, I don't want to see the bad ones!"

Jaina turned her head as if she couldn't bear to look at Nathan, even in human form. "What are you?"

Nathan met Mara's gaze evenly. He knew that she knew, she realized. He could tell by her reaction. Or lack of one. And he was asking for her help.

"He's a friend," she said firmly. "He's here to get us out."

Caren moved to the front of the group, as if to put herself between Nathan and the others. "But he's a monster!"

"No," Mara insisted. "The creature he just killed is a monster. You know him—he was one of the ones who held you prisoner here. Nathan and his people, they are . . . extraordinary. But they're not monsters."

The women murmured uncertainly.

"You're sure he's one of the good guys?" willowy Beth asked.

"I'm posi—"

Without warning, another creature leaped from the shadowed hallway. A giant rodent of some sort, the be-ing sunk two buck teeth into Nathan's shoulder and clawed at his face.

Nathan ducked, breaking free of the giant rat, but lost his balance and rolled halfway down the stairs. The rat pounded down after him.

"Nathan!" Mara caught his attention and tossed him her knife.

Nathan was just able to point the blade upward as the rat fell on top of him. The rat went limp and Nathan rolled the body off and clutched at his bleeding shoulder.

He stumbled down the steps to the women. Mara took pride in the fact that none of them recoiled at his nearness.

Her girls were survivors.

"Thanks," Nathan said, handing her back the knife she'd thrown him. "Now we have to get out of here."

The others nodded nervously in agreement, but Mara hesitated. It sounded like the fight upstairs had moved to the other end of the building. A strange blue light glowed from the hallway. The floor began to shimmy beneath her, as if a train were passing nearby, and even stranger, the walls began to pulse as if they were alive.

She'd seen a lot of weird things the last few days, but this was one of the weirdest.

Angela put one shoulder under Nathan's bleeding arm to support him. "Come on," she said, looking at Mara.

"You go," she said, her mind made up. If anything strange was going on, Connor was bound to be in the middle of it. "I'll be along in a minute."

"We're not leaving you," Angela argued.

"I have . . . something else to do." Her gaze never wavered from the blue-lit hallway.

Nathan's own gaze followed where she looked. He tried to pull away from Angela. "I'll help you."

"No," Mara told him. "You get the others out of here."

"They're doing fine on their own."

"They need your help," she said firmly, and shot him a glance that said they needed him for more than just escape. They'd need him to help them understand what they'd seen, when they were ready. To either accept it or forget about it. With a little Gargoyle memory-altering help.

Nathan hesitated a moment, then nodded sharply. "He's a lucky man," he said.

"Damn straight," she answered.

She glanced again at the fourth floor and took a deep breath. That was where Connor was—she could feel it.

That was where she needed to be, too.

*   *   *

Connor lay curled on the floor, struggling for consciousness, struggling to comprehend what Thaddeus—*Romanus*—had told him.

"I am your creator, made just like you a thousand years ago."

"How—?" He choked on blood. "How could that be?"

The house continued to rumble and creak around him. The floors buckled. The dog whined and put his paws over his nose.

"When I called the beasts and merged their souls with those of your forefather, I, too, was in the ritual circle."

Connor screwed up his face. "You got caught in your own spell."

"I became the wolf."

Connor shook his head. "I don't remember you. I don't see you in the memories I've been passed of that day. We looked for you after Gargouille was slain, but you were gone." He had to pant to catch his breath. "You . . . you ran."

Romanus slammed the end of his staff against the floor and sparks flew in the air. "Your dragon was slain."

"You were afraid. You couldn't face what you'd become."

"I had fulfilled my promise!"

"At the cost of our souls!"

Romanus looked over his shoulder as if there were someone there. He frowned and, for a moment, the house settled. But he lifted his hands higher and the shaking began again. The pressure built, threatening to cave in Connor's chest even more.

"You don't need to worry about your soul any longer, Rihyad. Tonight it dies for good."

Unless Mara was pregnant with his son, Connor thought, but he didn't speak it. Couldn't have if he'd tried.

"If it shuts this operation down, it's worth it," Connor said.

"You may shut this location down, but you will not shut me down. I will begin again, with a better bloodline this time. Stronger. More powerful."

Connor shuddered. He knew what bloodline Romanus wanted. A child of one of the Old Ones. First generation. "You'll never get Rachel."

"Not her. I will have her brother." He smiled. "Levi."

"No." Connor tried with all his might to lift his hand. To utter the words of the Awakening and bring his beast to life. Just once more before he died.

He couldn't let Romanus win. Couldn't let him get Levi. Who knew what he could do if he turned a first son of an Old One to his evil cause. That boy would be powerful, indeed.

Romanus lifted his hands an inch higher and the shaking of the house increased. The pressure hurt Connor's ears. Even such a solid structure as this one couldn't take this kind of pressure for long.

But someone, or something, seemed to be fighting him. Offering resistance. Sweat trickled down Romanus's temple. His hands sagged an inch and the muscles of his arms trembled as he tried to lift them higher.

"What's wrong, *Great One*? Getting tired?" Connor tried again to move his arm and managed to scrape his hand forward an inch.

A figure entered the doorway behind him. He was

able to turn his head enough to see her. His heart lunged. "Mara!"

Before Connor could warn her, Mara was tossed to the floor at his side, but the effort cost Romanus. His lips quivered as he gritted his teeth.

"Perfect. Now you can die together."

Connor grimaced. "If this house blows, you die, too."

"Fool," Romanus laughed sickly.

"Connor?" She reached for him. *No.* For the knife she'd dropped.

Romanus struggled with the unseen force that opposed him. The house shook as if ready to blow apart, then quieted. His hands lifted, then were pushed down.

With each molecule of effort he expended on destroying the house—with them inside it—his control over Connor faded a bit. He was able to crawl an inch, then two. Romanus didn't seem to notice.

His lips moved, chanting silently. His eyes were nearly closed. His complexion had gone pallid.

Mara was closer to the knife. She reached it with her fingertips, but didn't have the strength to use it. She pushed it toward Connor.

Connor clutched the handle, dragged himself to his knees, and made a desperate lunge for the magician.

Romanus sensed him at the last second. He opened his eyes wide, held up one hand, and in a cloud of foul-smelling gray smoke and a flash of fire—

He disappeared.

The house boomed as if its entire weight had been dropped six inches. The pressure was gone, but the structural damage was done. Dust crumbled from the ceiling. Nails popped from the hardwood floors. Glass shattered.

The invisible bindings gone, Connor stumbled back to Mara, one arm curled over his injured ribs, and reached for her with his other hand. "Come on. We've got to get out of here!"

The house fell apart as they ran, Romanus's scruffy dog whimpering at their heels. Stairs collapsed behind them. Beams dropped where they'd hung overhead only a second before. Gaping chasms opened in the floor where they'd just stepped.

When they finally made it to the front door, they ran through without a backward glance, and collapsed hand in hand in the snow while the big dog danced around them and lapped at their faces with his scratchy tongue.

TWENTY-SEVEN

Connor leaned against the window in Jackson Firth's room in the Chicago congregation dormitory. Jackson stood behind him, looking over his shoulder.

The man was getting around remarkably well for someone who was supposed to be dead. Connor had been sure he'd killed him in Teryn's office, but when Nathan had gone to move the body, he'd found a faint pulse. Evan Cain, a doctor and member of the Chicago congregation, had sewn him back together. Barely.

They weren't exactly sure what they were going to do with Jackson now that they'd saved his life, but Connor was glad they had. Saved his life, that was. Not being guilty of murdering one of his own kind— even if it had been necessary—was one less weight on his already heavy mind.

Until the Council decided what to do with him, Jackson was being held under guard. It was hoped he'd provide information that would help them track

Romanus, but so far that hadn't happened. Connor wasn't sure if the man was really that loyal, or just didn't know anything.

As he watched Mara walk down the sidewalk toward her waiting cab, he wasn't sure he cared.

Had she finished saying her good-byes so soon?

"You just going to let her go?" Jackson asked.

Connor shoved his hands in his pockets. "It's her decision."

"I wasn't asking what she wanted."

He turned. "What am I supposed to do? Kidnap her?" It was a mean-spirited jab, and he knew it, but he couldn't help it. He sighed. "There's no place for women here. It wouldn't work."

"Uh-huh."

"What's that supposed to mean?"

"Nothing." Jackson turned away and shrugged. "You're probably right. No sense trying to go against a thousand years of tradition."

Connor narrowed his eyes.

"Gargoyle tradition, that is. Mara's human, so she wouldn't understand that." Jackson looked at him sideways. "Of course, you're part human, too . . ."

Connor's jaw went hard. Was Jackson taunting him, or sincere? Did he think it was easy for Connor to sit here and watch Mara walk away? Did he think he did it because he didn't want her? Didn't want a life?

And why the hell did he care what Jackson thought, anyway?

He lurched to his feet and out of the room. "Come on, Wulf," he called to the big dog who seemed to have attached himself to Connor since Romanus had abandoned the animal in the collapsing mansion. Connor told himself he was going upstairs to his own room to read, but somehow found his feet pounding down the steps toward the front door instead.

Connor grabbed the door to Mara's cab just before she pulled it shut behind her. What did he want? They'd said their good-byes last night at the Good Home, the women's crisis shelter she and Angela had opened in Chicago just eight weeks earlier.

She and Angie had a ready-made bunch of clients—the women from the estate in Duluth. Of the twenty women there, all had suffered traumas and needed counseling. Seven had seen the Gargoyles in beast form. Fourteen were pregnant, six of them with boys. Colleen had delivered a nine-pound boy in the basement in Duluth.

Mara was carrying one of the nine little girls.

The sonogram yesterday had produced mixed emotions in her. It was a relief in some ways, knowing she wouldn't be faced with raising a child who could shift into another form at will and who would have a soul a thousand years old.

Or with having such a child taken from her.

Having a girl gave her more choices. She did not have to stay with the Chicago congregation of *Les Gargouillen*. She could go wherever she wanted. Start over with just herself and her very human little girl.

The trouble was, she wasn't sure where she wanted to go. She'd signed over the shelter to Angela yesterday as soon as she'd returned from the ob-gyn. This morning she was heading out to the bus station.

With no destination in mind.

Maybe someplace warm . . .

Connor glowered down at her. "You don't have to leave."

Yes, she did. Because last night when she told him their baby was a girl, he hadn't asked her to stay.

She changed the subject before she started crying. Pregnancy was making her very emotional. "Did you get word from the Duluth coroner's office?"

He nodded. "None of the human remains recovered appear to be Thaddeus. Or Romanus, rather."

She paused with her hand on the car door. "So he's still out there. Poor Rachel. I know she thought she'd be able to trace him through the name of the boat."

"She and Nathan have searched every registry they can find, but there's no vessel called *The White Whale* listed."

Mara ached for the woman she'd come to know and love like a sister since coming to Chicago. They shared something no other women in the world shared: they both loved a Gargoyle.

"If Romanus was telling the truth, he'll be looking for her brother," Connor said.

"Do you think he was lying?"

"No."

So now it was a race with Teryn, Rachel, and Nathan, against Romanus. With Levi's soul hanging in the balance.

"I'll be praying for them. For all of you," she corrected. The Chicago congregation had its own challenges in front of it. They'd rescued twelve infants and toddlers from Duluth. While they were blessed to have them, the care they required put a burden on a community already overtaxed by the destruction of St.

Michael's, and now the loss of four of their own in Duluth.

She sat awkwardly in the car, not sure how to end it. Not sure what he wanted. She wasn't sure he knew himself. "Tell everyone I said good-bye," she finally said.

Connor's knuckles went white on the door.

She gave him a moment to respond, to say anything, then gave the cabbie directions and tried not to look back as she drove away.

Connor stood on a balmy Ft. Lauderdale street on a Friday night, studying the single small window of an apartment on the third floor above Esplanade Street.

If he didn't move soon, the cops were going to roust him for loitering.

Let them try. He wasn't moving. He just wanted to catch a glance of Mara. To see how much the baby had grown. How her shape had changed with pregnancy. She was due in just a few weeks. He would be a father.

And yet still childless in every way that mattered. He hadn't raised a little girl in eight hundred years. Hadn't had a wife to love and protect. Hadn't built or maintained any kind of female relationship.

He wasn't sure he remembered how.

He was sure he wanted to learn.

Damned if it hadn't taken a traitor to his people to make Connor see that his loyalties had been misplaced. That he'd neglected his duty to a part of himself—the human part.

She passed before the window, shaped like a teardrop. The baby hung low and large.

He smiled. It would be a strapping, healthy girl. That much was for sure.

For months he'd denied that he cared how his daughter—or his lover—was doing. He wouldn't let himself think about what the child might look like once she was born. Would she have her mother's red hair or his dark locks? Blue eyes or amber?

Or would she be a little person unique to herself, with her own looks, her own traits?

He wondered if Mara thought about him the way he thought about her. If she remembered their days and nights together. If she woke up aching from the want . . .

He stared at her in the window as she moved about her little apartment. He thought about the first night they'd made love, after he'd been hurt. They way their bodies had fused and ignited one another. The way their hearts had melded.

Gently he pushed those memories to her. He saw her stop mid-stride. Her head tipped back. Her eyes closed.

Yeah. She remembered.

Then she turned and came to the window. She looked out, but she wouldn't be able to see him in the dark, inside his car.

She pressed her palm to the glass and he pressed his to the car window. Despite the distance between them, it was as if he were there with her. Touching her. Loving her.

He scratched Wulf behind the ears and dug a dog biscuit out of his coat pocket for his travelling companion. "What do you think, boy? It's now or never, huh?"

Wulf crunched his treat with a soulful look.

"Yeah, you're just full of great advice, as usual."

Swearing at his procrastination, he got out of the car and slammed the door.

She was waiting at the entrance to her apartment when he clomped up the last stair.

She opened the door, and he went inside without a word.

"You knew I was there," he said gruffly.

She busied herself arranging fruit in a basket. "For about the last hour. The memories were coming back too strong to just be . . . memories."

He uttered another oath. "I'm sorry."

"Don't be." She rushed off into the kitchen. Putting some distance between them, he figured. "Would you like something to drink?"

"Sure." What else could he say?

She came back out with a bottle of scotch and a shot glass and poured two fingers. "You go ahead," she said. "I can't drink with the baby."

"Then why do you have a bottle of scotch in the kitchen?"

"In case of emergency," she said, and smiled. "And it's a good thing I do, since you look like you're in dire need. Why are you here, Connor?"

He downed the glass for old times' sake. When he could speak again, he said, "Because I made a mistake. A big one."

She cocked her head, waiting patiently for him to continue.

"I spent my whole life being loyal to my people," he said. "*Les Gargouillen*. I followed the tenets of my congregation. Upheld the vows our forefathers made centuries ago. I was proud of who I was. What I was."

"That was a mistake?"

"No. But there was one thing I failed to consider. I may be a Gargoyle, but I'm human, too. I'm both man and monster. Flesh and stone."

He took a deep breath, gathered himself before he could continue.

"By staying so strictly loyal to one part of my heritage, I betrayed the other side. The human side."

He slid off the couch to one knee and picked up her hand. "I don't want to deny that side of myself any longer, Mara. When I thought I was going to die in that house with Romanus, the only thing I could think was that I wanted to live. I wanted a life. With you."

She curled one hand into a fist and laid it over her heart.

"But I wasn't sure you wanted me. I wasn't sure you could accept what I am."

"And now?" She sounded breathless.

"Now I decided the only way to know for sure is to ask." He pulled a velvet box from his pocket. "Will you marry me, Mara? You don't have to make up your mind right away," he added quickly. "I mean, I can move down here for a while. Permanently if that's what you want."

Flustered, he ran a hand through his long hair. "You can take as much time as you need to think about it. Just give me a chance to show you we can make it work. That's all I ask."

"I thought you asked me to marry you."

"Well . . . yeah . . ." Had he missed something?

She smiled. "Then shut up and let me answer."

He'd lived lifetimes that seemed to pass more

quickly than the seconds before she threw her arms around him and said yes to his proposal.

But he'd never lived a happier moment than when she finally did.

VICKIE TAYLOR

CARVED IN STONE

Six year old Rachel Vandermere didn't believe in monsters—until she saw one kill her parents. Now an INTERPOL investigator, Rachel has quietly amassed an impressive collection of evidence to support the existence of preternatural creatures. But she dares not go public until she can produce a living abnormal being to show the world—if only she can convince the enigmatic Nathan Cross to help her.

Disavowed from the Chicago congregation of Gargoyles, Nathan has given up life as a guardian of mankind for a more human existence. But when Rachel shows up at his door spouting her theories about monsters, he is thrust into the role of protector once again. For Rachel's diligent pursuit of the truth might just get them both killed.

0-425-20291-7

Available wherever books are sold or at penguin.com

**The search for Levi continues
in Vickie Taylor's next Gargoyle romance**

LEGACY OF STONE

As a child, Levi Tremaine discovered he possessed abilities he could neither understand nor control.

As a man, he isolated himself from "normal" society, preferring instead to exist in a shadowy world of deception and violence, among people as dangerous as he.

Now Levi is being hunted by the forces of both good and evil for the very abilities that drove him into hiding. Can he distinguish friend from foe in time to save his everlasting soul—and the woman he loves?

**Coming in December 2006
from Berkley Sensation**